TWO FOR THE *Love* OF ONE

MEG LUSH

M. Lush
XO

Two for the Love of One
Meg Lush

Developmental and Copy Edit: JBJ Editing
Cover Design copyright 2024 by Jo Kasunic

Digital ISBN: 978-1-7382910-1-4
Print ISBN: 978-1-7382910-0-7

Daux,

I figured out how to harness all my crazy.

Thanks for coming on the ride,
I'll meet you on the other side.

Chapter 1: Katarina

Patience is a personality flaw. An eight-letter word that painfully attacks my ego. Along with my other character weaknesses, the lack of it is by far the most annoying. Wanting the cart to come before the horse, or the crystal ball to be less fog and more future, is a surefire way to live a life of disappointment. If only I could steer away from all potential drama, heartache and its accompanying pain. Any situation that leaves you with that rock of self-disgust in the bottom of your stomach.

A heavy, mucous covered ball of muck that takes over your soul when you're filled with doubt, or even worse, have knowingly done something stupid, is beginning to form in the back of my throat. However, the sun streaming in from the hotel window warming my naked legs reminds me that things almost always look different in the morning. Stretching out, a moan escapes my lips as my eyes flutter open. My skin tingles and burns with the memories of yesterday, and I smile at how the intensity of the last few days ignites me as much as the hot summer sun. Tousling my short dark hair, I kick off the tangled covers and allow myself to bask in a fleeting moment of self-awareness. For the first time in my life, I am living it my way, but the verdict is out on whether or not it is the *right* way.

Have you ever found yourself so lost in finding who you are that you have to fly to find your own feet? I'd arrived in New York only a few days ago, but considering what had transpired since, you would think otherwise. Those days feel like months, and as I reach for my cell off the side table, all I can do is smile. Yesterday had been a whirlwind, and I am waking with a new excitement. Anxiously anticipating the text I've been waiting for all night, my heart pounds as my phone comes to life.

<BITCH!! You haven't called me yet?! What the fuck are you doing?>

My ride or die best friend Monica at 1:30am. Her complete disdain for a person's sleep schedule is predictable and definitely normal, so it doesn't shake me—yet anyway. I scroll through.

<Katarina, call me. I just want to make sure you're alive. I'm on nights, so text me if it's early that's fine.>

I furrow my brow. Mom's message came in after her night shift. She's never slept the same since my dad broke her heart. I was eight years old when he took a lover and moved away. She'd always joked she could never compete against another man, but I knew it still bothered her. My heart aches for her, thinking how lonely she must be with my brother and I both gone now too. But I can't think like that. I expect her to be concerned, but it isn't the text I want.

Flutters of uncertainty start crawling on my skin as I try swallowing the sour spit forming in my mouth. My thumb halts on the screen, and I bite my lip, unsure if I am ready for the last and final text.

<Welcome to The Hotel at Times Square, please let us know about your stay. Click the link below.> Received 10:43pm.

I frown, tears prickling at my nose. A mix of emotions including anxiety, embarrassment, and what the fuck consume me. Falling back aggressively, I lie there for a moment, staring at the water-stained ceiling and sigh. The lump grows bigger in my throat, acidity burns my tongue, and the headache creeping across my eyelids adds to the discomfort. I cover my eyes with my hands. Please tell me I'm not wrong; not *this* wrong. Not again. I find my finger and thumb stuck in my eyeballs as tears start forming and my nose begins to fill, reminding myself that Self-doubt always takes center stage. Well, she isn't coming on this trip.

I shake my head, letting out a long, shaky breath. *Not this time, Katarina, you've got this. Right?*

Jumping out of bed, I put a wide smile on my face and pad over to the mirror. My room is small with a queen bed, a few lamps, one side table, and a phone that doesn't work. The TV is set on top of an old cherry wood dresser, previously expensive, placed against the wall of cheap brown and gold wallpaper, ripped in spots. This may be New York, but I have no money, and this is expensive enough. The window has sheers and a blind that works, perfect. Outside the window are endless tall buildings—huddled close together with their water towers that make New York unique. My god, it is cool. The bathroom is off the front door, and all I can say about it is that it's clean and has hot water. I'd been able to find this place with the help of my older brother, Johnathan. Alone, with no plan and barely any money, I wouldn't have put myself here in the first place if my life hadn't come to a complete halt, filled with self-loathing and regrets.

Getting ready for the day, I leave my phone on the bathroom counter so I can talk over speaker and call Mom. It's clear she was sleeping before she answered.

"Hey, Mom, sorry to wake you," I speak into the phone, her picture staring back at me.

"It's fine, I'm glad to hear from you. You're making out ok?" she says in a sleepy haze.

"So far so good, nothing to worry about," I mumble through toothpaste spit. "Great first weekend, saw a lot and found the best little café." I decide to leave it at that, knowing she'll freak out or have something negative to say to add to my failing nerves. "I'll let you go, I'm just heading out the door, ok?" I lie, spitting out my toothpaste.

"Alright, proud of you. Talk later."

That was interesting. I don't hear that from her often, or ever. I chalk it up to over tiredness and laugh. "Ok, I'll call you later," I say and hang up the phone.

Staring at myself in the mirror, I try to focus on the spark in my green eyes. What was it that Monica had said? Right. 'Chase your dreams as stupid as they seem.' Right now, I am trying to remember what those dreams are, or if I even have any worth any salt. Why had I come to New York again? Ah, because Matt hates New York, and I hate Matt. It was surprising when he broke it off right after college graduation, I mean, who does that? And sure, it could've been the catalyst that sent me nose diving into this dark hole, but really, it had been coming all along.

"Katarina," he'd said, "we're just not working out anymore."

This part was true, but what he failed to mention was that he wanted to enter his post-graduate studies, assumed although not confirmed, with Carla Hennicky from down the street. Regardless, we had parted ways, adding 'single woman' to my repertoire of failures and sealing the deal on my lonely and pointless future.

Monica always had my back and came flying in with a joint and a bottle of cheap Merlot. Getting fully fucked up and emotional on silly smoke, she'd tried comforting me. "Bah, you don't need him, Kat. He wasn't your type anyway," she'd said, flicking her hand and dismissing any feelings that could've been circulating in the air like a speck of dust. She'd continued with the assumption, "I know you loved him, Hunny."

I hadn't really, but whatever. I wasn't invested in him. I was hungry and searching for what or who completed me. But I let Monica go on with her way of picking up the pieces of my shattered heart.

"You don't need him in your life, fuck him!" She took a pull from the joint and passed it over.

I shrugged. "Yeah, I know, but it sucks. With or without him, there's something missing. I just don't know what." Slipping inward I'd whispered, "I don't know where to go from here."

A new graduate in social work, I felt lost and defeated and definitely not an asset in my field. Hanging my head, I stared at the dashboard of her rusting out Pontiac, hoping the answers would fly at me through the air vents.

"You listen to me!" she'd snapped, grabbing my face, and squishing my lips together like a fish. "You need to know your worth and never settle. Life is vibrant and crazy and fucked up. Who gives a shit? Live your life on your terms, do what you want and go after your fantasies. You want to live out your fantasy, don't you?"

Trying to convince her I wasn't drowning in doubt, I'd muttered something that had sounded like 'yes, of course' to which she had shrieked back at me, "Okay, so whatchya gonna do about it, pissy pants?"

That had stopped me. What was I going to do? I was lost and broken, but not because of a boy. I had done it to myself. And she had made a good point: I wasn't doing anything about it.

"Fuck it," I spat. Monica stared at me, bewildered by my unusual outburst, and I stared right back. "I'm going to New York," I told her defiantly and with personal conviction.

Her reaction was to choke on her inhale. She stopped, looked at me with stars in her eyes, and the corners of her lips turned into a slight smile. She started to laugh. She laughed and laughed, holding onto her perfectly tight midriff, her blonde hair flowing behind her as she cocked her head back in judgmental joy.

It pissed me off but fueled me even more, and three weeks later I cleaned out my savings and caught a train to the Big Apple with her hooting up a storm of support. Up until meeting Johnathan in the city, I'd never done anything outside my hometown. He was on his way home from backpacking across most of Europe and agreed to meet in New York to help me find a hotel or hostel.

Although, I have a sneaky suspicion my mother had a lot to do with that. While he is the world traveller, I live scared of my own shadow, taking second seat to the darkness of my fears. I'm lonely and hate it, so I try filling the void with everything but the right things.

I had conquered the small-town college scene, gained experience in dead-end jobs, and had my fair share of one-night stands leading to nowhere. It was time to break the cycle and find a way to face my fears head-on. Deciding I wanted to do it right, I arranged for a work Visa so my mother wouldn't entirely lose her shit.

Turning on the shower, I glance at my reflection in the mirror. In that split second, I see her: the girl waiting. Big green eyes, short dark hair and the fit runner's body I work my ass off to keep up. With summer skies and longer days, my skin is kissed by what my dad would call 'little bits of brown sugar.' I scrunch up my nose, the little dots aren't obtrusive, but I hate them anyway. Is there anything else that can possibly make me even more different than my peers? Settling back into my current reality, I sigh and shake my head. Standing tall, I square off my shoulders and refocus on the today and now. The goal is to find a local bookstore more eclectic and inspiring than the regular Barnes and Noble, and that is what I am going to do. I love reading and cherish the 'escape from life' it equips me with. I want a life with adventure, but the reality is, when faced with it in real time, I close the book before the Chapter even gets started.

Although, this last weekend had been far from my comfort zone. My eyes spark and I begin to blush; a pair of hazel eyes shake my psyche. It isn't like me to talk to strangers, but now that I had, I find myself wondering what this Chapter I've stumbled into might end up looking like. I huff as a huge wave of self-loathing nausea plays in my throat. If I could just erase all my character traits—yes, all of them, even the good ones. I check my phone again; it is after nine and still nothing.

Sighing, I shudder away from all the negative narratives creeping into my cruel head. God, I wish I could stop doubting myself for one goddamn minute. But after what I'd exposed… I hesitate a bit with my thought. Can I trust another to keep my secret and to keep it from biting me in the ass?

I let the water stream down my body, playing over my first day in New York, a mere three days ago, but so much has changed. When I had been wandering around like a lost and scared puppy, in truth, I had been quite grateful for his invitation. There was something about him and the way we jived that I couldn't put my finger on, but it was definitely holding my interest. Had he seen something that morning I have yet to see in myself, or was I desperate enough to seek a truth in what might have been a well-played con?

After throwing on jean shorts and a black tank, I sweep one more layer of gloss over my lips as I mutter to myself about getting a grip. There's a reason he hasn't reached out, there has to be, and patience will be my virtue. Grabbing the room key and my purse with its usual ingredients, I head out the door, mustering up as much confidence my failing heart will allow.

Chapter 2: Katarina

Out in the hallway, an older man is struggling, trying to get into the room beside mine. Hunched over, he has his cane tucked under his arm, balancing a cup of coffee, awkwardly attempting to open the door with his key.

"These fucking imbeciles," he mutters. "I swear to God they're all fucking idiots. Living here as long as I have, you'd think they'd remember to replace my coffee packets. Fucking pain in the ass."

He drops his door key and curses again, so I pipe in, offering, "Hey, you need a hand with that?"

Bent down, he turns his head to look at me. "Fuck," he says, clearly to himself. Staring at the carpeted floor he retrieves his key while balancing his cane in his armpit. "Nope. All good, tourist. How long you staying here for?" His manner is patronizing, showing no real interest as he stands, avoiding eye contact.

"Couple months, for now," I reply, unsure of this crochety old man.

"Fucking great. New neighbours," he mutters. Rude and sharp he adds, "Well, keep it down, ok? Don't be bringing home parties and shit."

"Don't worry about me," I confirm, adding, "Great city, though, isn't it?" Unsure if he is a tourist or maybe a hotel employee.

Looking at me sideways, he grumbles, "It's a shithole." And is gone, slamming the door in his wake.

Taken aback, I start towards the elevator and mutter, "Ok. See you…"

Well, my first nasty American, and I'm living right beside him. Great. At least it is real. I don't want this trip being all sunshine and roses, anyway. That is not what I am here for. I want real life, all of it: the good, the bad, and the ugly.

Streetside, I begin the walk towards Gloria's Café. My hotel is located on 45th, between 5th and 6th, a few blocks from Rockefeller Center and Time Square, giving me prime access to anything and everything the city has to offer. I think of *him* and how he'd been so kind, taking me to all the touristy places, appeasing my wonder.

I roll my eyes. I must have reeked of ignorance and a lack of sophistication, making it nearly intolerable for another human. Maybe I will feel better today, venturing out alone just like I had the day we met. But there is something about how we connected that speaks to my journey of self-discovery. Our meeting felt invigorating, like he was meant to be here for more than just the ride. I check my phone again, still nothing. Unlike the last two days, we hadn't made plans to meet this morning, but after no response since we'd parted ways, I was beginning to wonder if I should doubt that intense connection. Is he ghosting me? Am I really that stupid? And why am I going to Gloria's now? If I am being honest with myself, I'm silently hoping to run into him, and that makes me feel juvenile, uncomfortable even. I remind myself that people have lives, people other than me, that is, and I desperately need to be un-desperate.

Arriving at Gloria's, I swing open the glass door of the corner café. The building is old, but this space is bright and airy. Not what I'd imagined in New York where everything is old and dark. The scaffolding outside the windows retains the ancient architecture; it also shadows the inside by stealing the light.

The order counter is filled with pastries, cookies, and sandwiches, while the remaining space holds tables for two strewn about the penny tiled floor. Glass windows grace the entire front of the café, and the few remaining walls are painted light green. I'd been introduced to Gloria a few days ago but wonder if she even remembers me.

I grab my latte and smile at the young man behind the counter before maneuvering to find myself a seat. Grabbing one by the window, I sigh and sink into the chair, watching the world pass outside as I contemplate the waves of my feelings. My thoughts are consumed by the weekend, and I struggle to find where I may have misread or misjudged any character, both his and mine. Surely, I'm not this naïve? Monica always has all the answers, so after I peel the lid off my steaming coffee, I dial her number.

Her bubbly little face icon stares at me, but there is silence on the other end, "Monica, you there?"

Whispering, she says, "Hey, girl, yeah. Can I call you later? I've got a bug."

I hold back a chuckle. Using the code we have for being indisposed, usually with a man, is her way of telling me to fuck off. I smile. "Yeah, of course. I've got a bug here, too, turned out to be a butterfly. Call me whenever," I say, a wink in my voice. I don't have a lot of friends, but Monica accepts me for exactly who I am. If I go anywhere, it is usually with her, which makes this solo trip even more daring.

I go back to staring out the window, the buildings are a mix of ancient architecture with the right amount of avant-garde. Incredibly, it all works together and is like nothing I've ever seen before. Filled with fancy businesses and million-dollar apartments, the city reminds me of a grandmother's living room you aren't allowed to touch. I feel small and insignificant, like I am intruding on the history and culture of the city. It is massive and intimidating, and once again I realize how, in so many ways, I am lost.

My god, how am I going to do this alone? Lifting my head high, I look up and forward; there is no looking back now. It doesn't matter where you are in this city, there are people everywhere. The homeless scatter around every inch with their cups and dirty blankets. It bothers me, but it is a real part of life. What had happened in their lives to bring them here? Can I help them? And what makes them any different from me or any of my loved ones?

Outside, there is so much going on, too many damn people.

When I'd been to Time Square, dancers had blared music from a vintage boombox gaining the attention of tourists that had crowded around in a circle. Policemen leaned against buildings or rode horses, watching and protecting. There was a Statue of Liberty impersonator posing with tourists. Characters such as Spiderman and Penguin, and girls dressed like Japanese anime selling lit up balloons. But the lights! Oh my god, the lights were bright and high making my head spin. They flickered constantly with advertisements on the latest stars, movies, and Broadway shows. A huge set of red stairs sat in the middle of the two streets of the square filled with tourists. It was beyond what I'd ever dreamt about.

Three days ago, I had walked toward Central Park. It had been hot, and the smell of the streets permeated the air. The city was jarringly busy as people hustled to work, bicycle taxis whizzed by, and runners deafened by headphones took their morning run. I had clearly been in the way. Tightening my purse across my body, I'd been making sure it was zipped closed with my passport, cash, and ID safely tucked inside.

Everyone had their purpose that day, from the artists sketching to musicians playing their chosen instrument. The traffic, along with people fighting for their space, was pure chaos. Trying to get my bearings, I'd almost not heard the voice cutting through the commotion.

"Hey, red shirt!" pierced the air, above all the other noise, catching my attention. Looking through the crowd, I wondered what all the yelling was about?

"Hey, red shirt, short hair!"

I had distinctly heard someone above the buzz of the city. Expecting a street performer trying to get the attention of a paying tourist, I had turned to see the most handsome man standing still against a building wall. He was leaning with his foot propped up, clad in expensive black leather boots with his hands comfortably resting in the pockets of his gray pants. He was tall, with a crisp white dress shirt and a reckless mess of dark curls. He was the only other person standing still.

Him and me.

But where I was lost and confused, he was clearly sure of himself, his surroundings, and what he was looking at. This man in his late twenties was distinctly staring in my direction. Calm and confident, he had a smile on his face that lit the day up even brighter than it already was.

Chapter 3: Katarina

"Hey," he'd shouted a little softer, "Red Shirt."

I was getting knocked around, and as I looked down, I realized I was wearing my favourite Queen's University shirt in red with black jeans and beige Converse. My hair, as it had been since college, was short and textured, some of which was probably sticking straight up. This man, whoever he was, was talking to me.

"Can I take you for a coffee?" His eyes gleamed, demanding my attention.

I squinted in response. *What the actual fuck?* Did this man—this very handsome man—just ask me out for coffee in the middle of New York City?

"I'm sorry?" I said, moving a little closer as I was bumped from behind by a group of schoolgirls in uniforms heading to summer school, or cutting it.

I knew there were a lot of crazies in the world, New York City being the mecca of such personalities, but I didn't expect one to look as put together, clean, and handsome as this man leaning coolly against the wall.

People were still knocking me all over the place as he just leaned there, rested and content with, I swear, a snicker under his breath.

"Sorry... were you talking to me?"

Calmly he replied, "Are you wearing a red shirt and have short hair?"

I flushed, feeling embarrassed. "Well, yes, I suppose I am. I do."

"Well, then, I'm talking to you," he purred with his head down slightly, his eyes averted upwards so he could still see me, like he was hiding.

"Did you just ask me for coffee? Is that what you said?" Sauntering closer, I questioned him with a standoffish, challenging tone. As striking as he was, this was New York after all, and I knew enough to be on guard at all times.

I put my hand on my purse and glanced down to make sure it was still zippered. He noticed and said curtly, "I'm not trying to rob you. I'm simply asking to take you for a coffee." He looked quizzically at me, still leaning against the brick building. "What's your name?" he asked, pushing off the wall and challenging my personal space before resting back on his side so he could stay against the wall, but giving me room to join him. I did and got myself out of the way of fellow New Yorkers.

"Katarina," I said, looking him over questioningly as we stood a few feet apart.

"Katarina..." he whispered to himself as he tilted his head and looked downwards at the pavement. He grinned, and I could see him turning it over in his mind, almost as if he were re-mouthing the word. Taking it in, putting it in a little box with a ribbon only to pull it out again later and savour it all alone with a cup of tea and a cookie.

Looking back up at me, he cast a winning smile as his curly hair rustled in the wind, a loose curl fell into his eye. His soft lips curved, showing strong white teeth that were as perfect as the stars in the sky. I'd never seen teeth like that before, and I must have looked as stunned as I felt when he reached his hand towards me and said, "Nice to meet you, *Katarina*."

Feeling like a dumbed-out schoolgirl, I took this stranger's hand in the middle of the noise of New York, and shook it, our hands holding the moment. It was slow and savoury: up, down, up, down, up, down, while the world paused, quieted, and waited for us. His hands were soft, fingers long. Friendship bracelets of some kind adorned his wrist, making me pause as I thought they were odd, juvenile. Taken aback by the boldness of this stranger who had stopped me on the street, I jolted back to reality, and in a slightly annoyed, awkward voice said, "Thank you. And you are?"

"Ben," he'd replied. He had a gorgeous mouth, flawless skin and tousled curls of glorious rich brown. I could see he had hazel eyes, shining like I imagined the pond in the middle of Central Park on a sunny day would. The name shocked me.

"Ben?" I questioned with a confused look. Given his stature, clothing, and overall demeanour I had expected a name like Roman, Xavier, or... or Julian. Something more distinguished.

Then, like the idiot I am, I blurted out to Mr. Handsome, "Ben? You mean Benji, like a pet? Or someone's dog?"

Still holding my hand, he pulled his away and stuffed it into the pocket of his grey slacks. Throwing his head back and shaking his curls out of his eyes, he nodded with a chuckle and said, "Yes, yes. I suppose you're right. A lot of people name their pets Ben, or Benji."

Our eyes connected, and I felt my heart flutter.

"Although, no one ever said it to me before... at least not to my face."

He turned and gave me a sideways teasing smirk, and I wondered if he always did that? Look at people from the side, sheltering them from fully seeing him. A sly glance to test, as opposed to a full-on study of the person with whom he was engaged. I'd later find out exactly how he looked at people, and how he looked at me.

Trying to gain my composure, my face turned bright red, matching my shirt, and I said, "Shit, I'm sorry. I didn't mean to be rude or hurtful. I'm just…" looking around, tears almost formed in my eyes, "as cliché as it sounds, in a strange city," I continued, suddenly feeling exasperated, accepting that I was lost, overwhelmed and a bit confused.

"I don't know anyone else here, you're pretty much the first person who's talked to me. I just got here yesterday." I wondered if he'd noticed my ignorance. Was I as exposed as I felt with this stranger, and could he see right through me?

Rocking back and forth on his feet, he nodded. "Ohhh, I see. You rarely see people twice in this city," he stated. "I thought there was something different about you. Tourist for sure, but also… different, like you belong here but don't know it yet. That's why I blurted out my invitation. I hope I didn't scare you."

"Scare me? Belong here? Definitely not," I replied, laughing awkwardly and shaking my head. No way. I'm not scared at all. Serial killers are all devilishly handsome, wearing perfectly pressed white shirts open slightly at the neck, soft pants, and sexy leather boots, and yell out to you in the street as you walk by. "No, not scared... just taken off guard, really. As I said, I haven't met anyone yet. I'm just trying to learn my way around." I point out towards the craziness.

"Understandable," Ben replied almost to himself, with a curt nod pushing himself off the wall. "Well, if you decide to accept my offer, and I don't repulse you by the time we're done, I could show you some great spots—help you get around without getting ripped off—and take you to the best place to get a morning coffee and pastry... if you eat gluten that is?"

The truth was I was starving, and although there were places to eat absolutely everywhere, I had no idea where to start. If I were being honest with myself, I needed the opportunity to sit somewhere a little quiet, gather my thoughts, and just look at a fucking map for a minute before I started wandering aimlessly around.

"Well?" He prodded.

I was still nervous, but also realized everyone around me was whizzing by; he had been the only one willing to offer any help, so I agreed with a slight shrug. "I guess it won't hurt. There are enough people around that if I start screaming my head off, someone will notice."

He grinned and nodded at this, chuckling a little. "You'd be surprised," he said.

I wasn't completely sure if he was joking, but I figured he must have been teasing me back after the whole "Ben the dog" comment and his wink my way.

Returning with a shy smile, I felt alright about my decision and drew my first boundary. "As long as you take me somewhere populated, just a little less hectic so I can adjust to all this?" I motioned again to the sights and sounds that made up the city.

"I can do that. I won't take you down any dark alleys, but," he winked, "you will have to stick close to me until I navigate us out of here." He raised his eyebrow and gave me a crooked smile.

Laughing, I blushed, embarrassed by my first impression and how I was coming across. "Lead the way, Ben, I'm all yours."

Taking me by the elbow, his hand was surprisingly warm and soft on my bare skin. He steered me so I was beside him.

"Let's see if we can turn this into a day of it," he proclaimed confidently and without hesitation. His manner struck me and made my stomach flutter a bit.

Closer to him, I looked up and noticed how much taller he was than me, about a foot or so, with a chiselled face and strong jawline. He smelled glorious, a little woodsy and hot like he'd just chopped trees in a forest, and his skin was still glowing from exertion. There was an added sweetness of a warm subtle spice drifting into my nose, like that of a fall drink I'd wrapped my hands around.

We began weaving through the other bodies, and I felt discombobulated. In the most pressing of times, he'd slip his long fingers down my arm, grabbing my wrist with a strong grip. Owning the city like a captain of his own waters, he pulled me behind him as he made his way through traffic. His scent wafted into my nostrils, so I had no choice but to breathe him in and all the complexities that came with him.

After a few minutes we turned a corner, putting us on a wide main street where the panic and crowds seemed to stop. There was a break in the tall buildings, opening to the sky above us. He quickly looked both ways and darted into traffic, crossing the double lanes, pulling me close behind. Dodging cars was exciting, and on his arm I felt safe. As my nerves jittered, and my toes skipped, I grinned like an excited girl scout. Safely across, we entered a glass door with a name etched on the front that I didn't catch.

He shouted out, "Gloria! How are you?" He waved his hand in the air.

An older woman with short curly hair, greying at the temples, lifted her head from behind the counter and replied, "Benjamin! Great to see you." She returned the wave with a friendly smile.

"Nice place, you must know her?" I nodded my head towards the older woman he'd greeted as Gloria.

"Yes, I know her well. She sells pastries my parents' maid, Nancy, makes." He smiled down at me. "I honestly think Nancy just enjoys making them, and without anyone home, there's no one else to make them for. Her husband Geoff drives for us, and he drops them over every morning. You need to get here early to get one, but Gloria usually keeps a few for me. She knows I love them."

"Driver?" I questioned, who the heck was this fancy guy? "You have a personal driver?" His hand grazed my back as he ushered me towards the counter. A warm shock of tingles electrified my body, making my cheeks glow. I hoped he wouldn't notice. He dropped his hand from my back, and I instantly longed for another moment of his touch on my body.

"Nah." He smirked rolling his eyes. "Not really, my parents aren't as important as they'd like to think they are." Clearing his throat, he shook his head adding, "Geoff just likes to help out. Mom and Dad live in the Upper East side. It's impossible to get parking."

He seemed agitated, so I broke from his gaze muttering, "Oh, I get it… I think."

"What would you like? Coffee? One of those sweet fancy things?"

"Coffee's fine, thanks." The menu board spanned the entire back wall with thousands of drink options, but I was a simple girl. Frowning, I was unsure why I was concerned with what this man thought of me, but I was.

"Coffee it is." He placed the order with one of the baristas. Turning back to me, he said, "I hope this is safe enough for you? The baker has a mean streak in him if you're not careful." He smiled at me as he teased, releasing any unnecessary stress I was feeling. I was extremely over cautious and realized how stupid I looked.

"It is," I replied sheepishly. His eyes sparked with mischief, and I tried not to show my embarrassment, so I turned away to hide my blush and looked for an empty table. Spotting one tucked in a corner by the window, I pointed and suggested the empty spot.

"Yeah. Grab it before anyone else does, and I'll bring everything over. Danish? They're the best, I swear."

"Yes. Please."

Setting my things down on the fresh white table, I pulled out the accompanying chair. I waited and watched all the hubbub until Benjamin arrived with our order. He sat down and flicked a lock of hair off his face. We hadn't talked on our walk to the café, given the crowded streets, and as we sat together, I found my mouth stuck with glue.

"So, Canadian, are you?" he questioned, taking me by surprise.

I was impressed by his solid intuition.

"Oh! How do you know I'm not from Florida or Chicago," I inquired, an interested smile crossing my lips.

"Chicago? Please, no one admits they're from Chicago. Why would you come to New York, anyway? Besides, it's obvious."

Offended, I took the bait. "Wow, okay. And what makes you say that?"

"Well, first of all, your t-shirt." He grinned and started to laugh.

Fuck. My face burned as I looked down. Feeling incredibly stupid, I noticed my t-shirt clearly stated Kingston, Ontario, Canada.

He continued to chuckle and said, "You also apologize a lot... Aaand you came over to me when I called out to you." He ripped his Danish in two and looked up at me ever so slightly.

What now? I raised my brows, insulted that he was insinuating I had been overly eager to accept his advances on the street. Was I the dog now? "What do you mean? I definitely didn't run to your side. Besides, how does that make me Canadian?" I ripped my Danish so aggressively that it flew everywhere, making him sit back in surprise.

"Whoa ok, crazy Canuck." He leaned back in his chair, his hands raised in defence. "I didn't mean to offend. I'm just saying Americans aren't that trusting."

Feeling my back stiffen, I thought seriously of just getting up and leaving him there. His chair legs tipped back down to the floor as he leaned forward, placing his hand over mine, looking me straight in the eye.

"I'm sorry," he purred, and I felt my face heat up like a volcano.

"It's fine." I mumbled, my mouth full of flaky Danish.

He pulled his hand away, and I stole an upwards glance at him; once again, I missed his touch.

The silence became awkward. Who was this guy with his pretty hair? He was cocky, thinking he knew who I was and why I was here. It seemed to me he was a pretty boy with house servants, a driver, and never heard the word no.

"I am sorry, truly. Don't feel embarrassed," he soothed leaning in closer. "It's a good thing. Canadians are so friendly. They welcome people for who they are and are less judgemental. Not that I've ever been, but I've heard from friends who have. Places like Toronto, that's the big city, right?" He teased and I gave him a friendly glare.

"Yes, it's a city. I grew up outside of there. I'm not as naive as you think, you know."

"Naive? I never said that about you. You girl, are saying that about yourself, don't put that on me!"

"Ok, fair. I'll give you that." I looked outside. "I love the energy of the city. You?" I sipped my coffee as our conversation softened. The Danish was incredible, and it must've shown on my face.

"Like it?" he said pointing at my plate.

"Yeah, it's really good. I like the cream cheese in the middle." This pleased him, and I felt my face blush this time for a reason I couldn't quite put my finger on.

"City life is ok if you can handle the calamity. Sometimes I wish I could shut it all down, you know? The noise, that is. Makes it hard to sleep."

I nodded in response.

It was a simple enough conversation, but there was something buzzing around us. An energy I couldn't explain. Maybe excitement, maybe fear. Maybe the vibe came directly from him but whatever it was, it was electrifying, and I think we both felt it. I thought fatal attraction was bullshit, and I was not a hopeless romantic, I had too many scars for that shit.

Most of the time, I was a good judge of character, but men weren't exactly my strong suit. Probably because I blinded myself from red flags to fill a void. But this guy felt different. I could sense a lonely boy inside a successful, good-looking man. Asking a random woman to coffee and his ringless hand, I assumed I was probably right.

"So, what brings you to New York?" His deep voice interrupted my thoughts.

I couldn't help being intrigued by this man, but was I going to expose myself to this stranger, let him inside, and divulge my reasons for coming here? The complexities that lead to me navigating my personal journey solo and for choosing New York as the epicentre to do it all? Believing I had to stand on my own two feet but was petrified to fall? If being truthful was the best way to start any possible friendship, then the moment had been given. The challenge was trying to express myself while keeping my heart and soul guarded. At the time, I'd chosen to jump in with both feet and throw caution to the wind.

"I came here to figure some shit out, I guess."

His face had been expressionless, so I looked toward the window and continued, "I'm a social worker, specializing in young people. But I'm young…" I'd looked down and twisted my hands. "I gotta find a way to grow up and grab life with less fear. Give myself some ground to work with. Before I go around trying to save other people, I need to save myself."

His head was cocked to the side, a peculiar look in his eyes, but I went on, "I figured being alone I could experience things without a safety net. If I live outside my comfort zone and push myself, I can mould my personality before exposing who I am to the world. And if I stay neutral, I can change my narrative whenever the fuck I want. Be whoever I want—especially when no one knows me. In a city as big as this, I can be someone new every day." Turning to look directly at him, I pointedly added, "I want to offer something, be someone who makes a difference, and I don't really care how cheesy that sounds. There aren't enough people in the world who are genuine enough to really give a shit about helping others and not wanting anything in return. But if it's gonna work, I need to suit up with some armour first. I don't expect it'll be easy."

Something flashed in his eyes that I couldn't read, but I felt inclined to continue. "I hate being alone and decided I need to conquer that fear before I ever find true connection." An imaginary blast of air left my chest like a release valve. I had just expressed what my intentions were, and in turn, realized what I hadn't yet really figured out. My reason why was in front of my face, and all I had to do was grab it and make it happen.

"Hmm," he said and sat back in his seat.

Was he interested or bored? I didn't know. I was suddenly feeling awkward that maybe I'd been too personal. Shaking the thought away, I realized that this was part of the fear: expressing myself regardless of what is accepted or unconventional. For the first time ever, I felt confident and careless of what anyone else thought.

"Well, before you go saving yourself and conquering the world, you need to know the best places to eat. Would you like to meet Gloria? She won't provide you with any netting, but if you ever feel scared, she will keep her door open and always has a fresh pot of coffee. Do you know where you are now?"

Thankful for the change in conversation, I sighed and put on a smile.

"Well, no, not really. But I think I could be near my hotel considering New York square is… that way?" I pointed.

"It sure is. We're at 49th and 6th." He smiled. "We'll figure out where your hotel is from here. Show me your map."

I took out the tourist map I'd picked up at the hotel lobby and was delighted when he scraped his chair over and huddled in closer. The heat between us made the butterflies in my stomach explode. His cologne kept me fixated on his skin rather than the map. New York was a grid, and I could easily get around where I was going to be living for the next few months.

After a while, he tipped back on his chair and said, "So, it's a gorgeous day. I suggest we start at Central Park."

We?

He looked at me full on, probably waiting for my reaction. When I stalled, he said, "I've repulsed you? Shit. I was hoping I wouldn't. I just thought Central Park is so big it's easy to get lost... I mean, it's safe, don't worry, but you can spend a lot of time wandering aimlessly if you haven't been before. There will be a lot of musicians and performers there today too, and I'd hate to see you get swindled into dropping twenty bucks for a photo op."

I thought about it as he got up, grabbed my dishes, and just walked away without warning. I realized I didn't want him to go. When he returned, I was ready to accept his idea, but he was preoccupied by his phone and very jittery. Nevertheless, I'd already decided I'd love to have him show me around.

"I'd like that!"

"What?" He wore a scowl and furrowed brow, spitting the word at me while he'd stayed focused on his phone.

"Umm... I'd like you to join me in Central Park today. I mean, if you want to…" I trailed off, wondering where the light in the air had gone. I realized I had no idea who this man was and what had brought him to the city on a Friday morning. I was glad we had met, but at the same time I was beginning to doubt my ability to make my own decisions. Perhaps putting my trust in people quite so quickly was something I should reconsider.

He looked up at me then, stress clearly in his eyes as they glossed over, his expression hard to read while he put his phone back in his pocket. With a sharp clap of his hands his eyes lit up like fireworks, and I jumped.

"Great!" He grabbed my arm, yanking me up to standing position. "Get your stuff. Let's go."

Not asking permission, and with all the confidence in the world, he pulled me towards the kitchen shouting, "Gloria, I'd like you to meet Katarina. She's from Canada!" Seemingly proud of his newfound friend.

"Katia-who?" she asked, moving towards us as she wiped her hands of flour.

"It's Katarina," Ben said to her when she arrived, casting me a big smile.

"Oh, that's different, although here in the city you can pretty much call yourself whatever you want. So, a Canadian, huh? Never been out of the city, myself," she said with a hint of a New York accent.

I blushed, hating my name and feeling embarrassed in front of Ben as it became a weird focus in our introduction.

"It's ok," I said, taking her outstretched hand. "I get it all the time." My name was often misheard or misunderstood, and when I met new people, I usually had to explain it. They would then feign interest or intrigue, making me feel exposed because it was different, meaning I was different. Too much onus on a name? Maybe, but either way, it made it hard for me to make friends confidently.

"Well, it's just as pretty you are." She pinched my cheek and added, "I'm always here if you need something to eat. I'll serve anyone, but the pretty ones always get served first." She winked at me and then cast a side eye glance to Ben, and I wondered how many girls Ben 'asked to coffee.'

"Thanks, I'm sure I'll take you up on that."

Ben was already walking towards the door, and I scurried to catch up. He was one of the few to ever get my name right in recent time, and I mentioned it as we walked out to the blossoming heat of almost ten o'clock.

"You said my name right."

"Yeah, why wouldn't I? It's pretty simple," he responded curtly. He seemed tense and nervous now that we were on the street.

"It's just that no one usually does, is all," I muttered. He was clearly not listening—his demeanor having turned cool. He looked agitated and annoyed, and I wondered what I'd said to make his mood change so quickly.

"I've gotta take this call," he said. "Shit. I forgot." Mumbling to himself, he looked like he could possibly be entering full on panic mode. Then he looked at me stone cold and ordered, "Just wait right here. Don't leave. I'll be right back."

Irritated and flustered, I didn't like him this way. It made me nervous, and I wondered where the guy I was with just a second ago. Taking off back into the café, he had whipped out his phone. When he yelled into it, looking panicked and angry, I contemplated walking away and moving on with my day without him. But I didn't have his number and wanted to at least thank him for the coffee. So, I had stayed against the window, waiting for this erratic but exciting stranger to come back outside.

And now I am waiting again. Filled with angst and uncertainty, sweating in self-condemnation. Something is screaming at me that my old habits are getting in the way again, as the world passes me by. I have to gather myself and my nerves if I'm going to move forward. Maybe delving into a best-selling novel will melt the hours away—and maybe my phone will ping when I least expect it.

Gathering my things, I kick my own ass and leave the corner café. I get as far as the outside window and rest against the same glass I had a few days ago. My journey of self-realization has grabbed a handsome hitchhiker, and the heavy voice of doubt starts to shout above the others.

I'm not looking at my damn phone again. The ringer is on loud and clear, set to buzz with every notification. I'll be getting more action from my mobile vibrator than my cell. He hasn't called, texted, or emailed, and any of the pigeons I saw in the city were not the mail carrier type. *You've done it, Katarina; you've royally fucked up.*

Chapter 4: Benjamin

I wish life had a rewind button, so I could reverse time by three days and avoid meeting her completely. Why I even started this mess, I'm still trying to figure out. But she had called to me, standing in the mayhem, just waiting for me to break into her world. The way she'd looked confused and maybe even overwhelmed stirred something deep within me. I'd wanted to help her, needed to. She'd looked so alone, and I'd studied her for a good minute or two, liking the way her big eyes took everything in and how the curve of her back made her butt stick out, high and tight, her breasts cut in two by the strap of her purse that she clutched for dear life. Soft hair dying for my fingers to pull on and a pair of lips so delicious I wanted to taste them even now. She wasn't from around here, that was for absolute sure.

I swallow my feelings and cringe. Being stuck here is a problem I can't figure out how to solve. A problem that is going to lead to other problems quickly. No one is going to understand unless I give everything up and that is not going to happen. Not yet, anyway. So, I sit in the dark, rocking with knees to chest, tears threatening to stream down my face, and I know I'm in deep. Too deep, and there is no way of getting out of it this time. I'm going to have to play this game he wants to play. If I don't, the consequences are going to be real. Real and life changing. *I might play along, but I won't forget mother fucker, there's no way I'm ever going to forget.*

To pass the inevitable beast of time that can be hours or days, all I can do is live within the walls of my memory. A memory that is too good to be true, but one I'm not willing to let go of. Her. The way she smiled up at me when I spoke had a way of crushing all the bricks I'd built around myself. Her walk was light and her hair a little messy like she'd just woken up. But she was so free about it, like a little bird. Free as a bird.

I smile. It sounds nice, to be free like that.

Steps come down the hall, and my heart begins to race, panic slowly creeping in. There isn't much around me but a pencil and notebook. I scramble towards them, figuring if he sees me writing in deep concentration he'll be appeased and leave me alone. I'll write, and maybe leave a little tidbit for the masked fools when there's nothing left to beat down. Words can build or break, but once they're out there, no matter the outcome, you can't get them back. It's better than nothing, so I start. And I start with the day my little bird flew into my shattered life.

I hadn't slept well—I never do, but that morning there was a consequence. Waking late had me increasingly moody and agitated. *Of all the fucking Fridays.* In shear panic mode, I'd shaved my face and threw away my tie. I had breathed deeply and reminded myself I was respected at work and had to keep it that way. The ladies adored me, of course, but a pretty face and a smooth attitude wasn't going to keep me employed. My brother's office was a phone call away, and the last thing I needed was my disregard for punctuality getting back to him. He had got me the damn job in the first place.

My morning spiralled further when the taxi, smelling of rotten cheese, forced me to jump out into the chaotic sea of downtown Manhattan, further blowing any chance I had of being on time. My irritation rose with the onslaught of New York City noise. No matter how much silence I tried to surround myself with, it was never, ever quiet.

After a few blocks of dodging human bullets, I stopped, leaned against a building, and took a deep breath trying to block it all out. My father's voice rang in my ear on how I should 'calm down' and I 'wouldn't be in this predicament if I were more like my brother.' The hangover didn't help, either. I rummaged around in my pocket, found two Advil, and swallowed them with saliva.

Dear old Daddy sure had things figured out. Raising children in the city required a 'certain style of regiment.' He'd nailed it down, perfecting it, and no one was going to tell him any different. His psychiatric clinic was built on 'carefully planned referrals, influential attention, and prominent circles. That's how you attract high paying patients and build a practice, my boy.' Thanks to him I was a self-made jackass with more than enough money, but no pot to piss in that was actually my own.

He and my mother, she was a peach, were highly regarded in the city, packing our home every Friday night with the very elite. Doctors, professors, behavioral medicine scientists, their wives and or mistresses, depending on the week, snacked, and nattered and drank my father's most expensive wine. Thank God I'd moved out nearly three years ago, even if it was his fucking name on the condo lease.

Shaking the memory, I had darted back into human traffic. I'd assumed the New Yorker position by hanging my head, and again started dodging people. The level of frenzy reminded me of my mother's eyes. She was stern and quick with a little bit of wildness hiding in the darkness. Straight and to the point, her tongue was fierce, and she had no time for nonsense. Having kids had ended her dancing career, and didn't we know it. But opening 'Vivian's School for the Dance' became her legacy far more than her performances ever did. She was a tough teacher but produced some of the most talented dancers in the city.

I'd attended the best private schools with all the other privileged assholes. My parents had insisted on hours of lessons so that we were cultured. We hated it. I was cocky and confident but lacked any self-control. I started smoking pot in the backyard. By grade twelve, snorting lines to get through rigorous testing was the norm. Popularity was never a problem, and I attended all the scenes just to get out of that house. I took care of my body with coffee and cigarettes and had a strong slim build;

I was good-looking, and I knew it. Pussy was never a problem—they all just wanted to fuck, and it was New York after all—fucking was art.

But that Friday, I was screwed if I didn't get my ass to work and not in a fun way. They were always on me, and I had to stay diligent. After stopping to fish some change out for a homeless kid in the doorway, I forced a frustrated breath out, trying to shake my mood. When I opened my eyes, it was a whole new world.

Red Shirt. Short Hair.

Everyone else was running around like the New Yorkers they were—except her. Instantly intrigued, I was attracted to her like an invisible string pulling me to her body. Knowing I'd never see her again if I didn't move fast, I threw on some charm and called out to this beautiful stranger.

"Hey, red shirt!"

I can't believe she actually took me up on my initial invitation. I had felt the usual rush of emotions I experienced on days like that. Stress married to anger, circling around to agitation that inevitably invited anxiety and worry to jump on the train for another ride around town. I was giddy like a schoolboy and with that came a multitude of other emotions jumping alongside each other in the inflatable castle. Almost like I used to be when I was living by the seat of my pants, showing up at home wasted with half my clothes missing.

That was long ago, though. I was better now.

Between my brother's support and my father's prescription pad, I was a model citizen.

As we'd moved across the city, I got excited when the crazy ideas dominated. This young woman I pulled along behind me knew nothing about me, and that was the best part. I could be whoever I wanted to be, who I'd always wanted to be, and she wouldn't know the difference.

When we'd made it to Gloria's and talked, I was enraptured by her voice. She spoke so easily about herself, like she wasn't scared of who she was. She'd liked the Danish, and I'd beamed with pride that she was impressed. I didn't want to let her in, though. We made plans for the rest of the day. Well, I knew it would be the rest of the day, even if she didn't. She'd soon figure it out.

Then, the meeting I was missing had reared its ugly head as my phone buzzed insistently in my pocket, and almost sabotaged the whole plan. I mean, I had to leave her there on the sidewalk for a few minutes. *Don't you dare leave me.* I could feel the switch flick as I started yelling and screaming at my poor assistant who was only doing her job because I wasn't. Panicked, I sought out the privacy and safety of Gloria's bathroom, sinking to the floor.

Breathe, Ben. Breathe.

I'd sucked the stale air in as deep as I could, letting it out in a rush. Eyes closed, I'd tried to calm my racing heart. I told myself the call was over and to move past it. It dawned on me that it was now the weekend.

The weekend.

My eyes flashed open with animated excitement. Three days of freedom!

I had so much time before facing the team on Monday. *Relax, this is perfect.* I relished in the realization and relaxed my shoulders. After scrambling my ass off the floor and gathering my fragmented brain, I'd splashed water on my face, ensuring my eyes returned to normal before I ventured off to show this new sexy stranger the city only I could show her. Smiling to myself, I'd hailed a cab. She was mine; she'd said so. I had no idea what I was feeling at that point, but something strange was definitely happening. The way in which my name blessed her lips made me feel like a new man. A man without all… this.

My Mother insisted on calling us by full names like it was some title of authority and respect. Anyone who did differently was met with a glare that could eat them alive. Always correcting every fucking thing with that clicky snake tongue. *Fucking pretentious bitch.*

When Katarina said my name, it was like the purr of a kitten with fresh milk.

We'd started at the park and the little angel was mesmerized. She made me laugh as her eyes bulged out of her glorious lashes, and she practically skipped along the cobblestone pathways of the Literary Walk. She stopped in the middle of the path and stretched out her arms, beginning to spin. I laughed, the American Elm trees towering over us, stretching unapologetically, and framing her in a way an artist could only wish to paint.

"Stand there," I'd told her, to which she obliged. "Pass me your phone." Our fingers grazed each other's, and wild shocks had electrified my skin. She'd shuddered, looking at me and then quickly looked away. What was that? I didn't know but wanted to feel it again. I needed to hold onto my image of her and had to find a way without being too obvious. "Let me take your picture and then you can take one of me, ok?"

"Yeah, ok." She'd agreed, positioning into her spot and casting me a wide smile.

"Now hold it there and let me get one with my phone. You make New York look good." Finishing our photo op, we continued to walk, her eyes everywhere, but mine only on her.

"Where's that sound coming from, Ben? The singing?"

I looked around trying to locate the source, a gust of wind filled my nostrils with her sweet scent of vanilla and cocoa. I felt happy. And for the first time in a long time, I felt alive.

"Probably Bethesda Terrace," I realized, breaking my trance. "Most likely a Broadway singer practicing or making some extra coin. We can go check it out. It's just up ahead." I motioned down the path.

"Please, yes. Please!" she squealed; her eyes had widened like a child I'd just offered a lollipop. Her laughter echoed through the trees, a sound I was coming to love almost as much as the singing.

"This way, come."

The stunning Bethesda architecture came into view: three arched entrances at the base of a wide staircase that led to the historical site.

"This is Bethesda Terrace, like I was telling you. It was one of the first structures built in the park. He's singing in the covered Terrace—that's how he's making his voice echo like that," I explained.

"When we walk through, the fountain is on the other side. It's called the Angel Fountain, and the pond is just behind it."

She walked ahead, towards the singing man. He seemed lost in his own world. Tall and slim, he paced in slow circles, his hands flowing along with his harmony. A young man with a tan colored fedora and blue billowy shirt. The mixture of his voice along with the location created a scene straight out of a classic romance film. A small change pot at the edge of the space he'd claimed as his stage was surrounded by patrons tossing in change or small bills.

I'd stood still, watching her intently. She was gorgeous, and the sun's reflection off the floor of the Bethesda made her glow like an angel. She was so pure, clean, and innocent, but also sexy and mysterious. I knew she was having a good time. The day was all so natural, the two of us easily fitting together. When I did touch her, to grab her hand and lead the way, she took mine and trusted me, believed in me. There were sparks in my gut. She made me feel human yet extraordinary. I felt like I could be a regular guy with her by my side.

We talked about everything. Where she lived, her mother and her brother. She skirted over her father, but I didn't question her. She liked to talk and laugh. I could listen to her all day. I learned about her reasons for wanting to come to the city, alone and on her own, and couldn't help but feel she was convincing herself at the same time. I was intrigued by her and impressed by her capabilities to be daring even though she didn't realize she was. At times I thought I could sense the weight she was carrying with her and how it followed her like a cloud, no matter how much she tried to shake it.

I knew all about dragging weight around like a ball and chain.

She fit in here, adapted quickly. New York suited her but didn't own her like so many of the city's lifers. She brought something to it, a light and energy that most New Yorkers were too busy to deliver themselves. She was a social worker and that made sense to me. I could see her helping people. She was genuine and cared, and believed she could show people the way to finding themselves without trying to fix them as though they were broken. Unlike my father who tried to change who you couldn't help but be.

"It's pretty cool, huh," I'd said to her, coming up behind maybe a little too closely. I'd taken a deep breath to smell her body, her essence.

"It's mesmerising." She looked impressed.

I was doing something right, making her feel good, and that made me happy too.

We wandered throughout the rest of the park, stopping at Azalea Pond where you could look across the water and see the city buildings beyond. She asked me to take photos for her and I did, anywhere and everywhere she wanted. Taking advantage, I took a few with my own phone when she wasn't looking. I wanted those for myself.

When she was hungry, we went back up streetside so we could hit one of the food trucks. To me it was the same old shit I'd grown up with, but to her it was exciting, making me laugh. She settled on chicken shawarma, saying it was the best thing she'd ever had. I rolled my eyes and told her I'd have to take her to some places to eat, my god.

It was late afternoon, and she was clearly getting tired. We were at Strawberry Fields where the Imagine mosaic tribute to John Lennon was inlaid in the ground, and a view of his home, The Dakota where Yoko Ono still resides, sits up on the hill. It was always a busy spot, and I wanted a moment alone, so I took the opportunity to lead her down to Sheep Meadow. I loved how she looked at me—into me—when I talked. I told her how it had been a pasture with sheep at one time. I don't think she believed me, but it was true. Now, it was a common spot for picnics and kids playing, not to mention the incredible views of the city.

We'd plopped down under a tree. She was leaning back on her hands with her legs straight out, taking everything in. The only thing I wanted to look at was her, so I propped myself up on one elbow facing her. Not wanting to come across as too forward, I maintained a friendly distance, picking at the grass.

She'd noticed my bracelets, and I'd wished I'd cut the fucking things off. I had no idea why I still wore them. *Yes, I do, who am I fooling?* They keep me grounded; lost in memories I actually want to hold onto. But still, they open up questions to those who take the time to notice, and, in this instance, I wasn't sure I wanted her to notice, so it made me nervous.

"What are those bracelets for?" she'd asked, and I'd felt the need to clarify they weren't from an ex-girlfriend or someone of the sort. How could I respond to her without saying too much? It was the truth that struck me as the only option, so I went with it anyway, hoping she wouldn't dig too much deeper.

"When I was younger, I had a hard time concentrating. I, um… needed help sometimes," I'd told her, dodging her eyes but still feeling her staring into me. "My parents worked a lot, so I spent a lot of time alone at home, with Nancy and my brother. Nancy would sit with me in the kitchen, and she taught me how to make these friendship bracelets to help me with my focus." I glanced up at her, not sure if I was ready for the way she looked at me so intently, paying such close attention to my words. "These are just a few that we made together a few years ago when I was staying with them. At home. My old home." Fuck I was saying too much. "I just haven't taken them off." I finished quickly and looked out over the park.

I'd been uncomfortable as shit but kept going. I'd never spoken to anyone before in this way, but I was drawn to her soft voice. Taking a chance, I felt that I could control just a little more info without making a huge mistake.

"I guess she was like a nanny to me," I'd told her. "She took us to the park and stuff, threw us birthday parties." Shrugging, I'd swallowed the sour lump in my throat. "Her and Geoff attended the school stuff my parents didn't make. You know." It was her soft eyes, the ones she focused on me so intently that quickly had me looking away again. It was like she could see right through me, right into my heart. It had freaked me out, and I wanted the conversation to stop, but instead, I kept rambling. "I dunno, it just kinda made sense, I guess."

I liked how she helped me to remember those good times. Katarina did that to me. Staring at the grass, I'd been unable to hide my smile of fond recognition of my life as a boy with Nancy. I remembered how she'd make breakfasts on Sunday mornings, allowing my brother and me to have her Danishes, fruit, and crispy bacon my mother would never let us have.

"That's cool. Maybe you could make me one. Now that we're friends," she'd said, hopeful, like it was a question, bringing my thoughts back to her. Katarina's eyes glittered with girlish excitement.

"Of course. Yeah, I can do that for you, sure," I'd answered her and shifted to smile her way. But that had been about as much as I could handle, and I shut down, wanting to move on from the personal questions

I didn't know how to answer. I'd suggested then, "Do you wanna get out of here? I can take you back up to your hotel." Even though I'd wanted to spend every moment with her.

"What are you doing tomorrow?" she'd asked. "I want to see the rest of the city. Take that tourist bus thingy and get a better sense of what to do here. See all the sights." She smiled and looked over at me, her cheeks pinkening. "You know, touristy stuff." She'd laughed.

"Want some company?" I'd asked her, sure of the answer.

"Do I?" She sat up, crossing her legs, happiness in her voice. "Hell yeah! Are you sure it won't be too boring for you?"

"Yeah, it's boring." I smirked. "I've seen it a thousand times. But with you I think it'll be ok. I'll make the sacrifice," I joked, casting her a sideways smile and raising my eyebrow. She laughed again.

"Ok, it's a date, then. Thank you, Ben. I appreciate it."

I didn't mind, I was bloody thrilled.

That was the first time I'd left her and was comfortable heading home. I'd had things under control. *Little bits and pieces, Benjamin. Do not obsess.* Meeting this woman had shifted something in my life, but I had to take small steps, patience, patience. The turtle wins the race or some shit. So how did I get here, to this point? Probably a bad idea, but I had allowed myself to absorb the electric feeling that had buzzed through me when I saw her standing like a goddess of sweet calmness in my world full of dragons.

Chapter 5: Katarina

Staying static against a café window in the middle of New York City isn't going to solve my dilemma, so I abandon the glass and start walking. My footsteps find me at an intriguing bookstore, so I venture inside with a little more spring in my step. I swing the door open and am comforted by the soothing and distinct smells of paper books and ink that are unmistakable in any book lover's dream. The signature surroundings fill me with a soothing calm in my heart. *See Katarina? You don't need a guy in your life for happiness.* But then shameful anxiety takes over, and I do what I've been fighting against all day. I pull my phone from my pocket, checking its status. Fully charged, no messages, no texts, and no pigeons. *Fuck!* It is almost eleven, even a dimwit knows that by now something is up. I'd shown all my cards and had been played. What am I going to do now? Racking my brain to put together the missing pieces, I go over every detail of Friday.

When Ben had come out of the Café that morning he'd been agitated and aloof. What the fuck was I missing? He'd shifted into a smile fairly quickly, and I couldn't deny how much it had made my heart glow.

"Hey, so sorry about that," he'd apologized, and I'd looked up at my stranger, his gaze staring into me. "Ready to go?"

We'd started walking, and as I followed his lead, I couldn't help thinking how different he was. He'd told me he worked at some magazine… what the heck was it called? *The New Yorker*? No, *The Manhattan*, that's right.

I pull out my phone and google the location. It is a few blocks northeast. If I grab a cab, the driver will surely know which building the offices are in…

What the actual fuck am I doing? I'm just going to show up at this guy's workplace? Can someone say psycho? Jesus, I need to get a grip. My smalltown girl is showing, and I have to stop.

He'd grabbed us a cab that morning and while sitting beside him in the backseat, I couldn't help myself glance over and look at his hands. They were large and clean with long fingers and impeccably manicured nails. Clearly, he took very particular care of himself, unusual for most of the men I knew. He was tapping his thigh as though humming the beat of a song and looked nervous, like he had a tic of some sort. Rubbing his thighs, it looked as though he needed calming, like this action was slowing his speed, which I'd thought was so interesting.

"How long have you lived here, Ben?" I'd wanted to know where this man had come from and how he was going to fit into my future.

"All my life," he'd answered so quietly I barely heard him as he stared out of the window. I wasn't sure if he was proud or sad about his hometown when suddenly he shouted, "Stop here!" to the driver, making me jump.

The driver had then pulled to the side, and Ben threw him ten bucks as he got out of the cab. "Keep it."

I shimmied over to his side, and he held out his hand. "Let's go."

I'd stared up at him standing outside the cab, the wind blowing his curls while he stared back at me. I took his hand, warmth had filled my body, and my knees felt weak. We were back at the same entrance where we'd first met, and as I got out of the cab the smell from the food trucks hit the air. There was too much for us to look at, but Ben only looked at me and was clearly right at home.

We'd walked into the park—it was breathtaking. There were people everywhere, and I couldn't stop gaping. An old man struck me as he sat in the noise quietly reading a book. Dogs chased frisbees, little dogs and big dogs, groups of them being walked by their sitters. Lovers. Lots of lovers, laughing and kissing as they held their partners' hands.

The trees created a canopy of movement and shade over the entire scene. Squirrels were ballsy, coming right up to tourists and striking a pose for their fans. Bicycle riders toured the pathways peddling freezers filled with ice cream treats while others were scattered on benches and large rocks, drawing, dreaming, or writing.

The eclectic sound of musicians, either playing solo or in groups, created an ambiance that was indescribable. It was easy to tell who the artists were, the locals, and tourists by their clothes, behaviors, and mannerisms.

Roads and paths spread every which way leading to new, stunning destinations. Horses pulled carriages over the cobblestone pathways filled with tourists and kissing couples. Ponds shimmered in the sun, and fountains and statues dotted open spaces. Where there wasn't trees and gardens filled with flowers, grass fields were busy with people playing sports or giggling children around jungle gym structures. It was magical.

"Stand there," he'd ordered, and I'd obeyed.

When I'd passed him my phone, our fingers had grazed each other, my whole body tingled, and I could feel a surge of electricity spread across my hips. Stopping, he looked up at me, and I thought he had felt it too. With a big smile on his face he'd said, "Let me take your picture." He'd been flirting with me as he snapped away, pointing out new positions and holding my gaze.

When I'd heard singing, I'd asked him where it was coming from, and he'd led me to Bethesda Terrace. "Ready, Katarina?" he'd asked at the top of the stairs, and I'd gleamed. Oh, how I was loving the way my name rolled off his lips.

Lost in my memories I frown at how much I am missing him today, remembering how, when he'd grabbed my hand, I'd let him without hesitation. We'd walked down the stairs under the Terrace, and he'd let go of me as I wandered inside in awe. It was gorgeous, the most beautiful thing I'd ever seen. There were carvings of plants and birds in the concrete archways and along the walls. There were ornate and colorful inserts of marble and tile. The ground was a mixture of little red tiles in a squared pattern, creating the perfect spot for an artist to cordon off a space for himself. It oozed culture, and the ceiling was the most amazing thing I'd ever seen. It was lit up by hanging brass lamps, pointing their light upwards to create a soft glow, highlighting the patterned squares with designs of blue, burgundy, and green. It opened on the other side through seven more archways to a courtyard, and as he'd promised, the Angel Fountain and glistening pond. He took my picture as I sat on the edge of the fountain, then scootched beside me, turning the camera to take one of us together. When he had put his arm around me my whole body had shivered. He was just so damn easy to get along with, smelled so good, and I loved being with him. We were fast becoming friends, and I'd thought the attraction between us was mutual. It felt electric. I was comfortable with him, and although I kept my heart tight on her leash, I was vulnerable for the first time in a long time.

"It's beautiful," I'd said.

"It is, you're right. And I've seen some beautiful things," he'd replied, eyes twinkling and sparking like diamonds on fire. I blushed, not knowing exactly what he meant; I felt he was referring to me.

I hadn't wanted the day to end, but we'd grabbed a cab and headed back through the Square to my hotel. I was exhausted and ready to sit and relax with a glass of wine. When we got there, I'd asked if he wanted to come up and get a drink at the bar, but he'd declined. I won't lie, I'd been disappointed. He said he was going to head home but we made plans to meet the next morning.

"Tomorrow morning at eight thirty. Gloria's, ok?" he'd shouted from the back of the taxi as I'd jumped out.

"Yeah, see ya there!" I'd replied, and the car was gone before I could grab his number… but he'd shown up, and Saturday was another exploration of this man, my own self and how the two of us just… clicked like fucking magic.

I shake my head—I don't even know him. *There are a lot of people yet to meet, Katarina,* I tell myself. *Yeah. But people like him? People who aroused and interested me within what, seventy-two hours?*

How do I feel about this guy? This crazy intense attraction? It definitely isn't what I'd come here for. Or maybe it is.

I'd thought way too hard about my clothing that day, caring too much about how I was going to present myself to this man, and that was a red flag I was getting in over my head.

I'd entered the café, and he'd been waiting. As I approached him, he'd stood to greet me, and I'd found myself in his embrace. It took me by surprise, the hug—quick and confident, but also reserved. He'd smelled like heaven, and my body instantly went to feelings of ecstasy. Memories of the previous night's dream where it had been me, him, and well, nothing else. My knees were weak and once we'd broken apart, I'd sat down, practically stumbled into the chair.

"Where do you want to start?" he'd asked.

He'd become my tour guide, and I wasn't sure if he wanted the role, but he wasn't complaining, either. I'd explained how I'd wanted to chill out on the tour buses that take you around the city. After finally taking a run through Central Park that morning and all the walking the previous day, my legs had been killing me. I was pleased to find out that he loved running too, just another thing we seemed to have in common.

"Running helps me clear my head," he'd said, his expression growing distant for just a moment.

"Well, let's go on the buses, then. We'll get a two-day pass. That will give us today and tomorrow," he had suggested and winked.

I noticed he'd assumed we'd be spending more time together, but I didn't mind, at this point I didn't want to be with anyone else. Grabbing our things, he stood and pulled out my chair. We were getting along like wildfire, connecting on all cylinders with a buzz of flirtation.

I'd watched him intently—I couldn't stop. I'd noticed how when we were walking, he'd take my hand, so we wouldn't lose each other. I loved it when he did that. He was comfortable in a world that was weird to me. He was at ease in the mayhem, like he owned it, knew it, lived it and slept with it. I guess that's New Yorkers, composed in their own chaos. He got us passes from some guys passing flyers, and we'd jumped on a big red double-decker bus.

"Let's go up top," he'd said. "It's the only way you'll see anything."

He was spicy, and I could feel the electricity of him sitting so close to me. New York made me feel sexy and confident, and the independence of making my own choices was liberating. I was still afraid of being here alone, so I very much welcomed my newfound friendship. I didn't feel dependent on it, though. It was my choice to spend my time with him, and I liked his company, I still felt in control of myself.

Going through the city on that bus was so much better. We were up high, and I could see it all. Even though it was daytime, there were still lights everywhere in the Square. Models on billboards, TVs featuring today's hottest stars, and massive posters advertising Broadway shows. It was crazy and cool, and I liked watching the people below, mostly tourists and New Yorkers that worked in the city. It was alive, and I was alive within it.

We took a bus to the ferry to Liberty Island, but we never crossed. Instead, we spent our time at the Brooklyn Bridge, Battery Park, and Ground Zero. We saw all the sights there were to see, hopping off and on everywhere and anywhere I asked him to take me. We still walked a lot, getting up close to certain things I wanted to explore. When he was pointing something out to me on the bus and explaining what it was, he leaned in close and would put his arm around me, giving me more details.

By the end of the day, I was beat. He had paid for the passes and lunch before I'd even had the chance. I wanted to thank him. Hell, I wanted to *thank him*, but that was whorish, and I shook my head. I invited him again to come to my hotel, saying we could sit in the piano bar. It was small and quiet, no reservation needed. Plus, I could put the bill on my room before he even had a chance to pull out his wallet. He'd agreed, and my stomach had fluttered. I couldn't hide the pleasure from my face, and I'm sure he noticed.

Located at the end of my hall, the bar area was to the left off the doorway. It was sexy and chic, lit by Edison bulbs strung up above. Under counter lighting created a nice glow, inviting guests to sit and order their key cocktail. Between the bar and where we stood in the doorway, tucked in the corner, was a mini grand piano. Its shiny black exterior glowed from the lights in its tight space. Directly ahead were the dining tables and a glass garage door that opened to the outdoor patio, open to the sky above. A large bench wrapped around the exterior with tables and chairs that could be configured however you liked. It was a cozy space where you could have a bite to eat and listen to local musicians from eight to eleven each night.

We'd snagged a spot at the bar facing the piano. The lone male bartender, occupied with pouring drinks, gave us a quick nod indicating that he'd seen us and would be over to take our order. At the piano was my old man neighbour. His shaky fingers stroked the keys, endearing them to produce the most incredible, sulky but beautiful sound. I was impressed—and completely surprised—that this seemingly drunk and miserable person could produce anything sweet or elegant. I noticed Ben had gone silent, listening and watching with keen interest.

The day had left me knackered and sore, yet ecstatic and blossoming. Most importantly, I was ravenous, and not just for nourishment in the form of food. It felt like New York was acknowledging me, and I was flattering her right back. Already feeling different, I was flourishing in the city. Energized and sure of myself, I wanted more. I can't explain it, but I needed to fit in and belong. I needed this city to be mine and felt that it could actually be feasible. I'd gotten my feet wet and was proud of it. I hadn't just survived my second day; I'd survived it well. After meeting the most incredible native New Yorker, connecting with him and complimenting his space, I felt a maturity I'd never allowed myself to feel before. I glanced at him in the dim light—I'd opened up to him more than I ever had with a stranger, and it felt simply, *good.*

"What can I get for you two tonight?" The bartender had broke my daydream, and I looked up. Having missed his introduction, I was left with only the name Bartender and liked the way it sounded.

We ordered drinks, and while we waited Ben was distant. Probably just tired, I thought. The vibe coming from the air around him felt tense and uncomfortable, and I didn't know how to shake the situation. Music began to fill the silence, and I was thankful for the distraction. The pianist was creating a somber, yet incredibly beautiful mood, the tune hanging in the air as thick as the storm clouds rolling in. He was hunched over, a bottle of Irish Whisky, half empty, on the lid of the piano, but the quality of the playing was undeniable. I got lost in its ambiance; the soft glow of the lights illuminated him. I found myself yearning to know more about who he was.

"You know who that is at the piano, don't you?" I jumped when Ben broke the mood with his comment.

"Other than my neighbour, no. I don't think he wants to be known, to be honest. I ran into him the other day. He's not a nice guy." I felt bad for saying so and shuddered.

"That's Max," the Bartender quipped while polishing a glass from the other side of the bar. "His name is Maxwell Templeton, haven't you ever heard of him?"

I shook my head, and the Bartender moved in closer.

"He used to be pretty famous. He was a guest pianist for the Philharmonic, doing shows on Broadway, Christmas concerts, that sort of thing. He hasn't played professionally for like twenty years, I think?" He placed a glass of wine in front of me, leaning one arm on the bar as he continued his explanation. The two of us watched the old man hunch and sway over the piano while Ben picked at his napkin.

"He looks miserable, and he is. He comes here and just sits down and plays whenever he wants to, sometimes he'll ask if I mind." Bartender looked back at me. "I never say no. One time, the hotel manager asked him to get permission, in case we had someone scheduled." He laughed. "Max threw a bottle at the manager's head and split his eye open. Now we just let him play whenever he sits down."

My eyes widened in surprise. How could anyone live a life so angry? I assumed he didn't have many friends when Bartender confirmed for me, "He doesn't leave the hotel much. Sometimes he doesn't come to the bar for weeks, just stays in his room. Or he can be here every night at all times. We lock up the bar section, but you can access the patio whenever. No one ever says anything to him, though. He's kicked our hired pianists right off the bench. We've had three of them quit." He stopped and looked at me in a way that made me feel desirable, wanted.

Ben cleared his throat and shifted in his seat. I couldn't tell if he was loosening up, or getting more agitated, but the air in the room felt stagnant and hard to breathe. Bartender must have sensed the same tension and sauntered away, saying, "Catch my eye when you're ready to order," before leaving me alone with Ben.

After a few minutes of silence Ben said, "It's a hard story." And the air in the room shifted as he looked away from me and swallowed hard. "His name *was* Maxwell Templeton—doubt he'd ever admit it now."

Taking a sip of my wine, I pulled back to look at it. Even my wine tasted different, fuller bodied, smoother, sexier. I savoured it in my mouth, letting it trickle down my throat, closing my eyes as Ben began to fumble through his story.

"Rumour has it his lover left him, died maybe? I don't know. Either way, his lover was gone, and he took Maxwell's head with him." Ben seemed agitated, almost angry, as I tried to read his body language.

"After that, Max went crazy and started drinking, showing up to concerts shitfaced. If you ask me, he was torturing himself, becoming embittered and angry as a result."

"Why would you think that?" I wondered why he had such a vested interest in some random pianist.

"Because people are horrible to themselves, Katarina. Especially if they've done something wrong to deserve it." Ben shook his head.

"Deserve what? The way they're treating themselves or the way someone is treating them?"

Something had been really upsetting Ben that night, and I couldn't decipher if there was more to the story than just a fallen musician. He continued on about Max as if he were disgusted.

"He became unreliable. Ruined performances. That costs a lot of money in New York, so, eventually he became this…" Ben nodded at the piano.

"He's broken. Lost everything including his home. He must live here if he's in the hotel. Don't know how he pays for it."

I guess I understood Max's pain even though I couldn't relate. The sad look in his eye and why it was there. The anger, too. Pain he must be living with every day of his life. My feelings toward Max started to shift, and I felt awful. If it really was true about his lover killing himself, he must be devastated. How could you live with yourself knowing that the one person in your life you were closest to, the person you loved and who loved you, you couldn't save? Even though you didn't hold the knife, you didn't hold the shield either. How did it feel knowing your love for them couldn't pull them out of their own darkness?

I could tell Ben was uncomfortable, but at the same time it seemed like he wanted to talk, needed to talk. I felt my training kick in instinctively, and as much as my heart wanted to reach for his hand, I held back, knowing that in vulnerability the gesture could send him back into his shell. I wanted to understand this man in front of me, so I bit my tongue and held my hands still.

"He used to be somebody, until he wasn't anymore," Ben muttered under his breath, and I had to lean in to make sure I'd heard him correctly.

What did that mean, exactly?

"Funny how people in your life can make or break you, don't you think?" At this he met my eyes, noticed me searching, and quickly looked away, sitting back into his chair. The veil of silence returned.

"I think that people around you are influenced by the energy you put out," I offered slowly.

He scoffed. "Yeah, I guess. But what happens when the only energy you have is toxic? Then what can you expect?"

I was getting uncomfortable and didn't know what to think of Ben's aggressive mood change. Trying to change the focus I blurted out, "You mentioned a lover." Realizing my mistake, I lowered my voice. "I assume he's gay?" I knew it was none of my business, but I was curious enough to dare to ask. I rested my chin on my hand and kept my eyes on Max who was slouched over, his soul bleeding onto the keys while his bottle sat on the lid, almost taunting him.

Ben chuckled. "He was part of New York's theatre and arts' scene. Most of them are, aren't they?"

This hit home for me. College had taught me about the complexities of society and how certain expectations on people cause judgement of others.

"Oh, I think I get it," I mumbled.

"I definitely don't," Ben spat, his demeanor agitated. "There's theories on what happened, but whatever did, it fucked him up." He pointed at Max with disgust. "The guy had everything, until he didn't. And it didn't matter in the end how hard he tried."

"Was his energy toxic? How do you know him?" I asked.

He laughed again. "I don't know him." Ben took a long swig of beer. A few moments passed and he shuddered, smiled, and his mood shifted gears again. "He was a famous pianist, Katarina. But fame and fortune ruined him. People ruined him."

I swallowed, took a sip of wine, and glanced back at the musician, trying to figure out what to say next. "I suppose people can do that, if you let them."

"Yes, if you're lucky enough to have a choice."

"He didn't have a choice?"

"Does anybody? Really? I'm not sure we can control our surroundings once the world knows what we truly are deep inside—what we're capable of."

I didn't like the way he was talking and wanted to change the subject, so I tried asking about any hobbies. "You seem very creative, Ben, and you know a lot about art, obviously." I smiled, trying to soften the mood. "Do you paint or play an instrument?"

"Yeah, I fucking play. That stupid piano was my muse as a kid." His eyes were cold as he stared at me, and for the first time all weekend, I wanted to be away from him. I didn't know what I'd done to upset him, but his eyes sparked with rage.

"My parents. They were the ones. They made me play," he muttered and started tapping his fingers on his glass.

I hung onto the droplets of what he was sharing. Talking about his parents obviously made him uncomfortable, so I'd dropped it, feeling I'd hit a nerve. The best thing to do in that situation, when you didn't have someone's trust yet, was to move on. College did come in handy for learning that.

I must not have upset him too much because he asked if I wanted to go to The Met the next day. I agreed to him picking me up at my hotel the next morning. I went with him down to the lobby, showing him my door at the end of the hall and making a joke about how lucky I was to be able to stumble home, making him smile.

It had started raining, and as I walked him out of the hotel there was a cab conveniently waiting there. He grabbed it so as not to lose it and was gone with a wave.

Chapter 6: Benjamin

I'm not clear on the time, and the day is questionable. It's been a blur between excruciating mental pain mixed with a tsunami of release, depending on the medium. The questions are the worst, but the self-reflection makes up for the exercises. I'm comfortable at least.

I've done what I was told to do and cut it all out. Stay in control but it doesn't feel like it's good enough. Up and down and round and round. I'm angry, scared, and all alone. The notebook has become my vehicle, my pathetic existence, my muse. With no other choices I write all my feelings down, trying to make sense of the demons inside. Spilling everything out with words, I try to find a way to self-analyse past mistakes, present predicaments, and future dreams. With paper and pen I do just that, but to her. All of it. Scribbling too fast, I hold my breath reminding myself to breathe. *Slow down Ben, it has to make some sense. Say it out loud if we have to.*

I'm never at peace with my thoughts, but I'm tired of blocking them out, not that it's ever worked anyway. *Don't run away from feeling. Don't push it down. Tell her. Share it. Admit it. Accept it, who we are. And all the reasons why.* Pouring out of me, I do just that, and for some reason, talking to the imaginary version of the woman I'm falling in love with makes it easier. I let it all out on those pages in the search for calmer waters, and I want to stay that way, empty and calm.

There are footsteps in the hall, then silence. When the flood gates open, I pour it all out. All the pain, all the truth. Digging as deep as my demons will let me, I challenge them all. I'm so sick of feeling confused and alone that I'm relentless on those pages. I just can't carry it any longer. *Who are you? What are you?* Resentments, fears and embarrassments. I'm ashamed, so futile, but I have to feel in order to be free of the chains that have locked me up all these years. I want all the feels so I can face it, and free it. All of it. The doors are opening now, their eyes peering out at me, every single one, and I can see them for what they are, what I am. I won't let them control me anymore.

Music plays in my ears and runs through my blood. Days and evenings intertwine, and I'm left in a state of numbness. Slowly they start to give in, and I realize they need to be destroyed before I can let them go. They are a part of me always, but if I can rule over them myself, we can live more harmoniously. *Come out, come out, let me see you, let me understand you, let me destroy you. I will break this habit of destruction. I'll break it for you.* Stuffing the pages under the mattress, I crumble, blisters on my fingers, and sleep just to dream about her.

We were sitting together on the patio.

"It's going to rain tomorrow. You can smell it. Clouds are rolling in." I pointed up and her head tilted back, exposing her neck. I couldn't help but imagine biting her there to see if she'd squeal.

We were at this rooftop bar in her hotel. It wasn't really on the rooftop, but I got what they were trying to achieve. The sun was setting, the air cool, and the clouds were making shadows to hide any secrets I might share on my face.

She was drinking wine while I had ordered a beer. I loved the way she made me feel that day, like I could break all my old habits. I knew it wasn't right of me, but I made excuses and reasons to shelter my guilt. I reacted too quickly when the Bartender eyed her in a way I didn't like. I can't remember the conversation; I blocked it out at the time. I knew I was about to let go and wanted out of there fast. Pressure was building and there was no way I'd be able to keep it up. But when I looked up at her again, and she'd smiled at me, I was able to soften, bringing myself back from the edge. The little door closed, and I cleared my throat to suggest a plan for the next day.

"So, listen… um… want to hit The Met tomorrow?" I had wanted her to say yes so badly. At the same time, I was terrified of hopeful feelings, they've never done me well in the past. "I figure if it's raining it would be a good time?" I added, hoping I sounded aloof instead of eager.

"Yeah. You sure you're ok? You're not sick of me yet?"

I hadn't liked how she was looking into me, and it made me nervous, but I told her I was fine.

Opening my mouth like a fucking idiot and telling her I could play piano had been a mistake. I groaned on the inside. I was getting too close to letting her in, and I didn't want to talk about that stuff. I needed to leave this part out of the getting to know you game. Shove it back in the door and lock it. But with her it was just so easy to talk. I squirmed and looked at her awkwardly to see if she noticed. Without skipping a beat, she just kept on talking. I followed her story, and she stopped asking questions. I listened, and it calmed me down. I could do this. Maybe I could let her in slowly a little more.

In the safety of the cab, I popped an Ativan from the stash I always kept in my pocket. I couldn't remember what I'd taken or not taken, but at that point it didn't matter. I left her there knowing we were meeting again the next day—if I could just get through the night.

Miraculously, I had slept fairly well and woke up fresh, purposefully getting to her hotel early. I had been waiting in the lobby for over an hour, an intense need to be there out of fear I might miss her. Finally, the elevator doors opened, and she graced the lobby. Katarina was a breath of fresh air blowing in off the glistening waters of an island coast. She approached me, and as I lifted my head, I could see her big smile and twinkling eyes.

"Hi," she said, and I couldn't help but grin. She was wearing the cutest polka dot blouse; I love polka dots. And I love polka dots even more on her.

"Two days in a row you came," she said. "I guess I haven't repulsed you either, huh? Do you want to grab a coffee from here? It's pretty much shit, but we'll be dry." When she leaned towards me to get a better look at the weather out the window behind me, I could see right down her blouse. Maybe she hadn't realized it or maybe she had, regardless, the view was beautiful.

"Raining a lot?" she'd asked.

"Mmmhmm." All I could do was stare at her neck while breathing her in, mesmerized by her and the fact that she was actually real.

I liked the distraction of the art at The Met. I was able to keep occupied and focused on what we were looking at. She stared at me when I talked, making me feel important, and I think I impressed her with my knowledge. The experience helped me keep my demons at bay and, so far, I'd had good control. We spent the entire day there, listening to the thunder rolling outside.

Chapter 7: Katarina

I'd had no idea what was coming over me, but I liked it. My body felt alive, my thoughts were wild and in full color, and my heart and soul felt it, too. Maybe the idea to leave the safety of my cocoon and find my wings was working, and I was actually succeeding. Good, Bad, and Ugly, right? As much as I had been spending all my time with Ben, it was what I wanted to do, and no one was going to stop me. I wasn't the same girl who'd arrived just a few days ago. The universe was looking down on me, and all the doors were wide open. When I thought of him, a smile crossed my face, and a surge of ecstasy tingled my hips. He had done all the right things, hadn't he?

We decided to meet in the lobby as it was pouring rain, a massive storm had moved in overnight. I overthought my outfit for the day, wearing tight blue jeans with a yellow polka dotted brown blouse. I had a bit of an obsession with those little dots and particularly with that blouse. I planned on grabbing a coffee downstairs while I anxiously waited to see if Ben was going to show up two days in a row.

When the elevator doors opened, Ben was already there, sitting in one of the lounge chairs by the front window reading a newspaper. His leg was crossed against his knee, and he wore dark blue jeans, a black t-shirt, and casual running shoes. His hair was wet from the rain, and he looked amazing. I confidently approached him, standing right in front of him. As he looked up, I felt a surge of heat as he stared.

"Two days in a row? I guess I haven't repulsed you either, huh? Do you want to grab a coffee from here?" I asked, motioning towards the lobby lounge. "It's pretty much shit, but we'll be dry." I leaned down towards him so I could look out the window for a glance at the street. "Raining a lot?"

"Mm-hmm." He seemed to moan, transfixed on my blouse. Inwardly, I smiled. I knew I looked incredible in this blouse, and by the nature of his reaction, I felt that he knew it too.

The Met was absolutely stunning. As we walked through it, I was astounded by how much Ben knew. He was cultured, smart, and he had an eye for beautiful things. Be it a sculpture or a painting, he could see the emotions in it—the intensity of the vibes that artist had portrayed in his moments of creativity. Going to The Met with Ben wasn't like going on a school trip; it was an adventure of the mind.

We left the Metropolitan Museum in the late afternoon to a crack of thunder right over our heads. It had been raining all day, but the sky was getting darker. We stopped to grab a quick hot dog from a vender as the streetlights flickered on, making the city sparkle. I could smell the rain from the sky, the sensual summer earth mixed with grease from the streets in the warm muggy air. It was a smell I wished I could bottle and place in a memory bank.

We were at the bottom of the Met staircase when the gentle drizzle turned into a downpour. I screamed and started to laugh, putting my hands up and ducking my head in a feeble attempt at protection, but there was no way of getting out of this rain. Ben was equally as wet as the rain came straight down on our heads. My makeup streamed down my cheeks, and he looked at me with hair in his eyes as he cast his head back, laughing uncontrollably. People were running, and cabs were full. All we could do was stand there looking at each other. Throwing away my half eaten hot dog, I envied the chefs crammed in their little food trucks, dry and warm, pulling in their overhangs.

"What are you laughing at, rat? Look at you! Your pretty hair is ruined!" I grinned at him. His black t-shirt was soaked through, sticking to his chest. When I looked down, I could see how my polka dot blouse looked clinging to me, and I wondered if he noticed.

"We're not going to get a cab, you know," he said, tossing his meal away too. "And your hotel is blocks away."

"Ok, well the rain isn't going to stop, and it's too late anyway. What do you suggest? You know your way around here better than I do."

He thought for a second. "My parents' place is nearby. I'll call Geoff. Hopefully he's home and can pick us up, come." He grabbed my hand and pulled me back up the stairs to the doorway to get out of the rain. He pushed me in before him, turning me to face him and stepped in to join the crowd that was trying to find shelter. We were very close, and all I could do was smell him, the rain making his scent even more pronounced.

He spoke into the phone, "Hey, Geoff, it's Ben. I'm at The Met, and it's raining like crazy. Can I get a ride?"

As the crowd jostled us, we bumped into each other. My body tingling with desire, I had to talk myself down from inappropriately touching him.

"Ok, he's coming," Ben said, sounding relieved. He looked down at me and grinned, his gorgeous smile and mouth so close to mine.

Geoff was there within five minutes. We ran down the stairs, Ben holding my hand. He opened the back door for me. "Shoo over." The rain was not letting up and thunder rolled overhead. He got in behind me and slammed the door.

"Holy shit!" he said, whipping his hair back, water splattering everywhere.

"Mr. Benjamin," Geoff said, looking back at us through the rear-view mirror, eyeing me warily.

"Hey thanks, how are you and Nancy? It's been a while."

"Nancy's good," said Geoff, still eyeing me questionably. "Where am I taking you, Benjamin?"

"Uhhh… Who's at the house right now, Geoff? My parents?" he asked.

"Not at the moment, but they're expected… later I think, but they are expected."

Ben looked dismayed and perplexed. Then, looking at me straight on, he said, "Take us to my parents' place, fuck it. We'll dry off, then we'll be on our way."

I think I might have sighed in relief. I hadn't wanted to end my time with Ben just yet, but the thought of bringing him back to my hotel room felt too presumptuous.

Whispering to me he asked, "Is that okay? You can borrow something while your clothes dry."

I nodded and smiled, turning away to look out the window so he wouldn't see how overly pleased I was.

"Sure, that's fine, thanks."

We turned down a street filled with massive trees and gorgeous brownstones. The rain had lightened up a little. Geoff slowed down and parked in the front of a house nestled in between the luxury apartments that made up the block.

"Back entrance," Ben spat, making me feel a little nervous, like he was ashamed of me.

"Very well," Geoff replied, and he continued to the end of the block so he could access the laneway running behind the buildings. The feeling of sneaking in by private entrance raised a red flag, making me think Ben was hiding something, but as he pulled me along by the hand, I stuffed my concerns aside and allowed my heart to flutter.

Garbage bins lined the alley, with a few stray cats milling around despite the continuing drizzle. Ben opened a gate to a pretty courtyard, with lights strung to illuminate the obvious entertaining space. His parents' yard was a fair size for what I'd imagine in a city. A covered, raised deck off the back door that spanned the width of the home gave a place for two to sit and have a smoke or a morning coffee. The yard itself was cobblestone, and there was a small garden along one side with a quaint tool shed. Potted plants dotted the deck and steps: tall and short, blooming with ferns and cascading tiny white flowers that were delicate and softly scented. Smaller pots along the back staircase held herbs like basil and rosemary, while the larger ones were busy growing tomatoes. To the side of the stairs, at the foot of the deck, was an impressive outdoor kitchen with a gas grill, stone prep station, and a small pizza oven. A wrought iron table sat in the center of the cobblestone patio with six chairs and an umbrella. Two lounge chairs to enjoy the sun sat along the back of the property beside the alleyway's private gate.

We entered through the back door into a beautiful kitchen, dark, with a small table under the window that looked into the backyard. There was an island in the middle that offered two more stools to sit at. Along the back wall, separating the kitchen from the rest of the house was the cooking wall, featuring a chef style fridge, gas stove, and dark wood cabinets. It smelled heavenly and warm, like spices and cider. I followed Ben through a small door to the rest of the house. The staircase was to my right, and I could see far enough to a landing that turned, continuing to the next floor. We stopped, and Ben stiffened for a moment, long enough for me to catch a glimpse of the front hallway through to a set of double wood doors with glass panes. We passed two rooms that seemed classy but staunch with a lot of solid wood and velvet cushions.

The front room with its wood burning fireplace and grand piano caught my eye most. The walls were stark white, but with the lack of side windows the brightness was needed. Dark paintings of flowing, faceless ladies dancing by the same artist hung as a statement to the décor. I followed Ben up the old stairs thinking how as a young girl, I'd wished to be part of an artistic family. The type that would live in such a home as this, where artwork told stories of artists' loves and losses, and tormented souls. Where there were books on every table, leather bound and tattered, having been read over and over again, passed down from generation to generation. The odd splotch of paint on the kitchen table normal and expected, where card games were played, televisions non-existent, and classical music or opera sung from the record player. Rooms full of culture, mismatched furniture collections with ancient artifacts and knickknacks purchased from travelling art or music festivals. Running my hand along the railing, I was in awe of his home and imagined a rich and brilliant childhood I was envious of. Landing in a hallway, he led me to the last door on the left.

"We can dry off in here," he said, letting me pass in front of him. The room was typically boy with navy blue walls and heavy wood furniture. Tall windows offered the only light in the otherwise dark room before Ben flicked on the lamp placed on a dresser. Books, puzzles, and small toys were neatly arranged on a bookcase covered in the slightest amount of dust; you could tell he hadn't stayed here in a long time. It was cool and perfectly tidy, and I quickly realized this was his room as a child, nothing like the man he was now. I felt intrusive, like he was letting me see a part of him he kept shut down and private. After taking it all in, my gaze landed on where he stood in front of another door.

"This is the bathroom, it's private," he said, opening the door for me. I smiled at him sheepishly, and he returned my nervous gaze. "I stay here sometimes… so I have spare clothes in the dresser.

"I'll change out here if you want to take the bathroom. There are towels in there, and my robe is on the back of the door. The top shelf has some pajama pants and T-shirts if you want to throw either of those on while I dry your clothes. Just pass them out to me, and I'll take care of it for you."

"Thank you," I whispered as I slipped past him, our eyes meeting for a split second as I closed the door.

Alone, I tried to relax. A large mirror hung over the old cream-colored vanity while the shower behind me stood in the corner. Looking at my drenched self, I wondered what the hell I was doing here. My New York guide had become my friend—a friend I was intensely attracted to. His smile, his eyes, and his curly locks had entered my dreams the last few nights, but I wasn't here to be with a man or fall in love. I was here to be independent and grow up on my own. Figure out what kind of life I wanted to live, who I was before I met anyone. I shook my head at my reflection with a scowl on my face, this was happening all wrong.

At the same time, I felt daring.

Removing my wet clothes, I looked into the mirror. Naked, I felt beautiful, mature, and sexy. I grabbed a towel from the cubby and put on Ben's robe. It was warm and had the exact same scent that had been putting me close to the edge all weekend. I popped the door open a crack and handed out the wet mess of my clothing to Ben's extended hand. I approached the mirror, towelling my hair, rinsed off my ruined makeup and reapplied the little I wore. I didn't know what to do with my panties and bra. Giggling to myself, I stuffed them in my purse.

I stood there, staring into my own green eyes, not knowing how to proceed. Should I stick with the robe, being clearly vulnerable, my nakedness the pull of a belt loop away? Or should I enter his room in his own PJs looking ready to plop down, share a bowl of popcorn, and watch a movie?

I decided at that moment I didn't want to do either. I took off the robe and looked at myself in the mirror again. My breasts perky, nipples hardened from the cool air. My slim waist curving into hips and strong legs I was very proud of. I felt confident, wild, and beautiful. I decided I was going to act on my feelings, as crazy as it was.

Keeping my heart in my purse, along with my panties, I hadn't committed to my feelings for him but was ready for his touch. I hoped he felt the same way because there was no stopping me now.

Chapter 8: Benjamin

This is getting to me. It has been more than a few days, and I am getting fed up and bored. What is the point of all this now that everyone has calmed down, me included? The only thing getting me through the hours is thinking of her by making bracelet after bracelet. Nancy has been kind, bringing me the childhood craft to occupy my time, and I had spent hours creating my own version of Katarina through the many colors at my disposal. At first the container of different colored threads had pissed me off, but I'd perked up once I noticed the pretty shades of green. Greens and golds, yellows and browns, just like her eyes.

The pills make me sluggish. I suppose they make me feel like I should, blissfully numb. I set aside the Danish, take a sip of the coffee Nancy had brought, and then pour the threads onto the bed, sorting through which ones make up my Katarina. My eyes dart from color to color, picking at them to decide which colors will make her eyes. I pull at the threads that will create the pattern for the bracelet. Moving my fingers, the threads of her colors start to calm me. Her memory comes into focus—her smile melts the ice; sparkling eyes chip away the bricks I'd taken years to build around myself. Her dark wet hair and a body full of vulnerability keeps my focus, a body she'd opened to me, and I'd fallen into her pit.

We were soaked to the skin, and although I had known it wasn't the best idea, I wasn't ready to be away from her. In that moment of desperation, I had taken her to the last place I should have. My emotions all over the place, and clearly not thinking straight, I had been giddy. It felt like I was taking home a forbidden artifact to show Nancy, not thinking of the consequences, or that she'd say I couldn't keep her. I was overly excited about my newfound friend, and I should've known it was dangerous. But we were getting along so well, and I felt I was really connecting to another human being for the first time in my life.

When we'd pulled onto my parents' street there was an instant sense of panic, but I shoved that shit down to the very bottom of my gut. In and out in an hour. We'd dry off, and I'd take her somewhere to eat, maybe hit a movie or a quiet club for a drink. I'd take her through the kitchen, sneak her in. Hopefully Nancy and Geoff would know enough to not say anything.

I'd never brought a woman home before, not even to my place in Chelsea, and I felt uneasy in my parents' space. My mother had told me to leave women alone, but I think she was just jealous, afraid of the affection they would show that she couldn't. That was what Alexander told me, and I was fine with it. She knew I was with women; she just didn't want to see it. Instead, I made alternate plans at swanky hotels or wherever the party was. I never let them in, the women. I was incapable of letting my guard down or giving my heart away, just my body for my own pleasure.

With Katarina in my childhood space, I felt exposed and vulnerable, like I was open to her in more ways than I was ready for. I was certain she could see inside me, and I wasn't sure how I felt about that.

"Thanks," she'd said as I held the bathroom door open, allowing her to breeze past me. Our eyes met, and I could tell she was a little nervous being here, but I tried to make her feel as at ease as possible when, I too, was feeling a little awkward. No one had made me feel like this, ever. She entered the bathroom and shut the door. A few minutes later she popped the door ajar, and her slim fingers handed me her blouse and jeans. No bra—I didn't expect it although I knew it was also soaked—

and no panties. Either she wasn't wearing any, or she'd stuffed them into her purse. I took her clothes as she shut the door and held them for a moment, lifting the blouse even closer to my nose so I could smell her sweet aroma mixed with the scent of the sky. I felt myself quicken inside and my cock tingle. I wanted this girl, and I wanted her to want me just as badly.

Chapter 9: Katarina

I opened the door in my full nakedness and entered his bedroom. He was standing near the closet with his head bent down, doing up his belt, not looking in my direction. He'd towelled his hair dry, and it flowed mischievously everywhere. When the door creaked behind me, he looked up, still holding onto his belt, and stared. I froze. His eyes were wide and gentle, moving up and down my body, taking it all in. Biting my lip, I stood with one leg bent nervously swaying back and forth, my arms clasped behind me. At first, he didn't move, and he didn't smile. Nor did he say anything. Suddenly I felt very stupid, and I stumbled backwards a bit, looking away and placing my hands on the wall behind me for balance. He started to move towards me, but then turned towards his bedroom door. Oh fuck! I thought, and tears welled in the back of my throat. I've really done it, he's walking out. Panic forming, I wondered how on earth I was going to get out of this house. I didn't need those clothes; I'd run back to my hotel in a towel since I couldn't get any more mortified.

But he didn't leave.

He walked to the door, pressed his hand to it, and clicked it shut. He turned the lock and paused for a moment before turning back to me.

"You are beautiful," he said, looking me fiercely in the eyes. He walked towards me, fully clothed, and placed his right hand on my waist, his other hand took the back of my neck, and he nuzzled his head just under my ear. Tilting my neck, I let him in. His lips were warm on my skin, and my knees weakened as everything else fluttered with burning excitement.

"I love your beautiful face." He moaned quietly, buckling his knees to lean into me at my level, the rough fabric of his jeans separating my legs just a little so he could get closer to me.

He grabbed my ass right where it separated to my pussy. His long fingers close enough to touch me, but not yet there. He couldn't be much closer, but I knew he was going to try. I was excited by his approval of my entrance as I felt the moisture start between my legs. He pressed me up against the wall—hard—lifting me as I wrapped my legs around his waist and my arms around his neck. He was ravenous and so was I. Not knowing what to expect, I was ecstatic that he'd accepted my daring invitation without hesitation. I realized that he'd been hiding himself and his emotions these last few days, too. That, or he was a slut and used to fucking random girls, but I didn't want to think about that.

Carrying me over to the bed, he lifted me higher, so my head was above his, looking down on his hair. I finally grabbed at it, gently pulling it as his eyes rolled back, and he let out a few grunted moans. It was so soft, and my hands were holding his head so his lips could kiss my chest just above my breasts. He laid me down softly, and I loosened my leg hold from around him, leaving me spread wide. Being a little shy, I tilted my knees together a bit. Lifting off me, he knelt with one knee between my legs, the other standing at the edge of the bed. His hands on my knees were warm and soft, and as he looked at me, he really looked at me, hypnotic, almost breathless. There could've been a marching band in the room, and he wouldn't have noticed.

I grinned. I liked that he was still clothed, it made me feel excited and vulnerable all at the same time. I needed him to take charge and control the sex we were clearly about to have. Our eyes met, and I could feel his soul stare into mine, ready to make love to it. He blew out his breath and had a look of disbelief in his eyes like he was the lucky one.

I felt desired like never before. I had never met a man as mysterious and sexy as Ben, exposed myself, and had him eagerly accept. Oh no, I was the lucky one. The way he looked at me, no one had ever looked at me like that before.

With a quick movement he removed his shirt, revealing his chest, sleek muscles, and strong arms. His skin was smooth, just a little trail of black hair guiding a clear path from his belly button to what lay beneath his pants. And his nipples were pierced.

My god, his nipples were pierced.

I whimpered and could feel my expression change to one of even more longing which he definitely noticed. Thick silver rings hung from each just waiting for my mouth to suck and pull on them, and I bit my lip. I sat up slightly, moving my hands so I could trace the belt line that hung just below the defined V of his hips. He nudged me gently with a flick of his hips and an evil little grin that caused me to fall back on my elbows and look up at him, as my breasts jiggled.

My breathing was heavy as he explored my body, he was doing everything I'd wanted him to do when I'd made the decision to enter his room exposed and naked. His mouth had no limits and his need to consume every part of my body made me weak. I anticipated his next nip; I liked it when he did that. It hurt just a little and made my womanhood buzz and tingle. But it was my turn now, he'd had all the fun, and I wanted to feel what had been nudging me through his pants for the last few minutes.

"Stop. Stop…" I breathed, panting for air as I lifted myself out of my ecstasy just so I could breathe for a minute. "Stop, please."

When he looked at me his eyes were soft like he was hurt or disappointed. Maybe he was concerned I wasn't aroused which was the complete opposite. I reached for his jeans and started to pull them down at the waist. "Let me," I said.

He helped me, smiling, knowing that I wanted more and wasn't actually asking him to stop or having any sudden regrets.

I sat up higher and had to reach down to grab his cock. Thank God for Pilates, my core tight, supporting my balance. He lowered a little towards me, on his hands and knees between my legs. With my right hand, I grabbed his balls. They were large, trimmed, and soft. With my other hand I grabbed the shaft of his large cock. It was so hard it felt like it was going to explode. I grabbed it, closing my eyes and moaning, my thumb playing with the dribble of wetness coming out the top. My knees tightened on the outside of his thighs. I was happy and excited, and I think that pleased him. He knew I was impressed, and he moaned too, clearly in pleasure from my grasp. He leaned in, kissed me softly, and licked my lips, teasing me with his tongue.

"I like that," he said, smiling and thrusting his hips towards my hands but pulled away suddenly, saying, "Not yet, not yet... just wait a little longer."

He slowly kissed along my neck, down my chest, my stomach, to the crease of where my thigh attached to my body. He nestled there, so close to my pussy using the tip of his nose to outline the area and nuzzle the few curls I always made sure to keep. He lashed out his tongue and started licking my skin, making me gasp out in pleasure.

My hips ached. It was a pleasure so painful my legs felt numb. Ben was insistent, wouldn't let me get away. It was just what I needed him to do. I loved how he controlled me, took me, and did what he wanted. I was his now. I never wanted to be anyone else's, and he hadn't even entered my body yet. I belonged to him, knowing not what that meant or where it was going to go, but knowing I would never feel this way ever again. He was burned into my heart and soul. It made me nervous how quickly I'd let him in. What if he didn't feel the same? I couldn't think about that now. I just kept going in blind, trusting his touch.

My orgasm was strong like I'd never come before. The dew of our lovemaking felt like droplets dripping down my thigh, but I was so numb with pleasure I couldn't really tell. He didn't let me go for a little while, letting me relax and savour the moment. There were tears in my eyes, leaking down the sides of my head, and my nipples were hard as rocks. I whimpered, and he released his hold on me making his way up towards my face, stopping here and there for a little bite.

Chapter 10: Benjamin

She laid before me with her legs open and ready, propped up on her elbows, making her breasts stick out. I had ravaged her lips, her mouth, her face, her neck. There were little red marks where I couldn't help but nip at her. I wanted to eat her so badly. I stared into her eyes, finding her soul. I wasn't letting go. It was clear she liked what she saw and that made me hard. Waiting for me to move on like a good girl, I could tell she was dying for me to ravage her breasts. I had, coming down over her and supporting myself with my arms. I sucked and nipped at her tits, grabbing them with my hands one at a time, squeezing until I decided to lay right down on her and bury my face in the softness of her beautiful breasts.

I'd always been confident with my sexual prowess, but with Katarina I felt nervous. Would I impress her? Would I give her what she clearly was asking me for? Had she ever asked anyone else like this? And had she been impressed or disappointed? What and who was I competing against? I had to make sure I gave her what she'd entered my room looking for. I had to.

I lifted up so I could loosen my belt and undo my pants. Her nakedness was unfair, and it was my turn to feel her hands on my skin.

I leaned over her, coming down on her with my hands and grabbing her tits hard, squeezing them together as she lay on her back. I stayed there, ravaging, sucking, biting, pulling at her nipples. She moaned—oh how I liked that sound. What could I possibly do to make sure I heard more of it? *Tell me Katarina, tell me how I can please you.*

Her hands were all over my back, her nails lightly scratching me. It felt so good my nipples hardened, and all I wanted was to keep her there with me forever. She grabbed my hair, yanking my head off her tits and sitting up. It hurt so good I almost felt like crying, but I fought her back down. I wasn't finished yet, but she was. She grabbed at my jeans and pulled them down. I was between her legs, my cock rock hard and bursting to be allowed out.

I liked the way she smelled. Her scent was soothing, subtle, and sexy. It made it hard for me to keep my come inside my cock, but I had to find a way to settle myself down. There were voices in my head arguing now, one side saying keep going while the other, very annoying one, was saying stop, this isn't a good idea. Maybe it was the fact that I was in my childhood home, but I threw that voice into the back of my head and slammed the door. I knew what I wanted, and I wasn't going to stop now.

I laid my body down, my face between her bent legs, with my hands circling the inside of her thighs to her bottom, so I could grab her hips and pull her in closer, control her, if she tried to squirm away. I heard her gasp and felt her legs start to shake while I ground my body into the sheets, trying to get my cock to relax a little so as not to screw this all up. Her warmth and her wet scent were making it harder for me to stay in control.

I dove in. My mouth enveloping her pussy and sucking the juices out, her moaning filling my ears. She tasted so good, better than good, a taste I couldn't even describe. I wanted it all over me. All over my face, my fingers, my cock. I needed to keep her wetness to myself and never let anyone else ever have a taste. Not now that I had it. Not now that it was mine. I licked her pussy inside and out, finding her clit almost instantly and hearing her moans of pleasure continue. She came with the most beautiful sounding sigh, shaking and whimpering, and I was so glad she had before me. I was glad that I had pleased her. I held her hips to me so she couldn't get away and lightly licked as she softened down into the afterglow of orgasm, pulling gently on my hair.

"Do I need to be protected?" I whispered in her ear. I wasn't afraid for my body. It was my heart I was afraid of. What was she going to do to me, this girl, this woman, in this bed where it had only ever been me before. I had let her in and allowed myself to be open.

She shook her head. "No, no it's ok... I'm taken care of," she whispered, looking into my eyes.

That's not what I mean, Katarina, I implored back at her, but it was too late. My hips buckled, and I entered her all the way in and deeper. She gasped, moaned, and cried out. Shit, I hope I didn't hurt her, I was just so ravenous I couldn't be stopped now.

"I'm sorry, I'm sorry," I said, but she just moulded into me, wrapping her legs around me, her arms along my back pulling me into her.

"Don't be, this is what I want, Ben. I need this, I need you." There were small tears in her eyes, and the love was so intense. I felt it too and was confused by it but kept going. How could two strangers make love like this on one of their first meetings, only days after knowing each other? It wasn't human. *Please don't hurt me, Katarina.*

I thrust inside her, in and out. Holding the ins and quickening the outs, grinding into her like a mortar and pestle. My fingers linked into her fingers, my body fully on top of hers, hands above our heads, smothering her as her hands clenched onto mine. My cock was at peace, enveloped inside the warm folds of her body. He was happy, singing and dancing, running and jumping for joy. I kept thrusting as she moaned, releasing her hands so she could grab and scratch at me. She took my hips and held my pushes into her, scratching at my back on my pulls, finding my hands controlling hers, taking them away again, clasping them from time to time. With one final push I had made it last. Lord knows how I'd done it, but I'd made it last until she let out one more orgasm. As I felt her pussy contract I exploded into her, a burst of hot semen penetrating her, making her officially mine. I groaned, *oh my god woman.* I was on top of her in utter and amazed joy, a smile on my face so big I felt goofy.

We settled in mutual ecstasy and laughed, even whimpered a little, the moment was that special. My face nuzzled into her neck, I liked it here as it was as close as I could get to her, smelling the heat of her skin's glow. Leaning up on my elbow I caressed her face, wiping away her tears gently and said, "I hope it rains again tomorrow."

I was thankful for how natural I felt with her. It was like nothing I'd ever experienced before, but at the same time as comfortable as if we'd been together for years. I wasn't scared, but there was something knocking at that little door in my head. I shook it off and ignored it, not letting it ruin my moment.

She laughed at me, not feeling the awkward silence that usually happens just after you've exposed your body, naked and raw, to someone for the first time.

We laid in each other's nakedness for a while, not caring about our sweat and stickiness. She stared at the ceiling, her body relaxed, firm but soft, melded into mine like two pieces of a puzzle. We laid there a while longer, quiet as the afternoon turned into early evening, soon to be night. The house was quiet too, but I couldn't be sure for how long.

It was getting late outside, the clouds making it darker than it really was. I didn't want to move. I didn't want the day to end, but I was tired and getting hungry. We'd walked for three days, made love exhaustingly, and I had nothing left to say right now. I'd already said everything with my body.

"Maybe I'll go back to my hotel," she offered, breaking the silence.

"Ok." I shifted away from her body, smiling. "Let's go. I'll borrow the car, so we don't have to walk."

Standing, I grabbed my robe, left the room, and came back with her clothes. Before she had her shirt on, I grabbed her and drew her closer.

"Katarina," I nuzzled into her neck, "let me smell you one more time." I was quiet as my thoughts left the room, my gaze unfocused.

"You ok?" she asked.

"Yeah, yeah. Yes, I'm good." Shaking myself out of my weird trance, I nodded, and my eyes brightened. "Let's go, are you hungry? We can grab some pizza before I take you back."

"Sure! Sounds great, I'm starving."

The intensity of our moment had passed.

Chapter 11: Katarina

Because of the rain and it being Sunday, Ben was able to find a spot to park not too far from one of his favorite pizza places.

"You can't sit inside, unfortunately but trust me, it's one of the best places in town."

We ate our pizza outside the little hole in the wall of a NYC pizza joint, sheltered by the tattered overhang. It was probably the best pizza I had ever had, and I would never have even tried it without Ben suggesting it. When we were done, and it was time for him to take me to my hotel, I felt sadness creeping in. I didn't want the day to end quite yet. Everything had been perfect, from the museum to the rain, to the sex, to the pizza. He was beginning to feel more like a best friend than a stranger I had just met three days ago.

"What are you thinking, Katarina?"

"Just that I'm glad I met you. I wasn't expecting you to be part of my trip, and so far, you've been my whole trip." I laughed. "I'm so thankful for these last few days. I wouldn't have wanted to discover New York any other way. Thank you for spending your time with me."

"It's been my pleasure," he answered, and I got the impression that he wasn't ready to leave quite yet, either. I looked at him to see if he was having regrets. "I wish I could crawl inside you, then I'd know you more than I know myself."

He took my hand and traced the tips of his fingers up my arms, one by one, sometimes with a jump, like hopscotch, until he reached my shoulder. Then his finger skipped across my nose, the others waving like a childish tease in my eyesight. I laughed, looking at him.

"What are you doing?"

"Connecting the dots…"

What? I looked at him sideways. "Connecting the dots? What are you talking about?"

He nuzzled down into me. "Mmmmmmm hmmmm… I'm connecting the dots on your skin, like little drops of brown sugar. Your skin is glowing and so soft."

I smiled inside, my heart glowed. "Brown sugar." I smiled. "My dad used to say that about my freckles. Saying I got them from my mother. They still loved each other right to the end, regardless." I looked over at him and reminisced. It felt like he had always been there, like Ben was close to my history, to who I used to be years ago.

"Well, he's right. They really do look like brown sugar." He smiled and I felt a lump form in my throat. I turned towards him, shame in my eyes. He must have sensed the energy shift because he gave me a questioning look. The time had come, I had to divulge the truth and tell him the secret that I was so ashamed of, no matter how many years I'd tried to come to terms with it.

"Was," I said, but he didn't understand.

He crouched closer into my vision as I hung my head, trying to hide. Lifting my chin with his finger, he forced me to look right at him.

"What do you mean?" he demanded.

It wasn't something I talked about with many people, my father. Many times, I felt the entire town knew about what he had done. I hated the statistics and all the stupid questions I would get about him, feeling their eyes on me at school, always judging the girl with the gay dad. I was never ashamed of him and who he was, but what happened to our family was tough in an era when people just didn't understand. But I was vulnerable at the moment and felt the urge to open up everything to this amazing man I'd literally just exposed everything to.

"My dad died when I was fifteen," I blurted out and could feel my throat turn sour with tears. My nose filled up, and I pulled away. I wanted Ben to know everything there was to know about me and prayed he wouldn't judge me for something I never had any control over.

He shrunk back and looked away. "Katarina, I'm so sorry. That must've been incredibly hard."

I smiled weakly at him. He didn't know the half of it.

After a moment, he sighed and turned towards me. "Can I ask what happened?"

I wasn't fully sure he wanted to know. The air had changed, and I felt like he was only asking me because I had forced it into our conversation.

"Well… He fell in love with the wrong person…." I glanced up at him. "Man, I guess." My voice faded to a weak whisper.

He looked at me quizzically.

"My dad fell in love with a man who was sick. He had AIDS and never told him," I sputtered out, ugly tears running down my cheeks.

There it was. Was he going to ask those same dumb questions, wondering if I or my mom had AIDS too? Was he going to be that guy or was he better than that? I couldn't look at him, waiting to see what his silence would turn into.

"I'm so sorry," he muttered as I glanced in his direction, his eyes dark and closed off.

I'd gone too far, and he was uncomfortable now. I'd ruined our moment. *Why did I pick now to tell him my dark secret?*

"Shit happens to all of us, Katarina. Don't let it define you." He stood up and grabbed my hand, leading me towards the car without another word.

We pulled up to the front of the hotel. There was no parking, and the doorman was already heading towards us to tell him he couldn't stay there. He smiled at me. "Text me your number quick before I get in shit here." I did as I was told and sent him a private text that I hoped would make him smile later when he saw it. His phone lit up in the console, and he said, "I'll text you when I'm home. I have to work tomorrow and at least four days this week, but I want to see you again as soon as possible." His left hand drooped nonchalantly over the steering wheel, a sly grin on his face. A large silver ring adorned his first finger that I'd only just noticed. He smiled his sexy smile, staring right into my eyes and making my tits start to buzz. Leaning over, he kissed me, one last, strong, passionate kiss, moaning and as he pulled away, sucking in the air between us with a shudder.

"Talk soon Kitty Kat." He breathed.

"Ok," I smiled.

Today had been the best day of my life.

Jumping out, I ran towards the hotel, and he sped off in his family's black town car with a toot of the horn and a wave out the window. It looked as sexy as he did, shining in the wet night.

Drifting into the hotel, I was grinning from ear to ear, lucky to get right onto the elevator. Getting off on my floor, I turned towards my room and could hear the piano playing from the rooftop patio. Max was there. Grumpy old Max playing his sad piano songs and hating the world. I would've enjoyed a nice glass of wine to sip by myself, reliving the amazing day I'd had with Ben, but realized the patio would be empty because of the rain and opted out. I didn't want to be at the bar where the piano sat, topping off my evening alone with Max and his negativity. Instead, I went to bed waiting for the text Ben had promised.

Chapter 12: Benjamin

Making my way through the rain slicked streets, I was preoccupied by our conversation.

My god. I closed my eyes, a sense of panic and fear coursed through me like hot lava. I couldn't help but feel the reality of what I'd just done. Something just as awful, just as selfish. I was being punched in the gut with my truth. She had told me her secret, clearly the one thing that she was ashamed of, and I had withheld mine. I wasn't ready to share the truth about myself; it scared me too much.

I could tell she'd been struggling to open up to me but was trying anyway. Sharing her secret with me made me feel guilty for what I had been hiding from her. I wanted us to be equal, but she was stronger when it came to sharing her past. I'd forced a smile towards her, afraid of what tomorrow or later tonight might bring me. My body was infatuated with her, obsessed, but it was my mind I was afraid of. There were too many doors that could open at their own will. Each with different behavior controlling thoughts.

As I pulled back up to my childhood home, I felt uneasy. I remember how it loomed in front of me like a mean giant, judging me like I'd done something wrong or been a bad boy. I hadn't wanted to go in without knowing who was inside, but I had to drop off the keys. The large trees had towered over me in the darkness like monsters' limbs clawing at me as I approached. I'd felt scared by the dark windows. The odd one lit up like watchful eyes.

Call the cab first, the voice had said inside my head.

Fuck yeah, Ben. No one could blame me for not thinking.

I'd grabbed my cell and should've stopped short when I noticed the forty-seven missed calls. Unfortunately, I hadn't. Still mixed up in the glow Katarina was bringing into my life, I lost all sense of reality. I hopped up the staircase like an eager trick or treater on Halloween, hiding behind the mask I'd been wearing for days. *I'll just pop the keys in the front door on the table and get the fuck out of there before Mother or Father hears me.*

What a stupid plan. I wish I could take it all back.

I could've been safe, the inside set of doors were closed, the hallway in darkness. But what I hadn't considered was just how angry my father was. As I'd turned, the second set of doors had opened, and he'd been standing there in a fit of fury.

"Benjamin!"

Shit!

"Geoff told me he picked you up with a woman today. What were you thinking? What were you doing, bringing her here? What happened with your meeting Friday?" he'd whispered through gritted teeth, his ears red and on fire as he'd stood there scolding me like a lost child. Had Alexander told him I wasn't there? Idiot Geoff had mentioned a girl, and I knew the rest would unfold terribly.

Fuck!

Father had put me in a position I didn't like with his accusatory tone, and I didn't know how I was going to get out of it. I tried innocence and honesty, not exactly my style. Then started mumbling, "Dad... Father, I mean, I just had a really great weekend. Can we talk about this tomorrow morning? I need to go home so I can get ready for work."

"Oh, now we're prepping for work, are we?" He'd raised his voice as though mocking me. He glowered in the doorway, and even in my heightened state, I saw the signs of him getting angrier. When he stepped out into the foyer and got right up into my face and challenged me, I felt helpless and confined. Two things that have never sat well with me.

He said, "We've told you about women before, Benjamin. They're not a good idea for you."

My jaw tightened then, and my eyes sparked with fury. He was so condescending, like he thought he fucking knew everything.

Why the fuck had Geoff said anything? Why hadn't Alexander just called me, my own brother? He fucking knows how Father gets! But I forgot about the missed calls; I hadn't looked at my phone in three days, not since I'd stopped answering it on Friday.

Plus, I'd never brought a girl home before, and that's why Father was so pissed. What he hadn't seem to have thought about was how I was supposed to react to his judgemental tone. I'm a grown fucking man! Alexander, on the other hand, was looking out for me, so that's fair. But even he'd been stupid, and that's why things had gotten so messy.

I'd had one leg out the door, ready to bolt at the first sign of my cab arriving, when he'd said the thing that snapped the beast.

"What were you thinking? You stunned asshole."

That's when I'd turned on him, rage in my heart, my eyes blazing with fury, "I was helping her, Dad!"

"Jesus, Benjamin! How can you help this girl when you can't even help yourself?"

"Fuck you! Fuck you!" I became so angry I hadn't given a fuck if Mother was home. My thoughts started to boil over to the point I became blind, and I blasted down the stairs, not knowing what had happened or been said. My Father just couldn't leave it alone.

I start to unravel as the memory of that night plays on repeat in my mind. I grab onto my ears and begin to rock back and forth, trying to tune it out, but it burns in the back of my eyelids. I can see my father's face, hear the words that had taken me down the path of self-destruction.

I hate how my father can so easily make me question myself, my motives, and my capabilities. Just the memory of it makes me question it all again: the crash, the spinning, the panicking. I can feel the loss of control returning, the walls around me closing in.

I start banging my head as the feelings of anxiety flutter through my chest, even though the moment had passed many days ago.

They think I can't handle it. Well, I don't know if I can, either, but I am going to fucking try. I am better, and she is… different. They know about her now and are going to ruin it for me. *Fuck!*

And now, here I am trapped in this fucking room for fucking what? I'm fine, *fine.* I go to work, do my shit, and take these fucking kaleidoscope of rainbow pills! Well, mostly, anyway.

I don't care that my mother is delicate. That's the real reason my father was trying to hide me from her that night. She is a heartless bitch, and at some point, he is the one who needs to come to terms with that. Like I give a flying fuck if he's disappointed in me. He's always disappointed in me! What the fuck do I care. But, when he'd yelled it into the street as I fled, a part of me had died that day.

I play with the threads on my bed, picking them up and starting to make knots as the tears run down my face. *I am a pretty useless piece of shit, aren't I?* Fuck me, what a buzzkill. I need to get better at blocking out the negatives and keep the positive thoughts at the forefront of my brain. She's the only one who can help me do that. A smile spreads across my face, and I wipe away the tears, swallow hard, and try to concentrate on the memory of her, but the demons won't let me. I am fixated on the anger.

Why the fuck had he done that? If I'm such a ticking time bomb, like he seems to think I am, then how the fuck are these types of conversations supposed to go? He ruined my day, my most perfect weekend with her, and the fallout hadn't ended there on that street in that rain. He calls himself a father, but he believes that I can't be normal. I think he needs me to be weak, to feed his own ego.

At some point, I got into a cab and made it home, that much I remember. I sat angrily in the back seat, glaring out the window, the rain drops masking my hot tears. With my chin on my clenched fist, I watched the haunted houses blur by when I was stopped by the scent of my hands—the scent of her. I remember looking at them, my hands that had traced her beautiful body. My fingers, still graced with the scent of her warm skin, stopped the rage.

I try to find that solitude now and close my eyes, soften my breathing, open my fists so my fingers can be open to my nose. I imagine her sweet smell. My dick gets hard, and I moan. Frustrated, I get up to pace the confined room. Stopping at the mirror on the wall, I brace the sides with my hands and stare at myself. I can do this, I tell myself. I can do this for her. I grab the pen and paper off the desk and begin to write more of it out, my doubts scratching at the windows.

Chapter 13: Katarina

The day passes quicker than I would like, and as it becomes late afternoon, I find myself heading back to Gloria's. The thought of running into Ben clearly enters my mind. My stomach fills with butterflies, and I wonder if he really is avoiding me. What if last night was on me and not him? Was I the only one that had felt it? No way, I have to be wrong. I wasn't alone in that room. He had been with me the entire time, inside me, my soul, and I was in his. I'm sure he'll call soon.

The café has died down now that the workday is in full swing. There are a few people grabbing coffee break orders to take back to the office for the afternoon crunch. I spot Gloria, and without thinking, pop my hand up and yell, "Hey, Gloria!"

She looks confused and I begrudgingly realize I'm probably not the only girl Ben has introduced to her. Gulping down the lump of embarrassment, I address the counter and try to smile. "Hey, um, can I grab a coffee? I, uh, was here the other day and you said…"

"Oh yeah, you're one of Ben's friends, right?" She winks at me, and I wince at the mention of 'one of.'

"It's nice to see you're making out on your own." She says like it is a question, raising her brow and wiping her hands on her apron.

Just like Ben is, I thought to myself, imagining her snickering at me and the stupid fool I've been. That is how my mind works, self-sabotage and made-up realities that haunt me, keeping me even farther from believing in myself. Ignoring the dark devil on my shoulder, I take the opportunity to ask what I am dying to know, hoping I won't sound too desperate and naive.

"Have you, um, seen Ben today? At all? Not that I'm looking, it's just I. Well—" My voice betrays me as I squeak out the words, trying to act nonchalant and not overly eager to know his whereabouts.

"Ben? Oh no, I haven't seen him today. He usually calls if he's coming by."

I feel a sigh of relief and a shudder of hope that if he hasn't called her either, maybe he hasn't even picked up his phone today, but I know I am grasping.

"Plans today?" she asks.

"Yeah, I've been to the bookstore and wandered around Fifth. I'm thinking of going to the financial district and checking it out."

She nods and carries on. "I don't read much. I'm way too busy here," she gestures at the café, "but good for you, and you are on vacation after all, right? How long did you say you're staying?"

I start to relax, I like her, she seems interested and very kind.

"Well, right now I've got a place for two months. After that, I'm not sure. If I like it, maybe I'll stay and find something in my own field. I'm a social worker."

"Social work huh? I don't know how you can stand people that much." She chuckles. "You must have a lot of patience and a big heart. Not sure you'll feel the same way after being in this city." She winked. "What are you going to do in all that time?"

"Get a job, hopefully." I laugh. "Ideally, I'd like to really get to know New York, not like a tourist but like a New Yorker."

I hope I don't sound as lost as I feel but as the confidence drains out of my voice, my heart starts to crumble with it.

"What kind of job do you want? I could use a hand here, you know. My sister usually fills in over summer to help with all the tourists, but she took off to Europe, lucky shit. It's not glamourous but you'd meet every personality New York has to offer. Kurtis, here, can show you how to make the drinks. Weekends off. What do you say?"

I shake my feelings off and think about it. I do love the café; I'll meet plenty of people, and it is close to my hotel.

"I'd need you from nine until about two, during the late morning and lunch rush, Monday to Thursday, and the odd Friday when the students bail on me. I won't hold you to it. If you don't like it, no feelings hurt."

It seems more than fair to me, giving me lots of time to myself, too. The only issue is running into Ben if he really doesn't want to be run into. I decide against cautious judgement and say, "Sure." I shrug my shoulders. "I'll take it if you don't mind having me."

"Great, done and done. Start next Monday?"

"Absolutely." Grabbing my coffee, I hit the street heading towards the Square to take on the city solo.

With the job search settled, I allow myself to relax a little even though Ben still hasn't called or texted. I can't deny I am allowing his absence to take up too much space in my head rent-free. I've texted him and could texted him again, but I want to see if I can feel him out, and not come across as needy, so I wait. It kills me. Confuses me. Hurt me. But I just wait.

I travel on the tour bus round and round, not really looking at anything and never getting off. Tears of guilt, shame, embarrassment, and disgust run down my face as I sniffle into my sleeve, trying to hide these emotions from strangers as they laugh and giggle, pointing at New York's scenery. What the hell is happening to me? I am here for a reason I'm not fulfilling.

Or am I? 'You came here to figure yourself out,' I hear my mom's voice whisper in my thoughts. 'What is this experience teaching you? Showing you about yourself?'

Lifting my head up to the sky, I take a deep breath in and blow it out. I gave everything I am to a man—a man I'd opened my entire being to and he'd taken it and used it. Fucking played with it, pissed on it, thrown it away. Hanging my head, I start to cry harder in earnest. I try brushing my tears away in anger, knowing they'll keep coming back again and again.

I am exhausted and beaten, and all I can think of is quitting and going back home. This was a stupid idea.

Still no call.

What will I even say if he does call? How do I feel? I am so insecure, and I've never felt this bad before. Laying on my bed, I inventory all my feelings, alone, betrayed, used, confused.

Really confused.

Chapter 14: Benjamin

By the time I had arrived home that night, after my father confronted me, it was well past midnight. My body and soul were full, but my head was a mess. What had I done? I try to explain the feelings of doubt and fear that kept taunting me, teasing me with their evil laughs like doors that open and close inside my head.

My condo was cold and lonely, abandoned as always. I don't let anyone in, and other than the maid, few souls have ever spent time in my space. I prefer it that way. I can keep out the noise. The nights are the worst, I'm surrounded by windows in the condo, but the night sky makes it feel like a cave. Big black voids to nowhere, reminding me how my mother and father have made me feel. Empty and good for nothing.

I think about the place I call home. Dark hardwood floors throughout and the furniture is sparse. A soft brown leather sofa and a Persian rug I think my dad picked out. The living/dining combo is surrounded by those dark windows except for the corner beam, which is floor to ceiling brick, holding a gas fireplace and mounted TV, not that it's ever on. There's a round glass coffee table with a few books and an NYC paper the maid probably left. I stick to my worn out, dark blue armchair. I found it in the parking garage, and it's my favourite piece because it feels real. I use it so much when I sit and stare out the vast windows.

The place was furnished by some designer when my father bought it, so I guess someone was in there before I moved in. It's minimal, like me, and I'm not sure if I like it that way or not. I need little light, but I like to flick on the small lamp in the evenings. In the mornings I use the same space to read the paper, the sun beating down on my back. The shades can be pulled down by the press of a button to dim the light, creating a warm glow in the daytime. I don't keep many things, maybe a candle or two. I prefer things dark and moody, especially when I am in one of my multiple mood swings.

The kitchen is rarely used. All new white cabinets, stone counters, and black stainless-steel appliances. The island separates the dining room area that holds a large wood table with six chairs that have never been sat in. Dark wood bookcases line the wall at the edge of the dining room, leading down the hallway towards the bedroom and ensuite bathroom. It's possible there is a guest bathroom in the same hallway, but I don't really know. The whole place is painted white, any and all art reminds me too much of home. There's a record player and records in the bookcase, the melody of music keeps me calm.

My head hurt, and I was starting to feel sick. Father always made it hurt, talking to me like one of his patients, never supportive. Not how a father is supposed to speak to his son. He makes me feel like no matter how I try, it doesn't matter. The doubts and negative vibes scramble up my thoughts. I wasn't thinking clearly at all. I needed Advil. Making my way to the bathroom, I smelled her on my hands again, and I softened. I was ok.

I had looked at myself in the mirror. It was better at home, but my father's words just kept berating me, knocking me down. All I wanted to do was change from what and who I've always known, always been, always reverted back to. Eventually.

I let you in Katarina, shared my bed with you, shared my soul with you. You made me feel like I could belong, that I deserve to be here. If I could just be with you, someone who doesn't know me, the old me, we could wash away the memories. You'd be someone I could work for. Someone I could stay strong for. I could start over with you.

My mind started to giggle. *No, you can't, silly,* it taunted.

I texted you back but paused with doubt winning over the physical function of my hands. I looked at my stupid self in the mirror. My words, my feelings were worthless after what you'd said to me.

<Leaving you tonight. Excited for our future tomorrows.>

It burned into my truth and all my failures like a scar. *A future? Fuck me, Katarina.* With me, there is no future.

Over medicated, that's the fucking problem. I needed to take those pills away. She could never know. Clouded and confused, I decided that these little pills—blue, yellow, pink, don't forget the white ones—those little bastards were the problem. I don't need them. I can't be like that if I'm going to be with another human being in a relationship.

Just stop taking them, Bennie, you'll be ok, you'll be fine.

My history blared in my face, all the mistakes, deficiencies, and struggles. I hated looking back, going back to when I was broken and falling down.

I am what I am, that's right. I am what I was, always will be, I can't change.

The voices agreed.

I started to unwind, a nervous wreck. Panic and doubt mixed with fear, the lies of hope and happiness. Back and forth, up and down like a fucking roller coaster. *Step right up, join us on the magical ride of Bennie's Brain!* I was stretched out too thin, grasping for something that could ground me. I needed a safety net, protection, someone to catch me when I fell. Could she protect me from me? Nervous and scared, I started twitching on the floor, cold sweat formed everywhere. Everything hurt. Her love and her scent were still on my face, my hands, my cock, and I wasn't ready to wash her off yet.

Ben, you need a shower, buddy to warm up, then get into bed.

I managed to crawl to the bathroom and as steam filled the room, I headed back to grab a bottle of wine, okay two. Leaving one on the counter, I popped the cork and brought the other into the shower with me, chugging back the dark liquid and burning down the lump that had grown in my throat. As she rinsed away, I instantly regretted it and started to cry.

Finally! Fuck, let shit out, Ben! I began to believe she had never happened, and that it was all in my head. I cried more.

You don't deserve someone like her, they giggled and taunted.

I crawled into my bed and hid under the covers. *Not good enough! Not good enough! Not good enough!* they sang.

I know. Shut up! I know, I know. I pulled at my hair, just wanting to make it stop. *Make them stop!* Mother and Father were right, I'm not good enough. Alexander too, that guy was right, I don't deserve her. I'll wreck it, break it, smash it into a million little pieces just like everything else I touch. She felt like forever to me but that wasn't real, not for me, anyway. The only forever for me was pain.

Infatuated and obsessed with what I couldn't have, I couldn't stop tossing and turning. *What you're going to find out, Katarina, if I'm not ready for this? The worst of me.*

The little bastards weren't letting me sleep. I was desperate to sleep. The bathroom lights were bright and blaring. I stared into the medicine cabinet full of different medications.

Confused, I sat on the cold floor and leaned against the shower door, legs sprawled out. I could still feel the turmoil inside me. I wanted to be good. I wanted to be better. But everyone told me I'm not, it's not possible. Was it true what they said? Pulling myself up off the ground, I knew the first thing I needed was sleep. Sleep, so my brain would stop, and I could think clearly. Pills scattered on the floor in the bathroom. *Shit.* On hands and knees, I picked up a few. *Time for the green ones? No, the blue. I don't know, whatever. Pop!* I drank from the bottle of wine. If I could just sleep, I'd sleep all this shit off and start again tomorrow. Petrified by the thoughts and the voices, I don't know how much I drank. I think I fell down; something hurt.

Someone was in my apartment. *Fuck!* I sat up, groggy as shit. What the hell? Broken glass was all over the floor, and I was lying in it, oops.

"Hello? Benjamin? Benjamin where are you?" Angry people were yelling, livid.

Then I realized….

Father.

Father was there. What time was it? I should have been at work. I had to go to work. Katarina. Did I call her? Oh god, what did I say?

"Mmfffff." I pulled up on the bathroom sink and fell just as Father entered.

"Benjamin? Oh Christ, Benjamin!" He was yelling, standing in the doorway. "What did you take? What did you do, Benjamin?"

"Fine, Dad," I shook my head. "Father, whatever. Fine. Just don't… feel well. Gotta go. I'll be ok."

"Go where? Work?" he yelled at me, very angry. "It's *noon* Benjamin. Why do you think I'm here?" His face was boiling red, and his expressive hands were flailing.

Dammit, calm down!

"It's this girl, isn't it?! This fucking girl!" he screamed at me, and my head instantly started to throb as I tried shaking it no.

"Remember the girl you brought to our house? Benjamin! She's the reason you keep doing this to yourself. Why do you believe you can handle things when you can't! When will you learn? My god, Benjamin. When will I have to stop fixing you?"

"Fixing me? What are you fixing?!" I found my voice and screamed back.

"Jesus, bringing her home. Idiot," he muttered and tried to pick me up off the floor.

Struggling, we both started fighting each other with our arms everywhere. Pushing him off, I got up on my own, pulling up on the sink, groggy and spinning.

"No. Not her. This is not her fault. I just got confused. You have me on too many pills. I took the wrong ones. I'm ok. I'm sorry. Just. I'll shower. I'll be ok."

"You can't even stand. For crying out loud, Benjamin!" He took a deep breath and calmed down while I gripped the counter and swayed, trying to find focus.

"Benjamin, Benjamin, Benjamin. Benjamin. What have I told you? The medication you take is what you need," he soothed. "There's nothing wrong with what I've prescribed. I know what I'm doing, unlike you. The problem is not the meds. The problem is that you don't listen. These girls, you can't have relationships, son. We've told you."

I shook my head and protested. "Wrong, you're wrong. I've never even had anyone that means anything, so how do you know?" I glared at him. "You don't understand. Why do you always take the best things away from me?"

"I don't know? I'm a *doctor*, Benjamin! I don't know, but you do? Look at you! I had to come here and pick you up off the floor." Matching my glare he whispered, "Just like your damn mother. Now listen, I have told you—we've all told you. Relationships are not for someone like you. Give me your phone," he demanded, extending his hand.

I glanced toward the floor where my phone was mixed in with the broken glass. It was closer to him than me, and unfortunately, he noticed too.

"Screw you, I'm almost thirty. You're not taking anything. I'm not a fucking teenager." Wobbling, I could barely stand straight.

"I'm taking your phone, and you're coming under my watch." Faster than me, he grabbed it, placing it in his suit jacket pocket.

"We're going to your brother's. Your mother doesn't need this, you and your shit again." He shook his head, his face red with anger. "Fucking child, you'll do what I say because my name is on this lease, and why is that little man? Because you can't handle it."

My eyes were brimming with tears of frustration and spite, reality set in.

"You're going to need to detox again, and you'll participate in sessions. Every day. While I try to hide this from your work. Dammit, Benjamin. I don't even know what to say!"

I explode. "What are you talking about? What shit are you making up in *your* head? You act like I'm an idiot, well I'm not! News flash, *Doctor*, I've been, and I still am *fine!* For years! *Years!*" My reflection flashed out of the corner of my eye, and I noticed how undone I actually looked. "Stop micromanaging me and doctoring my brain with all your fucked up shit. Leave me *alone!* Take your pills and *fuck off!*" I stood, ripped the entire medicine cabinet off the wall, and hurdled it toward him.

"*Benjamin!* Calm down! This is your spiral, remember? Don't pretend you don't know. This is how it starts. I'm calling Alexander and he'll come to get you. You'll stay with him until we get you straight again, cleaned up."

I knew I was done; I had no phone, and he owned my place. I didn't have a choice.

"Get dressed," he bellowed, and I hung my head in defeat and complied.

"Hey, brother."

Alexander was in my room. A bag was packed. I was weak, sick to my stomach, my head, and my heart. My head hung low; I sat on the side of my bed.

"Hey, brother," I responded quietly, closed off.

"Let's get you to my place. It's ok, Mother isn't going to be involved this time. Father and I will take care of work. Let's go, I'll fix this."

I lifted my head to the side and glared at him. "I don't need your fixing Alex! What I need is for all of you to *Leave me alone! Stop!* Stop trying to *fix me!*"

"Benjamin. Dude. Buddy. This doesn't look good right now. What happened? Why are you spinning?"

"*Why?* Why am I spinning? Father! That's why! Always preying on my weaknesses to make him feel better about himself."

"Jesus, Benjamin, you could've died!" He threw his hands up. "Thank God you didn't. Do you even know what you took? Sleeping pills, it looks like." He picked up one of the many bottles scattered on the bed, the same ones that had flown everywhere when I'd ripped the cabinet off the wall. "With a lot of wine, too." He shook his head and turned to me, kneeling in front of me. "Who are your demons, right now?

What are you dealing with?"

"Demons?" I glared. "Right here. The demons are right here. You two." I point out at the air. "You fuckers!" I hung my head down again, pulling at my hair.

"Ben, calm down," he soothed, resting his hand on my knee. "You're on the verge of a psychotic break, you know that, right? We have to get your control back before you hurt yourself."

"Do I have a choice, Alex?" I looked up at him. "Father has my phone, and my bag is packed." I sighed "Let's just do this. Get it done so I can come home."

I felt alone, ashamed, and broken, holding my head in my hands while my younger brother looked at me with pity in his eyes. I hated that. I knew I had failed, the failure that I was, that I've always been, always known.

Geoff came to pick us up. He was quiet in the car, looking without speaking. He'd been here before, picking me up from whatever hell hole I'd found myself in. It had been a long time, though. A long time. With Alex in the back beside me, and my father in the front, I stared out of the window of the backseat, angry as hell. I wasn't in a hole this time; I was just confused. I thought I could be capable. I figured I'd done well this past weekend with her, but my doctor told me I was wrong. Was I? Or was he?

Miserable in self-loathing, disgusted with my coping combo of red wine and sleeping pills, I realized I was where I needed to be. I needed a life worth living, successful and worth sharing with someone—someone like her. I'd take one more day, or week, with my father to straighten my shit out. I was willing to do it if it meant I could be with her. Would I be able to fix myself this time if I tried? Really tried? My family didn't know, couldn't know how important she was to me, or they'd sabotage it. I had to do this on my own, and I had to succeed.

Chapter 15: Katarina

It's been five days. Nothing. I left the ball in his court, and he's decided not to play. Last night I sent a question mark in a text after having too much wine and still nothing. I'm not texting him again.

Now I'm mad. *No, fuck you, you idiot you're mad at yourself.* Maybe I am mad at him, too, but is any of it his fault? No, not really. Me and my blabber mouth and stupid moment of idiocy had gotten me here, what did he have to do with it? Did he ask for it? I practically threw myself at him, but he allowed it didn't he?

I'm drunk at four in the afternoon and have lost control of rational thinking. Time to reassess. Studying my wine glass at the bar, I wipe my nose again, realizing, there are no more tears left to shed, and I pick up my heart. I call Monica and tell her some things, but not everything. Mostly things that don't matter. She says he's a dick and to find another guy to fuck, move on. She doesn't get it. She seems so juvenile to me all of a sudden. So fucking stupid. I feel older, harder, stronger in a weird way. Something has changed in me. I understand my capabilities, or lack thereof, and my pain, bit by bit.

What did you want to find, Katarina? The good? The bad? The ugly? I'm not scared. I'm terrified.

The days continue to start the same and every morning I exhaust my pain, shoving him down along with my feelings. All the way down. I run, faster than I've ever run. I am so angry, and I allow myself to be. I feed on my pain and make sure to eat every single bite. I cry, allowing myself to be ashamed. Face it head-on. No one, no man, will ever have this control over me, ever. My control is my responsibility, and I can't give that away. Lesson one, Katarina.

I've been frequenting the local bookstore as a daily routine after work. It is kind of out of the way from my hotel and serves as a way to pass the time. Time seems like a cruel joke as it continues to leave me with too much to think about. I am lost in my own little world, staring at new releases, when I am jostled to the side. Unexpectedly, I hear a voice beside me.

"He likes you."

I jump, alone in my own memories, I'm surprised to hear someone talking to me in a city that doesn't know my name.

Max is standing beside me. He's not the type of guy I would take as an enthusiastic bookworm and wonder if he's here in his own travels or following mine. This is last place I ever expect to see anyone, especially the angry pianist from my hotel.

"What? Who?" I stutter.

"That guy you're daydreaming about. You're in my way. Move over or hand me that novel there."

I move numbly and in shock. I begin to stutter another answer when he again snaps at me.

"I said he likes you. And you like him. Be careful with that shit."

Emotionally exhausted, I feel like my eyes are bulging out of my head. The audacity of this asshole has every pin pricked in my soul, and suddenly my anger fully erupts. The emotional roller coaster I've been on comes to a crescendo, and I spit at him, "I don't know who the fuck you think you are and how who, or what, I'm into is any of your business. Clearly you don't have many boundaries, or friends for that matter. Have you ever wondered why?" He looks at me with a menacing squint and I match his glare, countering back with, "I don't need your bullshit, neighbour."

Finally, he shows some emotion as he raises his one eyebrow and smirks.

Irritated, I continue, "Your name is Max, correct? I'm Katarina and although you seem so willing to share your opinion, it's not needed or wanted. Now if you'd please, *namaste* the fuck away from me."

Turning on my heel, I stomp away, leaving him standing unfazed in my wake. I make my way to the checkout with a book in my hand I'm not even sure I want but don't even care. My heart is pounding in my chest and I'm shaking like a leaf, but a huge grin forms on my face. *Holy shit! Did those words just come out of my mouth?* I have never, ever, said something like that to anyone, especially a stranger. I'd stood up for myself, and I'm absolutely giddy.

Leaving the store, I'm quite pleased with this new version of Katarina. Her boldness, daringness, that trust in herself! And the confidence! Wow! I like how I feel and what I am now capable of doing. The city is rubbing off on me, and I'm okay with that. But I'm heartbroken and sad, too, and just as quickly as my emotions have me up in the air, they come crashing back down again.

I frown. One minute Ben had me gliding through air, and the next I'm back to being just so damn confused. *What is it with the people in this city? What is it with me?* I roll my eyes, I pride myself in ensuring my surroundings are authentic and simple, and it doesn't seem like I am in the right place for any of that. No one seems to give a shit what others think of them and act any way they please. I've never been that cold hearted and simply can't understand it. As for simplicity, yeah right, not in this place as horns blare in my ears and flyers pepper the streets.

Outside, I'm engulfed by the sea of New Yorkers as I stumble along, unable to shake Ben out of my mind. Old man or not, the asshole is right, and it pisses me off that Max can see right through me.

Deciding I could use a drink, I hail a cab and head back to the hotel.

Nothing is ever enough. As the weekend hits, and I find myself emptily flirting with strangers at bars, my depression hits new lows. After making friends with a few people from work, I'm getting out of the hotel apartment and gaining a deeper knowledge of the city, but by the end of the evening I'm still alone and disconnected.

I find myself bringing bottles of wine back to my room, just like Max. Sunday mornings we seem to arrive at our doors at the same time, both of us miserable. His bottle brown. My bottle red. I am mortified by our similarities—the fact that life is winning over us, and we can't seem to shake our depressive little stories.

"Screw you," I spit out.

"Screw you too," he mumbles right back.

We enter our rooms and shut the doors, leaving the rest of the world outside to carry on with, or without us.

Chapter 16: Benjamin

The thought of scratching lines of time on the bedpost makes me laugh. I figure it's either the weekend or close to it, if I've been here since Monday. When the door knocks, I jump but am fully alert. It's time to go down to the bottom of Hell and dive back into the darkness. These meetings with Father are exhausting and downright annoying, but I think I've been proving myself. He seems pleased so far.

"Draw me a picture, Benjamin."

It's dark in Alex's office, the blinds drawn shut. A large desk and full bookshelves line the back wall. Father sits in a brown leather wingback chair. Across from him, I slump on the matching loveseat, smelling the stench of his judgement.

"No."

Irritated, he repeats himself, "Draw me a picture, Benjamin. Show me a picture of how you're feeling right now."

"No. I don't want to go there. I haven't been there in years, and I'm not fourteen." I glare at the pad of paper and crayons sitting beside him. Seriously? Fucking crayons?

He raises his voice, seemingly frustrated. Again. "You're there now. Don't tell me you can't feel it? Hear it."

Gathering my courage, I push back. "I'm doing this on my own, Father. I'm healing my way, like a grown man." I clench my hands.

His legs are crossed, pen and notepad in hand, and he's looking over his glasses. I hate those fucking glasses and want to ram them right into his skull. Staring back, I breathe in hard and change my focus. What color are her eyes? *Green, Ben. They're the most beautiful color of green.*

Breathe.

"Have you been feeling more confident with yourself lately, Benjamin?"

What's the right answer here? The one he's looking for. I decide to lie. "Not particularly." I've been the most confident I've felt in years.

"Ok then. That's good you recognize your limits. So why do you insist on doing things you can't handle?"

God, I hate this man.

He continues, "Can you face that, Benjamin? Draw me a picture of what that looks like."

"I don't want to draw a fucking picture, Dad!" My eyes fly open, and I grab at my hair and pull. *Fuck! Calm down, Ben. Calm, calm, calm. Think of her soft breasts, creamy skin with little bits of brown sugar.'*

He stares back at me, writing some bullshit in his fucking notepad. "What do you do differently from other people? How do you see yourself in comparison to others?"

Sitting back up in the chair, I breathe and fight back the tears of frustration forming in my eyes. "I'm not like other people. I don't… behave the same way." *Including love, I don't love like other people. They're not so lucky.*

"What makes you different, Benjamin?"

"My behavior. My abilities." *Not true.*

"How so?"

I stop and say nothing. Unsure of how to make him happy while proving to him that I can handle things better than he thinks I can, I get confused.

He redirects the question. "Do you consider yourself special in any way?"

You're damn right I do, and what's wrong with that? But I don't answer him.

"Benjamin? If you feel superior, would you agree you're in the middle of a manic episode?"

"Is being happy considered manic these days, Father?" I offer and glare at him.

"No, no it's not. But for you, manic episodes result in depressive episodes, and what happens during those?"

"I hurt myself." Right answer. He smiles. I close my eyes preparing for the onslaught of upcoming questions.

"Exactly, so what is good for Benjamin?"

Katarina. "Simple. Schedule. Routine," I say out loud.

"Correct. What is bad for Benjamin?"

You. Mother.

"Anything that breaks that routine." *Keep going, Ben, you've got this.*

"Correct. Why is that?"

"Breaks me, I can't handle change." *Right. Go, go, go!*

"Correct! So, what do we do, Benjamin?"

"Nothing. We do nothing." *Shit, Ben, wrong one.*

"That's not correct." He frowns. "What do we do, Benjamin?"

"We stay static." *Good, better.*

"Correct!" He smiles and makes another note. "Correct."

Thank god.

"Where do you live, Benjamin?"

"Chelsea." *Yes.*

"And what do you do there?"

Love. I love Katarina.

"I go to work and run. I play music and read." *Perfect.*

"Yes, and are those activities something you can handle?"

"Yes." I smile, he smiles. *I can handle anything.*

We do this every day, and every day I get better, stronger. I need to break the habit. When I return to my room, I write. I write to Katarina and spill out all my love. All my pain. All my fucked-up issues. I leave nothing unturned. I cry, so fucking much. As the hours pass into days, I make hundreds of bracelets. Green ones like her eyes with specks of gold. Black ones with brown like her hair. White ones with pink, like her lips and between her soft legs. Frustrated but relieved, I feel lighter now than I have in years, all of the weight stuffed under the mattress.

I know the excruciating work I've put myself through has come to an end when my brother comes to the door.

"Ben?"

"Yeah, come in." I am sitting on the bed, my fingers entwined in another bracelet with more scattered around me. I've been up and dressed for a few hours and finally shaved my face.

"Hey man, how you doing?" Alex stands in the doorway, leaning on the frame.

"I'm good." I raise my head to address him and then return my attention back down to my string version of Katarina, securing another knot.

"Still making those, huh? Are there any other colors? Why are they all the same?" He sits on the bed and starts fingering the bracelets.

"I like these colors," I reply and eye him touching my Katarina. I don't like it but make sure not to react and keep my cool. "What's up?" I ask.

He stops touching them and looks at me. Thank God.

"He wants you to go home today. Father. It's Friday morning. You know that, right?"

"Mmmhmm."

"Cool, he thinks you should go home and get back into your routine before heading into work on Monday. Sound good?"

My eyes light up, and a grin forms on my face. *Katarina, I'm coming. I'm coming to find you.*

Remaining as calm as possible, I nonchalantly reply, "Yeah, sounds good. Maybe I'll just go for a run first and get outside." I stretch. "Geoff can drop off my stuff? I'll run the Park and grab a cab home if that works?" First stop the park, she loves it there. If she isn't there, I'll try Gloria's, see if she's seen her. If not, I'll get a room at her hotel until I find her.

"I think that's a great idea. Run off some steam, buddy. Your stuff is here. I'm pretty sure your gear is in the closet. Don't forget your keys, and I'll grab your phone."

"Thanks man, that would be great." He leaves the room, and I jump up and destroy the closet for my gear, throwing it on in seconds. Before leaving the room, I stuff all the bracelets under the bed except for one. One I put on my wrist. The green one. I like the green one best.

When Alexander comes back, he has my keys and my phone. I can't wait to get my hands on my phone and see her picture. Being sure to control my nerves I stop myself from ripping the phone out of his hands before he hugs me and turns to leave the room.

"See you later and try to have a great weekend." He glances back at me from the doorway.

"Yeah, see you Monday." I sense a smile form on my face and feel the most like myself in days. Deciding to be a little playful and giddy, I offer him a strange look and say, "Is that what you're going to wear to work?"

He looks down at himself concerned, not realizing I'm messing with him. When he realizes I'm busting his balls, he laughs. "Screw you man! I've got better fashion sense than you do, bracelet boy."

We smile at each other, and for a moment it feels good to be normal again.

After he's gone, I focus on my phone, shaking with excitement. I unlock the screen, grinning in anticipation.

It's gone.

All of it.

Gone.

Her photos, my photos. Her number. Her texts. All fucking gone. *Fuck you, old man! Fuck!* I fly down the stairs and out the door. Panic never does stay at bay very long, and I can't run fast enough. I have to find her.

Chapter 17: Katarina

Life had become full of hangovers, but I eventually get my head out of my ass. With work, wine, and books keeping me occupied I'm forcing myself to get over it. It has been two weeks since I arrived in New York, and since I'd first met Ben. And a week and a half since I'd bared my body, my soul, and my heart to him.

Packaging the stupid bitch back up, my heart is currently resting, bruised, beaten, and mortified in the bottom of my gut, and she is going to stay there for a while. Possibly forever. As for my soul, I really don't know how it feels, it has never been involved before. I had thought his was involved too, but clearly, I was wrong. He is gone, and I am gullible.

Work is actually pretty great, and I feel like I know what I am doing. Gloria put me on the till to learn the menu, saying I caught on fast. The drinks aren't so easy, and by Friday I am glad for the day off. Everyday I've looked for Ben and haven't seen him once. I did recognize the driver, Geoff. He came in the mornings with pastries by the boxes. He has eyed me a few times, and I wondered if he wanted to say something; but he never did, and I didn't have the balls to talk to him.

"It's been a minute since Nancy supplied us so much Crombolini. The city don't mind though, nah, yeah. Keeps those crusties comin' in," Gloria would say when taking the daily deliveries.

I tried not to look too interested in their conversations, but it was killing me to know where the hell Ben was and why *he* wasn't coming in. He loves Nancy's treats and has no idea I work here. Unless Geoff had told him, and he really is avoiding me completely.

I am tired of trying to figure it out and determine not to waste any more of this trip waiting around for a man. I may have started my morning at the café in my usual jean shorts and for today, a red fitted tee, but I am going to bust out of this routine. Leaning on the fact that I am tough and resilient, I put a smile on my face and pick myself up off the floor. Even though I don't want to do it alone, I'm not quitting because I don't quit on myself. This is good stuff. My confidence building, I now know my way around by subway and can hail myself a cab. Maybe I will fit in here. Fake it till you make it.

Sitting at the corner table, the same one we'd sat at two weeks prior, I settle into the book I've bought from the local bookstore.

My nose catches a scent that makes every cell in my body start to vibrate, and I freeze. Without even having to look up, I know he's here. My skin starts to burn and prickle, and as I slowly lift my head and shift my gaze to the side, I can sense the silhouette of a man standing beside my table.

Because my face had been buried in the book, I didn't notice him walk in, but that scent is unmistakable. I can feel him, his energy vibrating with mine, and I instantly get warm. With my one hand wrapped around my coffee, I stiffen with anger, tempted to throw it at him even though it is extremely hot.

"Hey. Katarina," Ben says, breathless. He's been running, that is clear as I turn my head, watching his chest heave and fall with exaggerated breath. He is wearing a bright blue running shirt, long black running shorts. With his shirt soaked, dripping with sweat, wet curls and shining grin, he looks incredible.

"*Hey? Katarina?*" I respond, looking up at him in disbelief. Tens of thousands of emotions, words, and everything else bursting to get out of me and he says, *Hey? Katarina?* I stare at him incredulously. *Fuck you. And fuck you again.*

The thought crosses my mind for a split second that if he's this oblivious, maybe our engagement is normal for people here, and I was missing the beat, but I squash that. I'm not going to get into the habit of doubting my feelings. Discrediting what my heart, body, and soul know. And feel. Without a doubt. No, this guy is just an asshole, and I fell for him hook, line, and sinker. Ugly.

"Can I sit?" he asks. My eyes grow wide with disbelief.

"Yeah sure, sit," I challenge, and his face lights up like the fourth of July. The moment his hot ass hits the chair, I stand up, leave my coffee, and bolt right out the door at a pace that would make a Giselle jealous.

Fuck him. Fucking sit. Sure, you can sit, but not with me. You want to sit with me? Well, you should've called me a fucking week ago, fuck face. Fuck you. I'm not falling for his shit again. I might be dumb but I'm not easy, not that easy anyway. He is behind me, I know it, jogging to catch up and dodging people. *Good. Fucking run, you asshole.*

"Katarina!" He yells out, catching up. "Katarina, please, let me talk to you!"

But I continue walking, not even looking at him.

"Katarina, hey! I lost your number!" I can hear the panic in his voice, and my heart softens "I… I lost my phone... misplaced my phone…"

I quicken my step, and he's right on me, advancing. I can feel him starting to become aggressive. Ben is much bigger than me and he bumps his body against mine, steering me towards the wall. With his body, he pushes me into the alleyway. I'm pissed, but it's New York, and no one notices.

"What the fuck are you doing?" Turning on him I face him full on.

This fucker pushes me into an alley? Ironic considering the conversation we had when we first met regarding this scenario. He really does have a hard time keeping to his word. I'm not scared though; he might be an asshole, but I know he won't hurt me. We've already had sex, and I know he isn't a rapist. That I fucking know.

"What do you want? What do you want?" I yell at him, tears in my eyes.

He stares back and goes dark, pushing me with his chest deeper into the alley. The alley stinks, and I stumble back a bit figuring ok, you want to do this here? Let's do this here. "What do you want to say to me, Ben?" I glare.

Sheltered from the street by a large garbage bin, he comes at me and grabs my wrists, lifting my arms and staring down at me. Our eyes search each other, sparks flying and I've never seen his eyes like this. Maybe a little that first day, when he took off on that angry phone call. They are dark, cloudy, and he looks a little crazy.

He slams me up against the wall, just enough that his aggressiveness shocks me, and pins my hands above my head. Taking his hips, he pins mine against the wall so I can't squirm away, and I feel the juices of excitement run through my body. His arms are fully extended, giving me room to breathe so I'm not freaking out, in fact, quite the opposite.

"Ben," I say, "let go of me. Let go of me now." I can feel his cock on me. He's getting hard, and I start to soften, my hips auto lifting to meet his. His eyes, still firing like sparks, begin to water.

"Listen to me. Please don't run from me, and I'll let go of you," he growls, still staring like a wolf.

"Fine," I comply through gritted teeth, hoping to diffuse the situation. His black eyes are filled with dark passion, possibly hate, I'm not fully sure. He pulls his hips off a little and loosens his grip on my wrists, but he doesn't let me go.

Chapter 18: Benjamin

I am being way too casual, but I am scared shitless. Maybe I'm not—definitely not—ready for this. It is taking all I have in my brain, brains, to keep fucking calm. She looks at me and stops glaring, that is a good sign. No, she has a look of disbelief on her face, like I am out of my mind.

Well, technically I am. I am panicking now, repeating the mantra my father told me to use when I start slipping. It isn't working. I need to talk to her. I have to get her back into my life. I have to make her understand. Panic starts popping his little head out. *I didn't think this through. I should've thought this through. Oh hell, she's mad at me. Well, so am I, Katarina. Just fucking talk to me. Get her alone, make her look at me, make her listen, make her talk to me.*

"Katarina," I start, "just let me explain, ok?" I can feel myself starting to calm down. The anger, fear, and panic go back into their little doors and shut inside. Good. I'm good.

"I'm so sorry, Katarina," I plead. "I... had work." Thinking of the half lie on the spot. I have worked hard these weeks, only it was on my head. Why hadn't I thought this through?

"I had something at work, and it took me out of town." A full on lie and invisible eyes in the back of my head begin to roll. Fuck, I'm lying to her now. This isn't good, that's what Father says starts the trouble, lies.

"I was with my brother. We flew to Boston for some business. It was last minute. My phone, it fell out of my pocket in Geoff's car. I didn't have it, I didn't... I literally just got back late last night and went for a run this morning before coming to find you." Oh, the lies are flying everywhere now. "And then, and then I saw you through the window at Gloria's, and well now I'm here. Sweaty and stuff, but here, with you now, so…"

I risk the puppy dog eyes that used to help me dodge trouble for a while when I was a kid, and she looks at me questioningly. She isn't trying to leave, and she isn't glaring, so maybe it is working. I take the chance and lean into her, lower her wrists, caressing her arms.

She returns my look, still dubious, and hangs her head, whispering, "You know the name of my hotel, Ben. You could've called me there." She looks up, and I can tell I've hurt her.

Shit. She is right. I didn't think of that, and clearly am not thinking at all. "I'm sorry," I stammer. "I... I didn't think about that. Alexander was pissed that I bailed on him the previous Friday. It ended up being a whirlwind of meetings and trying to save my own ass. I didn't think of that, but I will tell you," I caress her cheek, hoping she can feel the passion, the real truth, "I couldn't stop thinking of you." Grinding my hips against hers just a little, I nuzzle her neck.

She is soft now, relaxed, and lets me. I feel her hips give and her head tilt into my face a bit. I did it. I think I saved myself with my Katarina.

"What are you doing running out here?" she chirps up. "You live way too far away to have run from Chelsea. Where are you coming from?"

Shit. I forgot I'd just been released from brother's close watch. I really need to think things through. "I told you we just got back late last night. I crashed at my brothers." I hate lying to her.

Truthfully, I say, "This morning my first plan was to find you. I have a few days off. Let's just grab a cab to my place so I can shower." I'm not letting her out of my sight, and I have to shower. I feel I can trust having her in my space, but can I trust myself? It doesn't matter, I need her in my space with me.

"We'll spend the day together." I give her my best look. "I've missed you. I want to hear about what you've been doing. Would you do that? Please?" Grabbing her chin, I tilt her face up to mine. She's so beautiful and her eyes connect with mine. She's searching, and I know she wants to believe me. I feel safe with Katarina. The one thing I've learned during my recent breakdown is that she is the only one that actually makes me feel calm and safe, normal. And I want her with me. Maybe her presence will chase all the other demons away.

Chapter 19: Katarina

I'm hesitant, determined not to be a fool, but I can't keep my guard up with him. My body literally melts into his, and my heart and soul go with it. My broken little heart is back where she wants to be, giddy with excitement and glowing with renewed faith in this man. She is an idiot.

I need to use my brain to decide if I've been wrong about him, something has to be in control here. Maybe I was wrong, but I'm also not a pushover. He hurt me, and what I've realized about myself these past two weeks is that I like to be in control, need to be in control, and I don't like surprises or distrust. I am getting stronger at walking away from bullshit that doesn't suit me.

Making the decision to go with him, at least for today, I say, "Yeah." I look down and nod my head. "Yeah, fine. I'll do that. Better than standing beside garbage bins, anyway." I squish up my nose at the smell.

He laughs. "Sorry about that." He smiles and winks at me, taking my hand and leading me out of the alley. Once out, he presses his warm body up against me, his scent wafting into my nose, and kisses me. Passionate and soft, wrapping his arms around me, he lifts me right off my feet.

"I missed you, Katarina, so much," he purrs and looks into my eyes.

One thing I feel I can trust is my intuition, the problem is I don't always follow it. But in this case I can tell that he is being honest with me, at least about his feelings. I don't think I fully believe the story about his disappearance, but at the same time, I just met the man, and I've never been a possessive person, especially when it comes to healthy relationships. I have no idea where this is going, but I do know where I want it to go. And if I want it to go well, I am going to have to let my guard down a little bit. I know he missed me just as much as I missed him. With our bodies close together again, I can feel it, just like I had when we made love. It is undeniable we have a connection, and I am going to see how deep we can go.

His apartment is bright, the floor to ceiling windows offering an endless view, making it feel like a castle at the top of a high mountain. Nothing like the character of his old home or his childhood room. There is a maturity to it, manly and mysterious, making it hard for me to read him and his style. His cologne permeates the air, making the apartment smell clean and fresh in his own manly way. Many books by various authors take up the corner wall, with a record player, a small collection of records, and a full wine rack. There is a sophistication to it. It is sexy, and the windows are so huge they make me feel like I am floating high in the sky. I love it.

"Nice place," I say as he drops his keys on the kitchen island.

"Thanks. I like to keep it minimal." Our eyes meet and he continues, "It's not huge. One bedroom and this area here," waving his hand around, "I read a lot, listen to records."

Sensing his nervousness, I try to relax. "Yeah, I bet. Nice TV. Is it big enough?" I joke. "You and your friends must have watched a few good hockey games here. Guys' nights and parties." I'm trying to learn more about him, but he isn't exactly forthcoming.

He laughs and shakes his head. "Not exactly. I'm more of a basketball guy, myself. Hockey's ok."

What?

"*Hockey's ok? Are you kidding?* I love hockey. My brother played. I am from Canada, right? Hockey, hockey, hockey," I say.

He offers up a weak smile and says, "Well, you'll have to teach me about hockey, and I'll teach you basketball. I'll be right back, just going to take a quick shower. I won't be long." Turning, he goes down the hall towards his bedroom and what I assume, is the bathroom.

Hearing the shower turn on, I wander around, gently fingering the spines on the books until I settle on last week's untouched newspaper that's laying on the coffee table. I plop down in the armchair and wait. After a few moments, my mind begins to wander over the last two weeks and how I've been on an emotional rollercoaster. Now here I am again, in Ben's company, like nothing has happened.

I want to believe his story about work but it's nagging at me. There is still a lot to learn about Ben, and I am determined not to let him, and his actions, control me that easily. No, if I am going to continue seeing him, I want to be in the driver's seat, at least when it comes to my heart. I know my heart belongs to him but if I have to, I'll take it away again, no matter how much it hurts. He needs to know that I am a strong woman and don't need a man to complete me. I won't be taken advantage of, and what I am giving him is my choice. My time is a gift, my heart and soul a treasure, one you don't abuse.

Before too long he comes out of the hallway, bare chested with those fucking nipple rings, towelling his hair with his strong arms. He's wearing dark blue track pants with NYU down the left leg and his feet are bare. Coming up beside me, he stands with his tight stomach a reach away. I swallow hard and look up at him.

Can I get you some water?" he asks.

Studying him for a moment, I can feel the heat off his skin, and he smells glorious, as always. At that moment I decide I need to teach him a lesson when it comes to me and how I expect to be treated. Teach him not to lose his damn phone again.

Feeling confident and daring, a new part of me I am starting to explore, I turn on him, still upset about the last two weeks and snark, "Do you have anything to drink, like really drink?"

Startled, he looks at me quizzically, "Uh, yeah… it's like ten in the morning, though. Um, I might have a few beers in the fridge."

His groin bulges beside me. All I have to do is sit up a bit more, and it will be in my face. I do and snap his waistband, exposing that he is naked underneath.

"Ouch, fuck. What was that for?" Ben looks at me a little mad, but still with a smile.

With my right hand, I grab his manhood hard and squeeze. Surprised, his eyes widen, and he throws his hands up. "Whoa there! What the fuck?!" he exclaims.

I stare back at him, biting my lip. I'm going to control today and make sure he knows exactly who he is dealing with.

"Don't lose your fucking phone, ok? Do you understand me?" I tug on his package just enough, keeping a hard edge to my tone. He looks surprised, like a lost little boy, and I can tell he realizes not to mess with me, but I'm not sure he knows how to take it.

"Ok, ok. I'm sorry. Are you still pissed? I can't tell."

"I'm not pissed, but I will be if you think you can treat me like shit and take advantage of me. Do you see this in front of you, here?" I point at my body and my heart, and he nods.

"Well, it's mine. My body. And I'll share it with you, but I'll take it away again if I need to. Don't hurt me again, Benjamin, and don't fucking ignore me." I squeeze a little harder.

Chapter 20: Benjamin

I feel like I am being scolded like a child, and I like it. She isn't making me feel inferior in any way, she just has the power. Not particularly of me, but of herself. She knows who she is, what she wants, and what she won't put up with. I like that kind of confidence. I like knowing that she is sure enough of herself to take charge of situations. This is what I find missing in the women I've known before who put all the pressure on me to make the decisions. With Katarina it feels more equal, like I can rely on her when I'm not having my best days—I just hope I can do the same for her.

I nod without saying much, and she releases her hold. As I head into the kitchen, I ponder over how different my emotions are with her as I stare at the lonely six pack in the otherwise empty fridge. Still contemplating, I grab two bottles, popping open the tops, keeping my head down. When I look up, she is still sitting in my armchair, but now wearing only a matching black bra and panties set, her clothes a heap on the floor. Shock waves course through my veins. With her legs crossed and her hands draped over the arms of the chair, she stares at me, and I can't help but stare back.

"Is this what you want, Benjamin?" she dares me, strong and independent. She knows exactly what I want but also knows it is hers to give and hers alone. There is no taking.

"Yes, Katarina. It's what I want. You're what I want," I reply, practically salivating to lick her skin.

"Are you going to treat me right, Benjamin?"

I like how she says my full name. "Yes, I will. I promise I'll treat you right," I answer her.

"Come here, then." She smiles. Having stood her ground and set her boundaries she is her soft self again, edging me on with her eyes while she bites her lip. I walk over to her, beers in hand, and pass her one. She takes it, shifts in her seat, and uncrosses her legs, leaning towards the couch. "Sit with me."

I do, sitting at the end of the couch closest to her. She takes a long sip of her beer, and I do too. It's cold and lights up my palate so early in the morning.

"Actually," she says as she shifts forward, "stand here for a minute, will you? Come here, let me see you."

I do as she asks and stand in front of her. She opens her legs so I can stand in between and sits herself up straight. As she pulls me in close to her by my pant leg, she situates her open thighs on either side of my knees, her face perfectly lined up to my crotch. Her hands raise and settle on my hips, pulling me into her and nuzzles her face right between my legs. She begins to breathe in deeply, rubbing her hands along my hips and the front of my legs. A quiet moan escapes her lips.

I smile arrogantly. "Like that?" I ask.

"Do *you* like it?" she snaps and flicks my hardening dick with her fingernail making me inhale a quick breath, she's a feisty little one.

"Oh yeah. Yeah, I do," I reply quietly, trying to hide my shock. Not knowing if I am allowed to touch her, I gently put my hand on her hair and start twirling it between my fingers. How badly I want to touch her. She rests her head on my hand, letting me know it is ok, and I am allowed.

Softly but quick, she pulls my pants down until just my crotch and ass are exposed. With her face fully in my private area, she begins to nuzzle my cock. She digs her nails, her glorious fucking nails, into my hips, controlling me and holding me where she wants. She starts to lick. Her tongue is cold from the beer. Oh my god, how I like that. Her mouth glides along the crease of my legs, my balls, and I feel her little sucks and nips as she explores. She moves her hands around, one on my ass, holding, the other massaging my balls and looks up at me.

"Move back," she orders, a nasty little gleam in her eye, and I do as I am told. Suddenly, she drops down to her knees. *Holy fuck that was hot! My god, I am the luckiest man in New York right now.* I tilt my head back and sigh. I can see out the windows, but no one can see us. Standing there, half naked in my living room, it's liberating feeling so exposed to the world. She pulls my pants all the way down, scraping her nails up my thighs and down the backs of my legs all while her face nudges into my crotch.

Then she grabs my balls and dick quickly with both hands and squeezes. Opening her beautiful mouth, she puts all of me into her wet warmth. Oh, for the love of God, her mouth is so soft, so juicy. She starts sucking, hard, slow, rhythmic, and I inhale sharply. I am tingling, on fire. My head tilts back again, my hands resting on her head, softly but firm. I never want her to stop. The sound of her sucking is glorious, beautiful, and sexy. I play with her hair, and as I am moaning, she is moaning too. She gets quicker, excited and greedy. Her hands stay tight on my hips, or grabbing my cock, and she keeps going rhythmically.

After a while, but not long enough, she pulls off, nuzzles the base of my cock and gives my balls a little suck. *Oh, fuck me, Katarina.* I look down at her with admiration. She's killing me.

"Are you enjoying yourself?" she whispers with a smile.

"Yeah, yes Baby. You feel amazing." I groan while playing with her hair.

"Sit down," she demands.

She helps me as I step out of my pants, and I'm fully naked. She kneels, still in her black lace bra and matching high cut panties, and I flop down on the couch, my dick hard as anything, waiting for her. Crawling over on her hands and knees, she makes no attempt to remove any of her underwear, but I can see the wetness starting between her thighs. Settled in between my legs, she grabs my cock hard and begins stroking.

"Pass me the beer," she says, looking me in the eye. I reach over and grab it, giving it to her. Releasing my cock and putting her right hand on my knee, she takes the beer in her left hand. Taking a sip, she lets droplets moisten her lips before diving right back onto my cock. Her mouth is wet and cold as she continues to devour me ravenously.

Grinding her body in between my legs, she begins to push herself up with her arms, her breasts grazing my dick as she slithers up my chest and starts kissing my neck. One leg at a time she removes her panties before straddling me. When she sits, my cock rests in between the folds of her wet pussy but not yet inside. It is so warm and wet; I can't help but stare at her mesmerized, begging with my eyes for her to put me inside her. She teases a sexy smile and begins to move her hips forward and back, pleasuring herself. Lifting my hands up her back, I go to remove her bra.

"Don't touch me," she snaps. "Don't fucking touch me," she softens and whispers in my ear, biting it and taking her left hand to my throat to squeeze, choking me just a little.

My eyes roll back in my head, and I groan. My god, could I get any harder? She holds onto me as she moves faster, and I don't dare move my hands from my sides. I just let her use me, take me, do what she wants to me. I deserve it, her soft anger towards me.

As she moves quicker, I am dying with pleasure that I can't fully grab onto. When she comes, she cries out, then whispers, "Fuck, me," to herself and begins to shake.

Her breathing heavy, she maneuvers her hips so I can lift up enough that the tip of my cock caresses her opening. She gasps a little, her eyes finding mine and bites her lower lip as she slowly lowers herself onto my cock. Surprised in my complete ecstasy, my back arches, cock tingles, and I almost cry. She pulls my hair, hard, and it hurts. I can feel tears in my eyes, and I grab onto her ass, squeezing her as she moves up and down on me, grabbing my nipples and pulling on the rings. It hurt so fucking good. She lets me grab her as she bounces and grinds until coming again. Then she is off, panting, leaving me gasping for air.

My eyes fly open, what the fuck? We are breathing so heavy, and I am literally dying to come, my cock bursting. I look at her. *What the fuck are you doing to me?*

Her eyes taunt me, smiling she presses down on my chest, forcing me to slide along the back of the couch. I lie on my back with my head resting on the arm so I can see her. Still straddling me, she snakes her way up my body, looking at me in between her licks and nips on my legs all the way to my balls, her face dives full in. She starts sucking on my balls. Oh, how she's sucking so perfectly, her lashes fluttering as she steals looks in my direction. I try to watch her while experiencing the sexual tension she's putting me through. Jesus, I want to come. She lifts her head, plays with me a little longer, and starts to suck on my cock again. *No, no, Katarina, don't do this to me!* My hands are on the back of her head again, and she is sucking hard and fast. I am going to come. *My god. Oh my god!* It doesn't take long, I explode. I squirm and shudder, I can't handle it, she is insatiable. I am crying. I know it and feel stupid but can't stop. I take a deep breath. I am in love. *Fuck me, I am in fucking love.*

"Now that, is why you don't lose your fucking phone," she says and snuggles into my arms. I already know that and don't dare say a word; I just grin and let our eyes say the rest.

We lie there for a while. She is in my arms, stroking my chest and fingering my nipple rings.

"I like it when you do that," I whisper into her hair.

But when she asks, "How long have you had them? What made you get them?"

I instantly panic, I don't want her to know my past, who I've been, and the types of people that have influenced some of my decisions. I stop for a moment and can feel myself stiffen. I don't want to lie, either.

Answering cautiously, I utter slowly, "It's New York. People do strange things. I was younger, maybe a little reckless." I look at her and offer a weak smile that she returns silently. Something tells me that she knows—she knows not to push me somewhere I'm not ready to go, and I feel comforted. I realize it may be possible that someone might be willing to take the time I need to let me open up.

I allow myself to start letting her in, full on, into my heart and mind, my life. The night turns into the next day, and the day after that.

We talk about everything. I tell her what I can about myself. Except my darkness. That I keep hidden. For me, when I am with her, that part doesn't exist.

I have to get a little creative at times when we talk about my childhood and my family. When we talk about the reckless years, I keep to the good stuff, the fun stuff. We both have funny stories about getting drunk or smoking weed; I just don't mention the other stuff. I tell her about the shows, the plays, and nightlife I used to go to. She is fascinated and wants me to take her to places. I tell her I will, knowing I'll never take her to the underground places of my past, my old places. When I touch her, my skin tingles, and I get emotional at times. She doesn't mind, though. She accepts me. We are raw and open together, with each other. I am falling, but in a good way. I am madly in love with her, and I think she loves me too.

We order Italian from a place I frequent, and I open wine as the sun is setting, putting on one of my favourite artist's latest albums. I always purchase vinyl if I can find it, preferring the organic sound. I hold her and dance with her, swaying her body effortlessly. It is just us and the only place I ever want her to be, with me. My hands continuously caress her as she stares at me. I love her eyes.

Chapter 21: Katarina

We spend Saturday in Ben's living room. We talk a lot, like we had the first weekend we'd spent together, but this time I am trying to learn more about him. His work, his interests, like running and art. We speak little about his family, he clearly keeps that guarded. I lay my head on his lap, and he plays with my hair when he reads. I encourage him to get lost in some classic movies, to allow himself to loosen up and share a laugh or two or escape in make believe worlds. We are equally infatuated with the other. Our bodies in complete sync, our love making becomes fucking and our fucking becomes love making. It is perfectly simple, perfectly natural.

We open one bottle of wine, then two, and eat dinner as the sun sets, listening to music. Folk, indie, and instrumental pieces. It was sexy and emotional, smart.

We dance, and he knows how to hold me and move me around. As I follow his lead, I begin to commit to the fact that I'd follow him anywhere. As night falls, the outside world disappears.

"Maybe I could take a shower?" I murmur drunkenly. Not stupid drunk, but we are well into our second bottle of wine, and my body has been ravaged all day. I am full in more ways than one and need a shower to perk me up.

"Fantastic idea," he agrees, nibbling on my neck.

I laugh at him. "Alone?"

"No," he says, "absolutely not. It's my shower."

"It's your shower? Really. Well, isn't that just grand of you. I let you do anything you want to my body, but you won't share your shower?"

"Anything?" He raises a brow.

This conversation is going somewhere I like. Intrigued, I begin forming all sorts of new ideas and thoughts in my head.

I don't know what to say. I assume he is referring to some kind of kinky shit. *Maybe, ok? Depending.* Or another part of my body. He's been everywhere else but one place… I wasn't sure. Trying to dodge the question, I say, "Fine. You can shower with me, but hands off."

"Haha, yeah. Ok. Sure. Whatever you say." He grins and starts pulling me down the hallway.

"I'm serious, Ben," I reply, giving him a teasing but scolding look.

"I know, I know." His look becomes serious. "I would never do something you don't want me to. Ever."

His room holds a large bed, a dresser, and a full-length mirror stands in the corner. Soft black blankets make his bed overly inviting. The lighting is dim, and candles burned low on his nightstand. They had been lit earlier, maybe when he'd showered, dangerously, confidently.

Tall windows, with a sliding door to a small balcony for two to have coffee, wine, or smoke, give a stunning view of the nighttime city. The bathroom is to the right, and I shake him off and shut the door in his face. I face the mirror with the shower behind me. I move towards it, turning the taps and the room quickly fills with steam. My body is sore but content and complete. I feel whole and crave the heat of hot water penetrating my skin, my face and hair. I step in with a sigh.

I knew Ben would come into the room. Quiet, but there, watching me. I open the shower door and look right at him, catching him off guard. "Come," I say. He looks at me obsessively, but I'm not afraid. He pulls off his shirt, drops his pants, and steps into the shower. Grabbing me, he holds onto me tightly, the hot water beating down on us, and he starts grinding into me. With the shower gel that smells incredibly of everything I crave in him; we wash each other and laugh. That is all. We take care of each other in this shower, massaging our sore bodies. When my hand reaches down to grab onto his stiff cock, he pulls my hand away and sternly tells me, "No, I want you in my bed. I'm taking you to my bed." And his eyes spark with gold.

We continue to giggle, smiling through our kisses. We are having so much fun, holding and washing and making bubbles. I wash his hair, he washes mine. It is sensuous and playful. I grab him again, but he stops me. He definitely wants me in his bed. He opens the shower door, pulling us both out of the rain, and passes me a towel.

"Are you going to turn off the shower?" I ask.

"Oh! Yeah, hold on."

We glow in the candlelight of the bedroom. The blankets are soft, and he walks up to me sitting on the edge of the bed, tips me back, and crawls on top of me. As one, we maneuver our bodies up, so I am laying on the bed, and he is on top of me, stroking my thigh.

We are close, so close, and slow. He is gentle with me, making love to me, teasing me. I can feel the energy in the room that we are creating. This place, this moment, is all ours.

We shut out the rest of the world. His apartment, his couch, his shower, his bed, are now ours. I feel so comfortable in his space, our space. His hands are wrapping around my ass, and he gently uses his fingers to caress down in between my cheeks, it tickles. He lands right on my spot, the one spot he hasn't explored yet. No one has. It was the one thing I'd never shared, my one piece of virginity.

"Would you let me?" he asks softly. This was what he meant by 'anything' from earlier. I can't deny it feels good, what he is doing, and I moan out a little as he presses. I am wet down there, so it doesn't hurt, nothing he does to my body hurts.

"I'm scared," I admit into his ear.

"Ok. It's up to you, I won't pressure you. I promised I wouldn't hurt you. I understand." He nuzzles into my neck, his hands not moving from where they are.

"Can we try?" I instantly decide. I want to give him this. I want to give myself this. I want Ben to be the only man that has ever had me this way, for it to be his, ours. I am scared and a little embarrassed, but I'm turned on and willing.

"You're sure, Katarina? I'd love to. I've never before. I've never asked, never wanted to. I… I just need all of you," he whispers into my neck, grinding his hips into me.

"Yeah, yeah, I'm sure." I grab onto him, holding him closer to me and kissing his neck, I know he likes that. He shifts, centering himself between my legs and lifting up. He goes down my body, landing between my legs and nuzzling, licking. He ventures everywhere lower, it is exhilarating. I moan and run my fingers through his hair. He comes back up, with his hands gently guiding his cock in between my ass cheeks.

Starting slow, he presses in, fuck it was huge. It hurt, but only for a little bit. He is perfect, nudging and pressing in ever so slowly so as not to hurt me. "Oh, Ben," I say, eyes wide. "Oh my god, Ben."

He continues going in deeper as my body gives in. It gets easier the more I relax, and it feels so fucking good. My nipples are hard as rocks, my hips are tingling. It feels like his cock is up inside my throat, and I can't stop moaning like a cat in fucking heat. He grinds, picking up speed.

I fucking moan.

"You ok, baby?" he asks in my ear, and I nod, so he keeps going. I don't want him to stop.

This has to be perfect love making, soul touching, heart surrendering love. I hold him and he holds onto me, kissing, grinding, legs between legs, hands all over everything, stroking. Slowly, he makes love to me in his bed.

My moans become deeper and longer. When my back arches, he shifts to stay with me. He gets himself all the way in as I sigh with pleasure. "It feels so good, Ben, so good." Tears of satisfaction and awe edge my eyes. The feeling is different, and I like it enough I know I'll want to do it again.

A couple slower thrusts, and he pulls out, finishing off on my stomach, I don't mind.

His smile is infectious.

Our silence speaks volumes, his leg drapes across mine while I twist his hair. Our bodies are at ease with the familiarity of each other, like they've been accustomed to each other far longer than a few days. Reluctantly, I move and shimmy out from under him.

"Washroom, water," I say, and he grumbles sleepily.

"Come back, don't be long," he mummers, snuggling down into his bed, waiting for me.

I ready myself for bed, grabbing a water and turn out the light. Blowing out the candles, I crawl in beside him. When I snuggle into his waiting arms, I kiss him, and his eyes open, the moonlight reflecting on our faces.

"I love you," I say. I don't care. I do, and I am going to tell him.

He's quiet but his eyes tell me everything I need to know as he looks at me in a way I can't describe but can feel how special it is.

"I love you, Katarina. I love you, too." He grabs my face and kisses me. All the stars from the sky fill the room as my heart explodes, my life can't be any better than this moment.

Chapter 22: Benjamin

When I hear her say she loves me, my heart bursts into a world I'm not accustomed to. I don't know what love means, what it's supposed to look like, and I definitely don't know what it feels like. But if it feels like a sweet explosion, a painful release of pent-up joy, ecstasy, that makes your heart sing, then that's what I want. In this moment, her 'I love you' connects my soul to hers, and I'm terrified. *No one loves me, no one loves Ben.* I tell her I love her, too because I do. I've never loved anyone, and I begin to believe in a real future with her, my Katarina.

When my body explored hers and she moaned the way she did, it took my heart away. All I know is that I want to make sure she stays by my side forever, and that I am the only one to please her. My entire purpose in life is now her, and only her. I will do anything to ensure her safety, her pleasure, and her happiness.

We wake up the next morning finding each other's arms and lie together, silently stroking each other's bodies. After a while, I have to pull away, groaning in fake agony as she pulls on my hand to stay with her. *Oh, trust me, girl, there's no other place I'd rather be.*

"I have to jump in the shower." I wink at her, hoping she'll take the hint. "Join me if you want to. I'll make some coffee after."

When the bathroom door opens, and I see her little feet through the steam, huddling by the doorway so as not to be seen, my body buzzes. I love the girlish games she plays, like she is shy in my spaces, but she isn't shy at all.

"Oh, joining me after all are you?" I shout out towards her, and she giggles. "I was just about to get out."

"I am." She appears face to face with me, the electricity heating our bodies more than the shower. "But as much as I want you to stay, I want coffee more."

I tilt my head back, letting out a slight huff, and push my urges down.

"Fair enough," I weaken and leave the shower, grabbing a towel so she can have her private space, some time alone.

By the time I return, two black coffees in hand, the shower is off, and the bed is made. She is out on the patio off my bedroom.

"Hey," I reach for the door and tap with one of the coffee cups "I see you borrowed some clothes." She has stolen a pair of my boxers and tied a white t-shirt in a knot at her waistline. "You look adorable in my stuff, Kay."

I sat with her on the noisy balcony, taking in the morning rush of life below us. It feels natural, and she is just so perfect, in every way.

"It's going to be hot today," I point out. "What do you want to do?"

"Nothing. Stay here if that's ok? I like it here."

We don't leave the apartment all day. After our coffee, we order bagels and fruit for breakfast from the café downstairs. Getting extra for throughout the day, she also got a carton of milk for her coffee. Hanging out together is nice: TV, books, card games. Throughout the day I find her, touch her, take off her clothes, and kiss her all over. She catches me taking her picture; I can tell she hates it, but I'm not going to stop and eventually she gives in with sideways glances and smiles, so I can snap my photo.

I make love to her on the rug, pushing the coffee table out of the way and tossing her to the ground to her squeals of delight. I allow my primal and obsessive side to flourish, it is exciting. When I grab her and turn her around, so her back is towards me, I yank down the boxers she stole from me and push her against the kitchen island. She screams out but pushes her ass towards me as I begin fucking her from behind. She likes it, I like it, and we do it again over the back of the couch.

Anytime we move around the apartment there is a touch, a squeeze, a kiss, a teasing pull to the hair. She is all over me, and I love it. We are playful with each other, we are sexy, we are serious, passionate, and fun. We are one.

"Come on," she says, pulling me up off the couch. Taking my hand, she pulls me over to the dining room table.

"Sit," she tells me.

I grab a chair and sit. She straddles me, standing, and I hold her hips, staring up into her eyes while her hands run through my hair. *God, I fucking love her.*

"You know you're the only woman I've ever loved, don't you?"

She shakes her head, and I decide to open up a little to her.

"Katarina," I start nervously, looking away, "I wasn't, aren't… I'm not an easy guy. I... I don't let people in. I don't have a lot of friends. I work, I read… and now you, I do you."

She looks at me without any judgement and smiles her sweet smile. "That's ok. We don't need anyone else, do we? I'm pretty simple myself." She settles herself on my knee. "I like being with you; I've never felt this way, either. We'll figure it all out as we go, I guess."

I nod and she searches my eyes while holding my face. I know she doesn't understand what I am saying, how can she? I just hope that by having her in my life, I'll be ok. Eventually, I'll have to tell her about the medication, that I need the stupid pills. She'll find them in the bathroom. Maybe by then it won't scare her off. I just have to time it right, is all.

She stands up and removes the boxers she is wearing and flips them across the room. Still wearing my t-shirt, her bare breasts poking through, she saddles up to me and hovers over me, lifting my chin up to meet her gaze.

"Now take your shorts off," she demands.

I do as she asks, and she sits down on me. Already hard, I am inside her instantly, and I grab her hips. Sucking in through my teeth, I turn my head and attack her neck, biting her hard.

"Ouch! Jesus, what the fuck is wrong with you?" Her eyes widen. "You're crazy!" She smiles and throws her head back, moving her hips as she starts to grind up and down on me. I pull off her shirt and hold her closer.

"You know you're the only woman who's ever been here before?" She shakes her head as she moves up and down, our faces touching, our breathing mixing together and getting faster. "No one has ever been here. I've never had a meal at these chairs before," I whisper in her ear.

"Really?" she exclaims, moving her head back to look at me again. "Well, can we officially call it our place then?"

She is joking, but I'm not when I say, "I hope so, Baby. I'd like that."

We find ourselves on every one of those fucking chairs.

Chapter 23: Katarina

I think he likes the way I wake him Sunday morning. Watching him sleep, he looks so peaceful, his soft lips, long lashes and messy head of curls. Gently, I reach over to move one of the locks off his face and he reminds me of an angel, a sexy angel sent only for me.

Lifting the covers, I pop my head in to see what is underneath. His arms are strong. I love the muscles and contours of his strong arms; they make me feel safe and protected. His chest is smooth and warm as I watch it lift and fall with his breathing. My eyes move down further, following the trail of black hair and landing on his cock. He is soft, and I can't help but get excited, I have an idea.

I scoot down, nestle in lower and start to lick, nip, and suck. Hiding under the covers, I giggle, I can hear him start to groan and moan my name as his hands land on the back of my head. I like how his hands hold me there, proving he likes what I am doing and keeping me from being able to stop. I am his girl and that's the only way I want it to be, his. Feeling the need to impress him and wanting to keep on impressing him, I continue.

"Mmmm, Katarina," he moans groggily. I like that and start sucking a little harder, moaning so he knows I am enjoying myself just as much as he is. His hands reach down as he takes hold of my head, gently pressing so I won't stop. When he touches me, my skin burns, and I am desperate for him to touch the rest of my body. He has me, of that there is no doubt. I want a man who controls me in the bedroom but lets me soar outside of it. Respect me, love me, and support me with my decisions. This man is doing just that.

Chapter 24: Benjamin

I wake up to her lips on my cock. At first, I'm not sure if I am dreaming, but as I open my eyes and feel her warmth, smell her scent and watch the covers move, I know it is real, she is real. My hands instantly go to her head and hold her there. Goddamn she is hot.

I love how this girl makes me feel. She puts me in a position of control. She allows me to take care of her and lets me feel like I am the only one who can.

Is she independent? Absolutely she is. But she also is a soft, beautiful woman who wants a man by her side, and that man is me. I know without a doubt how much she loves me and how much I love her. She continues, and as I get harder, she gets feistier. She is squirming all over the place, and I can tell she is touching herself. I'm not allowing that, so I grab her hair and gently pull her off me.

When she lifts her head and looks at me, I can see the animalistic passion in her eyes. Her breathing is heavy, and her lips are wet. She is biting her lip, and her eyes are begging for me to do something about it.

I flip her over onto her back. Ripping between her legs, and grabbing her hips, I pull her to me. Smothering her body, the blankets fall away, and it is just her, me, and the bottom sheet. She is excited. I mean, really excited. She won't stop moving, so I grab her wrists and hold her hands above her head hard.

"Stop it," I growl. "Stop it, and I'll take care of you, ok?"

"Mmhm," she whines, actually whines. She is frustrated and needs me to fix that. Leaning down over her, my hands still controlling hers, I kiss her. I can feel her melt beneath me like a puddle, and she stops squirming so much, opening her legs wider. I go for her neck, my favourite spot, and I bite her. She squeals, she likes that. Her breathing is heavy, and she is getting impatient, so I continue to tease her.

"Please, Ben, please give it to me…" she cries, kicking her legs.

Nope. I'm gonna make you wait. Forcefully, I pull her arms down to her sides and hold her there as I go for her breasts. I suck and lick, biting as I usually do. She is squirming again and arching her back, lifting her hips, trying to get me to put myself in her, but I keep hold of the control. I can feel myself fierce. I like how I have her, and there is nothing she can do about it.

I loosen my grip on her as I go down and bury my face between her legs. I don't need to hold her down now, she'll stay. She is gasping and grabbing my head as I take care of her needs, her juices flowing as I suck and nibble. When I put my fingers inside her and then bring them up to her lips to taste what I desire, she suckles them greedily. She is kinky and I like it. She is moaning deeply and lets out little screams when I lick her a certain way, I haven't heard her quite like this before. I keep at her, and when she comes, I hold her as she bucks, trying to get me off her. She is pulling at my hair, begging me to stop, but I won't, my arms lock around her thighs, and I'm not letting go. Her body lets go and gives up. She literally gives her entire body over to me and goes limp in my arms.

I have succeeded in my plan. She is numb and can't move as I meet her face to face and slowly enter myself into her. Moaning deeply, her eyes roll back, and as she arches, her body molds into mine. She is putty in my hands as I make love to her, move her, shift her, fill her up. Her moaning gets deeper and deeper and doesn't stop as we rock together.

Her body allows it, opens to it as I do what needs to be done for both of our pleasures. Our bodies together are one unit, but I am the driver this time. I love it when we come together. My body shakes and goosebumps dapple my skin. At that moment I know I have her as much as she has me. There is no competition between us; we are in this together.

I lift off her and lie beside her, pulling up the covers from the floor. She goes to freshen up and as she comes back, I reach out and grab her arm, pulling her back into our bed. This is the best way to spend Sunday mornings. She laughs and I smile at her. She is my best friend, and I can tell I am hers.

"I think I'm going to start looking for work here," she says to me as I hold back the covers for her to shimmy closer.

"Like real work. My work. Social work, somewhere."

Landing in the crook of my arm, she looks up at me dubiously, but I fully understand what she is saying. She doesn't plan on leaving anytime soon. What do I think of that? She likes it here. *You can stay here forever if you want*, I beamed inwardly. *Stay here forever.*

I take a deep breath. There is the slight hint of woman in the air. I close my eyes and take another deep breath. I like the way my room smells now, with her mixing in.

"I don't want you to go, Katarina. I want you to stay here with me. Will you do that? Will you stay?" I make my decision and jump up when she starts nodding that she will.

"Hold on, ok? Just wait here, and I'll be right back, promise."

I jump out of bed, throw on my robe, and come back to the room within a few minutes.

"Here," I say, flopping onto the bed, dangling my sanity in front of her face. It is a key with a green friendship bracelet attached. "Have a key to my place. Here, take it," I press. "It's an extra, and I want you to have it, it's yours." I feel like a child, so excited that she will be my new, permanent pet. "And I made that for you, like you asked me to." Motioning at the green bracelet made of string, I desperately want her around me all the time. It is bad enough that I have to work tomorrow. I also want her to feel safe with me, that I am committed to her. But she is silent, and I start to feel uncomfortable.

"So, um… just come here whenever you want. You'll be here most of the time anyway, won't you? This is our place now; how much longer do you have in that hotel, anyway?" I let out my breath when she takes the key from my hand.

"Ben, are you sure?"

"Sure, I'm sure." I jump off the bed with excitement and reach my hand towards her. "Come on, get up! I haven't fucked you in the shower yet!"

She starts to squeal and kick at me as I pull her up.

"Oh alright." She rolls her eyes as she gives in. "Let's go."

Sunday continues to be the same as the previous day, exploring each other's minds and bodies. Late in the afternoon we go out for a walk, and I take her to ZiZi, a Mediterranean spot and exclaim, "Now this is Shawarma!" I can feel my anxiety slipping in as the day goes on, and as we get closer to reality, I begin silently shutting down.

Monday, we both have to work. It is becoming so natural, and I feel incredibly comfortable with her, but that is also what I am afraid of. We bring out the best in each other, complementing each other so well. I am up earlier than her, trying to be quiet in my morning routine.

"I'll see you later? Will you be here when I get home?" I ask her, leaning over her and kissing her forehead, tempted to climb back into our bed.

"Yeah, sure. I'll be here."

Those words sing in my ears.

Leaving her is like cutting off one of my limbs, but it is day one of Ben 2.0 post meltdown, and I have to nail it. I fight my way to work in the usual chaos of the city, but it doesn't bother me like it used to. I just keep thinking of Katarina and the fact that she is in my bed and will be in my apartment when I get home. It calms me and keeps me in a good mood.

My office is all glass, like most in the city are, and I have my own private bathroom. Thank god, as that is where I go when I need to hide. I always wondered if my brother had planned it that way.

Once I dive into my work, I feel even more at ease. Working alongside the editors and designers for the magazine, I find myself overly agreeable. They seem to notice too, as I catch the odd raised eyebrow, smile, and whisper between employees.

And then the day is done. Just like that. I did it and did it well. *Now I can go home and see my Katarina. Wow, so normal.*

<Hey, babe, it's me. I thought I'd try making us dinner tonight LOL. What time will you be here?> Katarina texted me.

<Leaving in a few, I should be there by six.>

Is this what adults are supposed to look like? Feel like? I smile.

But then I read the next message.

<Brother. How did you make out today? I heard people were talking about you, you were in a great mood. Said the vacay did you some good. Ha Ha. That's good news buddy! That's good. Proud of you, pal. Listen, Father wants to see how you're making out, you know the drill. Wants us both at home for dinner with Mother Wednesday night. Seven. See you there.>

Fuck.

A bolder just came crashing down on my head. The last thing I want to do is be present in that world. *Mother's world. Father's world. Childhood home world.* I cringe and start to panic. Oh well. I have to. I need to. I have to prove to them that I am ok and with a woman, too. In a relationship. *Fuck them, Katarina is coming with me.* I am asking Katarina to come with me. Hold my hand and keep me safe.

When I get home, I am clearly preoccupied and agitated, but I can't shut it off. I throw my keys on the counter, practically knocking over some little plant she must have bought. It smells amazing in the apartment, and I realize she must have found the unopened box of pots and pans I'd stashed in the front hall closet from my brother. She also must have done some grocery shopping.

"Hey, Babe!" She's bouncing about, but I can't pull myself up to match her vibe. "How was your day?"

"Hi," I manage to say, trying to stop my hands from running through my hair, but it is futile.

"You ok?" She asks grabbing my face and forcing me to look her in the eye. "What's wrong?"

She holds my face in her hands. *Heck, she holds all of me in her hands.*

This woman can do anything, and my fears slip away. Well, mostly.

"I'm good. I'm good," I tell her and myself at the same time. "We just... well I just… well we… if you would… have to go to dinner with my parents Wednesday. Would you come with me?"

Anytime the subject of my parents came up over the weekend, I grew quiet, and I think she noticed, but never pried. I can't tell if she can read my thoughts now, but I can't hold back my mood very well.

"Well, I have a date that night with another guy." I can tell by her teasing smile she is trying to lighten me up. "So, I'll have to work around that. But yeah, sure, I'll come with you."

I am terrified but breathe a little more easily now that I know I won't be alone and am able to drop my shoulders and relax.

"Good, that's good." I move on. "Smells great in here. It's never smelled like this before. Where'd you get all this stuff? Hello, Katarina."

"Hello, Ben." She wraps her arms around my neck, and I hold her waist.

"I shopped!" she explained, clearly proud of her accomplishments. "You need a lot more things to make it a kitchen, but it's a start."

"We'll go out this weekend to get what you want. Let me get changed. Want some wine?" I let her go and pick out a Merlot I know she likes. "I didn't know you could cook."

"Neither did I." She laughed.

"I'm sure it will be great, Babe," I reassure her.

We eat and chat about our days. She tells me how she struggled to balance the groceries home, and I laugh at her. But I can't shake the doom I feel in my heart, I'm not fully present in the moment, and it is impossible to hide anything from Katarina. I doubt myself as I look at this beautiful woman's eyes sparkling in the candlelight. Am I good enough for her? Am I able to give her everything she needs? She completes me, but do I complete her?

"Are you satisfied?" I ask her, cutting the silence.

She stops clearing our plates and sits back down at the table. I stare at her while the blood starts to boil inside me. I hadn't been nervous to ask the question, but now, as she stalls, I am beginning to panic. It is a dangerous place for me, and I don't like this game she is playing, if that's what she thinks this is. Suddenly, I am racked with the fear of letting her continue, of possibly losing her if I can't control the anger that is brewing inside me.

She looks at me square in the face, right in my eyes and tells me, "No."

"No?" The hair on my body rises, my blood is right at the top of its boiling point. I raise my eyebrows and clutch the edge of the table. If she doesn't start explaining fast, I am going to flip the fucking thing over. *Don't play with me girl, you don't understand what you'll get.*

Determined to find out if this was her idea of fun, I struggle to remain calm. *What the actual fuck?* I was in a mood, and I knew it.

"Get your ass in the bedroom," I growl. "Now!" The anger boils up to the surface.

She jumps up and walks backwards down the hall, taunting me, pulling out my demons. I am afraid of myself but feel safe balancing the two feelings I have of love and anger.

"What are you going to do?" she pressures with a slick smile to her lips, "What are you going to do to me, Ben?"

She is actually enjoying this.

Stalking her down the hallway, my hands slide along the walls as I pursue her. She smiles provocatively, her eyes sparking, challenging me.

I push her with my body into the room and grab her by the throat. She gasps, smiles. Ripping her blouse open, the buttons flying everywhere, I tear it off her. I am aroused and uncontrollable, but she doesn't mind, she likes it. My cock is rock hard—she is meeting my demon straight on and standing up to it.

"I'm going to fuck you, Katarina. I'm going to fuck you hard!"

"Please do, Ben, please do," she tempts and winks.

Fuck she is ballsy. I shake my head and pull her to me by the waist of her pants, tearing at them. She's not wearing panties, that makes me hot. Her pants are off in two seconds. Pushing her down on the bed, I come crashing down after her. I can feel my rage. The rage caused by my panic, and I am using it to consume her. I push up her bra and start biting as she struggles to remove it from behind her back. My clothes are off, and I don't know if it is me or her who removed them. All I know is that I am on top of her and inside her within seconds.

She cries out, loud, and screams in excitement and pleasure. She is loving this as I grab her throat, pull her hair, and bite her neck.

My hips are moving so fast in and out of her, fucking her as hard as I promised I would when she says to me, "Who do I belong to, Ben? Do I belong to you?" Face to face she stares at me, challenging me.

"Yes, me," I mutter through gritted teeth as I thrust into her, scratching her and grabbing her hard, staring straight back into her eyes, sparking with pent up rage.

"Then say it," she grits right back.

"You belong to me. You're mine!"

"Yessss, Ben. I belong to you, now fuck me! Satisfy me! Satisfy yourself with me!"

I do.

I explode into her, and she smiles and laughs. "Fuck you, Ben, that was incredible!" she squeals, happy and out of breath.

My breathing heavy, I collapse beside her exhausted but calm, so damn calm. It was as if I'd run a marathon, making it to the end in first place, and falling onto the pavement. She rolls over onto her side and grabs my face, forcing me to look at her.

"Don't ever ask me that question again. You satisfy me. You fulfill everything I want!" She kisses me hard. "The only problem is I can't get enough of you, Ben. That's why I'm not satisfied. I don't think I ever will be." Panting she begins grinding her hips into me and nibbling my neck. I lie back and let her nibble at me.

That makes me feel good.

Complete.

Chapter 25: Benjamin

"Wake up, sleepy head." Soft hands press down on my chest, her warmth penetrating into my skin.

"Hmmmm. What time is it?" I roll over so my back is towards Katarina who is staring at me, perky and wide-eyed.

"It's six thirty. Come on, let's go! We're starting today with a run at the park before work. It's beautiful out!" she chirps.

I bury my head under the covers, but first get a peek at her. She is dressed and ready to go in black running shorts and a dark purple tank.

"Time to go, sleepy head!"

"Noooo!" I whine. "I don't want to. Come back to bed." I reach behind myself, fishing for her. I feel her crawl onto the bed. She whispers in my ear, "If you get up and run with me, I'll let you take me in the shower before work."

My eyes pop open. That sounds like fun. Rolling over on my back, I lift my arm so she can squeeze in.

"Come on, let's go. I want us to do things together that require clothes on, not just off. It's good for us."

As much as I like her clothes off, she is right. Relationships are more than just sex and require activities beyond what we've been enjoying. I stretch out my arms and give in.

"Fine. Alright. But I hate you."

"No, you don't. Let's go," she says, pulling me out of bed and throwing my running shirt in my face.

We take a cab to the park to save time. It's just after seven, and the sun is shining, but the heat hasn't hit yet. There are already people running or walking their dogs.

"Ok, this is your idea, Kay, where are we going?" I ask as I tie the longer part of my hair up off my face.

"Well, this path here looks good if you can keep watch on our time? Make sure we're back at the entrance so we're not late for work." She doesn't give me a chance to agree before taking off and yelling back, "Try to keep up!"

I hang my head and chuckle to myself, silly girl. You think you're going to outrun me, huh? I think not. This is my city. You try to keep up!

"You think you're pretty funny this morning, don't you?" I shout, catching up to her quickly. Her shorts are tight, and I smack her ass as I blow past her. It makes me smile when I turn to look back at her. She can't keep up with me. I like that I'm faster than her, more powerful, but I don't want to be a dick and piss her off, so I slow down to a stop and wait for her. I haven't felt this good in the morning in a long time, if ever. Getting out into the fresh air, running in the wind, I feel free, free because of her.

Out of breath, she catches up to me.

"Ok. Point taken," she says breathless. "I didn't know you were that fast, Ben. Learning something new about you every day." She's panting, her hands resting on her knees.

I put my arm around shoulders as she stands, and we walk a minute. "That's what this is all about, right? Getting to know what you can and can't do with me." I wink. "Follow me. I know a good five K route that will get us back in time. Should take us thirty minutes at your speed. Can you handle five K?"

"Oh, screw you!" She slaps me on the chest and starts bouncing, preparing to jog. Following her lead, I begin to bounce too, and turn backwards, taunting her as I begin to speed up.

"Ok then, come on. Let's go, sleepy head!" I face myself forward and start running, a little more slowly this time.

She's healthy and knows how to run well, maintaining a good pace and controlling her breathing properly. I love running together. We are compatible in one rhythm, and it strikes me. I've never enjoyed running with other people, it's always been a singular sport for me. Until now—we feel like a team, and I like the connection. Watching her from the corner of my eye, the sweat forming at the base of her neck and the bounce of her tits are enough to make any man's morning. But she is all mine.

This is good. We'd shared enough and gotten to know each other this week and I'm not feeling as afraid anymore. My usual triggers seem to be held at bay, and it's noticeable how my anxiety is lifting, especially in public places. The feeling is becoming addictive, and as the days have been passing, my need to have her with me at all times is becoming obsessive. I hear the warnings in my head and ignore them anyway. *I need more. I want more, and I want it all with her.*

We make it back to the entrance with more than enough time to spare. Our breathing returns to normal during the cab ride back to the apartment and upon entering, I flip on the coffee. She kicks off her shoes and starts heading to the shower. I follow her down the hall.

"Hey," I call out to her. I think she is forgetting something.

"What?" she looks back at me.

"I think you're forgetting our deal," catching up to her in the bedroom, I stare into her confused face.

"Deal? What deal?"

"You said if I ran with you that I could have you in the shower." All my focus is on her with full intentions to do exactly that.

She smiles and rolls her eyes. "Oh right. I guess I did. Well, never break a promise, right?" She flips off her tank and throws it at me.

Both of us in the bathroom, we struggle to get ourselves out of our own gear. It is hot and sticky and with the shower running, even steamier. She gets in first, stealing the shower stream, making me have to wait behind her as she rinses off.

Standing behind her naked body, I am already ready to go. The run gave me energy, and her wet skin ignites my passion immediately. I need to have her right now.

Turning her face towards me, her body follows. I grab onto her, pull her body into mine and kiss her hard, both of us moaning. Moving her so I can get some of the shower too, I wrap my arms around her waist and her back. As usual, she molds into me, and I use my knee to forcefully separate her legs. This causes her to lift her one leg up and around my waist as I grab the other one, lifting her onto me fully.

She's holding onto my neck for dear life. The shower making us wet and slippery so if she doesn't hold on, she'll slip. I would never let my baby fall. Taking my one hand, I put myself inside her and position us up against the wall. Thinking the cool tiles will shock her, she moans instead, and I raise my arm above her head for balance, putting our faces inches apart. She moans again.

I have her under my full control; she isn't getting away from me now. I start fucking her and she gasps, enjoying it. I thrust into her, pressing her body against the wall, and as she moves against me, I speed up. I like my face being so close to hers, and it doesn't take me long to let loose inside her. It weakens me, and I let her legs down while I regain and rest myself from the orgasm.

She hasn't gotten there yet and starts touching herself as she leans against the wall of the shower, closing her eyes. I'm not having that. I grab her between her legs and start rubbing her, she releases her hands and lets me, moaning out her approval. Using my fingers to play inside her, I grab her peach like a baseball while pinching her nipples with my free one, playing her like putty in my hand.

"Pinch me harder," she whispers, so I do.

When she comes, she literally comes in the palm of my hand. I lift my glistening fingers to her mouth. Taking the tip of my middle finger between her teeth, she bites it, her eyes open wide, staring into me with that look of naughtiness only she can give. I take my hand to her neck and squeeze just a bit as she enjoys the last of her orgasm, and we smirk at each other.

"Pass me the shampoo. We gotta get going," she breathes out, her body trembling.

"Yep. We do. You can't have me all the time, you know. One of us has to make some money." I grin, and she laughs. We are both going to be late.

Chapter 26: Katarina

I'm beaming at work all day. Even the rudest of customers can't get me down. I am in love and transparently happy—exactly where I want to be.

Gloria is in the back making sandwiches for the lunch rush when I get a brilliant idea. Grabbing one of the large totes she sells to tourists with *Gloria's Café NYC* printed on them, I ask her if I can have a few.

"Sure, take whatever you want. I got you." She gives me one of her grandmotherly grins.

"Thanks, Gloria." I pack a couple sandwiches, some grapes, and a couple cookies.

When I get back to Ben's place—home, I suppose I can call it now—I put my little package in the fridge and change into a dark green linen shift. I text Ben.

<Hey you. How's your day? I have a surprise for you tonight… a little date night. When will you be home?>

<Hmmmm, sounds good ;) I can maybe squeeze out a bit early. Meet you at 5? You're at our place?>

<Yes. Our place. See you then :)>

The local grocery store has a bit of everything. I scour the aisles for simple kitchen accessories, picking up a small yellow tablecloth, matching napkins, and two travel mugs. Feeling like a girl, infatuated by young love, I'm practically gliding through the store as the picnic I'm planning starts taking shape.

By the time Ben gets home, I am ready to go. The bag is packed with all the goodies and a bottle of wine we can hide conspicuously in the travel mugs. I add a deck of cards and a few celeb magazines to give us something to do while we lounge. Maybe it's lame, but I am as happy as a schoolgirl and think it will be fun to have an evening picnic in the park.

When Ben sees me waiting in the doorway in my little outfit, sunhat and oversized sunglasses he starts to laugh.

He picks me up, spinning me around in the air, and says, "You are absolutely adorable my darling! Whatever are you up to?" As if he's an Englishman and we're living in a country cottage.

"Taking you to the hills my love, for a little picnic in the park! Come, my sweet, I shall show you the way!" I mimic in kind and grab his arm, pulling him out the door as he quickly grabs his keys back off the counter.

"If you could live anywhere in the world, where would it be?" We are sitting on the blanket underneath one of the trees as the sun is going down. Ben faces me, laying on his side, propped up on one shoulder playing solitaire. I am working through a Hundred and One Random Questions quiz. We've eaten our sandwiches and poured our wine; Ben is eating a cookie.

"Italy," he says, looking down at his cards.

"Really, eh? Huh. I'd go to Greece," I reply.

"Sure, there too." He looks up, passing me one of his winning smiles. "We can do a cruise."

I scrunch up my nose in return. "Great idea, but I'm terrified of water."

"Really?" He raises his eyebrows. "Can you swim?"

"Nope. Don't want to," I reply adamantly, sticking my nose in the air before looking back to the magazine and taking a sip of my wine.

"Well, I guess I won't throw you in the pond as planned, then. You can't swim? Not even a little bit?"

"Nope, and I can't skate, either. I'm terrible at anything athletic other than running. That, I taught myself. My parents didn't get me into anything when I was a kid. They were too busy with themselves."

Ben is staring at me, listening intently. The mood turns somber, and I feel the need to explain, so I sigh and continue. "I guess the reality was that their life, particularly my father's, came before ours. There was no time or money left over after my brother's hockey, and even then, they relied on other parents for his rides a lot." Cringing at the memory of begging my mom for horseback riding lessons, I frown. "I became angry for a while and wanted nothing to do with the arts or my education, or my father, for that matter! High school became about smoking pot, being dark and miserable, and dating boys. By the time I was interested in becoming cultured and interesting, my dad was long gone. That's partly why I'm here. Why I want to stay here."

"Yeah, I know the feeling," he mumbles, going back to his cards.

When I lean over to kiss him, he grabs my hip with one hand and slaps my ass with the other. "Do you really like those magazines?" he teases.

"Um, yeah, duh." I make him a funny face, so he knows I am totally kidding.

"Don't you want to know who Taylor Swift is dating this week?" I joke, feeling comfortable being myself with him. These are the good feelings I trust myself in experiencing.

"Oh, my god, you're such a girl." He runs his hands through his hair, shaking his head. "A beautiful one, though. I think you're going to drive me crazy." He glances my way, his long fingers shuffling the cards in his hands.

"Good. I hope so. Gotta keep you on your toes," I chirp, following with the next question. "What's the strongest muscle in the body?" I smirk at him, curious how he might answer.

He raises his eyebrows at me with a dirty grin, and it makes me laugh.

"You're an idiot, Ben! That's not it!"

"Oh, no? Prove it." He challenges as he lunges toward me. Messing up all the cards, crawling on his hands and knees, he's ready to attack. He goes for my neck with an aggressive but playful bite, and I laugh as I fall back while grabbing onto him.

"Oh, my god, you're awful!" I squeal.

He continues to come after me as I giggle and laugh, trying to keep my legs together and skirt down.

"I could take you right here if I wanted to, you know."

I straighten my legs, shift, and lay back. He joins me by laying half on top of me, the sun reflecting off his hair.

"Wanna get out of here?" I ask.

"Yeah. Let's go."

Chapter 27: Katarina

Being in Ben's condo has changed my morning routine significantly.

We shower and dress, standing side by side in front of the bathroom. I brought most of my things from the hotel and am currently wearing Gloria's mint green uniform.

"So, dinner with the 'rents tonight, huh?" I say around a mouthful of toothpaste. "I'm not going to lie, Babe, I'm nervous as hell."

"Don't be." Ben grabs me by the waist and turns me to face him. "They're going to love you!" He seals his point with a kiss, toothbrush in my mouth and all.

"Whatever you say. Have you even told them about me?"

For just a moment, a shadow flickers across his face, but then he gives me an impish smile. "Naw, don't worry about it. Honestly."

"Well, let's stop on our way so I can get your mom some flowers. Will she like that?" I just want to make a good first impression. I know Ben comes from money, and I don't want his family to think I'm some kind of hick from the land up north.

"Sure. I'll see you back here later, and we'll go, ok? Love you." Quickly he runs out the door leaving me to fret on my own over the upcoming meet and greet with his parents.

The day goes too quickly, and by the time evening comes, I've imagined any and all scenarios on how the evening might go. I'm pretty sure of myself and my upbringing. I am polite, personable and can use the right fork, so I should have nothing to worry about. Ben, on the other hand, seems so nervous, almost agitated, pacing the living room. I ignore him, not letting it affect my mojo and choose slim black pants and sandals that show off my black painted toes. I know my green backless top makes my eyes stand out which makes me feel attractive and confident. I offer Ben a smile, and he returns it.

"Do I look ok?" I ask.

"You always look ok. Right now, you look stunning," he tells me as he grabs me by the waist and kisses me.

"Should we go?" I suggest, preferring he would take the lead tonight.

He's unnaturally quiet, blinking slowly, as though he is weighing his answer. Like this morning, the moment passes, and I wonder if I imagined it.

"Ready, Babe, yep," he says with a subdued smile.

Once downstairs we grab a cab, and I notice Ben's hands are clammy. He is picking at his black pants and acting out of character. I pretend not to notice. I'm nervous enough about meeting his family for the first time. I don't need to borrow whatever is making Ben twitchy too.

I recognize the front doors as we pull up outside, and I can't help but smile. My insides begin to warm as I remember the beautiful moment we shared just weeks ago that started our exciting love affair. As we approach the front doors, Ben grabs my hand and offers me a reassuring smile.

"It's okay, Baby. It'll be okay," he says. I raise an eyebrow and grin back at him. We've got this.

Before we're hardly through the first set of doors, the second set flies open, and an older man, obviously Ben's father, stands there with a middle-aged woman just behind him. The man stares at me, cocking his head to the side in a rather Ben-like fashion. His eyes widen, and I can't tell if he's angry or just surprised.

"Benjamin?" he growls. I swallow.

Anger, then.

The woman hiding behind the man looks at me and whispers in his ear, "Who is that? Why is she here?"

Stepping forward, it looks like Ben is about to challenge both of them. His hand is gripping mine tightly as he pushes past them, pulling me with him so we're no longer trapped in the entranceway. I can feel the tension mounting, and my heart speeds up in my chest.

"Be nice, Mother. This is my girlfriend, Katarina." Ben's voice is calm, quiet. Assured. "Look, she brought you flowers. Nice to have something pretty in the house for a change, isn't it?"

I gulp. Girlfriend? Yes, I suppose I am his girlfriend. They don't seem so happy about it, though. Maybe it's just me. I smile at them both, holding Ben's hand with my right while holding the flowers I'd brought in my left. His parents look nice enough, but something is clearly not right in this situation. I pass the flowers to his mother, and she glances at them before looking at me disapprovingly. Catching herself, she smiles, takes the flowers, and drops them on the side table.

"Thank you, dear." She's cold as ice, and I shift my gaze.

Ok, then.

Ben turns and muscles further into the hallway, pulling me into the sunken living room. Too loud, he shouts, "This is the living room. You didn't get to see it the last time you were here." He kisses me on the cheek. I'm stiff, and I know my eyes are wide as I nervously look around, trying to assess the situation.

Turning towards her husband, I notice his mother question him, "She was here, Roland? When was she here? Better question, why?" She seems genuinely confused and clearly unhappy about it.

Why would my previous visit be a problem, I wonder to myself and look to Ben for some guidance. Is there a favorite ex-girlfriend I am unaware of, maybe? I'm sure he's brought women here before, this used to be his home, too?

His father is practically shaking while glaring at Ben, holding onto his wife like she might fall down.

"Well. We're here, guys. Your invite, and you can't even offer us a drink? Not what you expected, is it?" Ben's tone is sharp. He puts his arm around me and kisses me softly on the side of the lips. His mother whimpers and turns away.

Ben turns his attention to a man in the dining room, and bounces up the few steps, leaving me with his parents.

"Alexander, brother!" Ben walks toward him and shakes his hand, pulling him into a half hug. "Come here. I want you to meet Katarina!"

"Katarina, that's different. It's nice to meet you," Ben's brother extends his hand towards me, coming closer so I can take it. Stunned, I take his hand, nodding a silent hello. He has the same build, same hair, but cut short. He's looking awkwardly—almost apologetically—at me.

What the fuck is going on here? Why is Ben being so rude to his parents and so jumpy?

With all of us in the living room, I find my voice and greet Ben's mother, "Hello, Mrs. Ford." I shift my gaze between her and Ben's father. "Mr. Ford. Nice to meet you." I lower my eyes from their stares and keep my hands clasped in front of me. I have the feeling they don't want to shake my hand.

They pause side by side and look at me, Mr. Ford's arm around his wife, he turns his eyes away, correcting me.

"It's Doctor Ford." He sounds annoyed and put off.

Shit! I'm awkward! Ben didn't say anything, warn me. I look at Ben in disbelief. *Really, Ben?* I wasn't expecting anything, but I definitely was not prepared for this.

Looking back to his father, I start to say, 'I'm sorry' when Ben hollers, "Nancy!" He jumps back up the two steps into the dining room towards the kitchen. "You here?"

He's being very loud and nervous. Not himself. At all.

"Come meet my girlfriend!"

When he returns, I sidle closer to him, not feeling comfortable under the glare of his mother's eyes. Standing beside him, I search for his hand to hold as who I figure to be Nancy comes into the room smiling at me. Shockingly and quickly, Ben grabs her and gives her a huge hug and kiss on the cheek. Unlike his mother, I notice, but I'm just thankful someone smiled at me, and I smile back.

"Ben!" she shouts looking at him with surprise, eyeing me again for a moment before she concentrates back on him. "I mean, Benjamin." She laughs nervously.

Mrs. Ford glares at Nancy as Ben releases his hold on her. Nancy looks down, seemingly knowing she's made a mistake of some sort. Avoiding Mrs. Ford's glaring eyes, she asks, "Should I set another place?"

"Yes, absolutely! Can you put those flowers in some water? The ones mother dumped in the hall. Kay, here Babe, have a drink." Ben passes me a glass of wine as Nancy turns and exits the room.

I take the wine that Ben has poured for me. Nancy quietly enters the hallway and takes the flowers I brought to put them in a vase.

"Katarina," Dr. Ford says to me, "please allow me to apologize. We, uh… we weren't expecting you." He glares at Ben. "We had some family matters we wanted to discuss with Benjamin this evening." He gives me a weak attempt at an apologetic smile.

"Oh. It's okay, Dr. Ford," I fluster, looking up at Ben. "Ben hasn't mentioned much to me about you guys. I didn't know." I look squarely into Dr. Ford's eyes, trying to show some form of confidence and a lot of class.

"His name is Benjamin. It's *Benjamin*," Mrs. Ford corrects me sternly, icy cold. I smile awkwardly back at her—fucking terrified.

"Sorry, Babe." Ben moves his body behind me, wrapping his arms around me. His body presses against mine like he's protecting me.

"This is my mother, *Vivian*, and my father, the great Dr. Roland Ford!" His voice is mocking with a false account of pride. "And you, Baby," he leans into me, nuzzles my ear, and says loudly enough for everyone to hear, "can call me whatever you want. I prefer Ben anyway."

Fucking awkward. Keeping my eyes on Roland, I move onward, attempting light conversation. "You're a doctor? That's wonderful, what's your specialty, if you don't mind my asking?"

He smiles at me, actually smiles. "I work in psychiatry. I have a private clinic in Queens."

"That's interesting, I have a degree in social work. I just graduated." I straighten up and square off my shoulders to show off some pride.

"Ah." Disinterested, he steers Vivian to sit on the couch, sitting himself beside her and resting his hand on her slim leg. The rest of us join them on the opposing couch.

"Katarina," Vivian says directly across from me, sitting forward and picking up her glass of wine from the coffee table, "that's an interesting name… Are you Swedish?"

"Uh, no, no I'm not. Scottish, Irish mostly." I smile. This isn't so bad.

"I see. Well, that's a Swedish name, that's why I ask," she snubs and takes a sip of her wine.

"Um, really? Oh, I didn't actually know that, although I should I suppose." I shrink back and laugh awkwardly, looking at everyone else's reactions and wondering if she hates everyone or if it's just me.

"Yes, really. I've travelled there many times. Tell me, Katarina, what do you know?" I feel like she's challenging me.

Taken off guard by the question, I stumble and stutter a moment. She stares at me, almost as if in combat, I find my voice and continue. "I, uh, I know that a name can define a person's personality. Quite well, actually," I speak little louder. "Vivian, in fact, your name is of Latin origin, meaning lively. It's unique and has only been a popular name since the 1900s." Take that, smarty pants.

She raises her eyebrows at me; Roland does the same.

"Well," she says pertly, "well, I suppose you're right." She smiles and sits up, quite proud. "I used to be quite lively, and I'm definitely unique. Wouldn't you agree, Benjamin?"

"Sure, Mother. You're unique, alright." Ben is quiet now. His mood is calmer and more collected than when we first arrived, so I begin to relax, too.

"Tell me, Katarina. What does your name mean if you know so much about names?" Vivian continues to challenge, but I've got her figured out.

"Pure. It means pure. Like a pure heart, or soul, perhaps," I respond calmly and lean a little closer into Ben, allowing him to pick up my hand and hold it.

"Well, I highly doubt that," she mutters into her wine glass.

Excuse me? Did anyone else just hear that, or only me? No one reacts, so I swallow hard and sit back, clasping my hands together with Ben's.

Roland pipes up, "Social work then? Interesting. What brought you into that field?"

Ok, so we are just going to ignore Vivian. I respond, "Well, my father died at a very crucial age. I was a teenager... it was difficult. My family was… damaged. We were close, but we had hard times and needed support. As I got older, I felt the need to give back, help people. Particularly children, youth, like I was."

"Still are, dear, still are," Vivian comments, rolling her eyes and taking another sip of her wine.

"Wonderful field, isn't it?" Roland seems comfortable now, clearly enjoying the conversation on his own field. "I'm sorry you lost your father. You must've worked very hard to get through those feelings, that pain and abandonment." He leans forward, taking his drink from Nancy, before she silently slips back to the kitchen.

"She's not one of your patients, Father," Ben comments with a glare in his eye.

I smile at Ben like it's ok and squeeze his hand. "I did. Although, maybe not always in the most constructive of ways." I laugh a little and shrug my shoulders, starting to feel some warmth enter the room.

Alexander, sitting on the other side of Ben near the empty fireplace, pipes up, "He must have been quite young, I imagine? Was he sick?"

"Alex!" Ben smacks his knee as his mother glares at him. I make the connection for her disgruntlement. I get it now; she doesn't like shortened names.

"It's okay Ben-Benjamin." His full name feels awkward on my

tongue. I look nervously out of the corner of my eye at Vivian. She's sipping her wine, engrossed in it. Dodged that bullet. "He was in his forties. He died from AIDS."

Roland leans forward, eyes wide and says, "Really? I thought that was more rampant in the eighties?"

"It was, he just had complications early on and didn't do well with medications," I explain.

"Dirty disease, AIDS," Vivian quips. "Dirty, dirty." Shaking her head, it seems she is more interested in her wine glass than our conversation. I'm not impressed, but I'm classy enough not to react. Man, she's snarky.

Ignoring her, I continue, "I worked with children during my placement. That's where I learned the importance of names and how they reflect personalities. The Dorian Gray effect, social scientists say. Correct, Doctor Ford?" I ask him, undeniably looking for approval.

"You are correct, Katarina." He nods, twirling the tumbler, filled with dark liquid, on his crossed knee.

"There was a young boy, very quiet, disturbed. He wouldn't open up to many people, but he opened up to me. His name was Ted, or Theodore if you will. He was obsessed with watching people and learning their mannerisms. His name means 'gift of God,' and he really was. He was very special."

"What happened?" Ben asks, his arm resting around my shoulders while rubbing my leg with his other hand. His parents, watching us peculiarly.

"He learned how to cope, in the end. As he worked with us, he began to open up, slowly. Even though he would lash out, his therapist and I just kept working with him. We earned his trust and got him to talk, deal with his monsters and insecurities in a positive manner as opposed to a destructive one. There's a right way and a wrong way to address the human psyche. Wouldn't you agree, Doctor?" I don't know why I want Ben's dad to approve of me, but for some reason, I need him to like me, to think I'm smart, to realize I'm good enough for his son.

"Absolutely, Katarina. You seem to have found the right field for yourself." Placing his empty glass on the coffee table, he gives me a small smile.

Roland and Alexander are both looking at me now, almost starring. It is a little weird, but as they exchange glances, I think they may have been impressed.

Then Roland asks, "Are you working now? Or planning on working?"

"I'm actually on vacation. I live in Canada, just outside Toronto. I came here to gain some worldly experience before deciding on my future. I'd like to start looking this week, or next, in my field."

"You're in the right place for that," Vivian mumbles, "little that you know."

What is she talking about? What does that comment even mean?

Ben reacts, tensing up beside me. He glares at her and says, "Mother, drink your wine."

"Dinner's ready, Doctor Ford." Nancy enters the room, breaking the conversation and tension between Ben and his mother.

In the dining room, Ben pulls out my chair. I sit down, and he leans in, kissing me from behind on the cheek. On instinct, I turn into him. His mother cringes, and I sense the tension between them growing all over again.

Ben isn't acting like himself, and although there are bits and pieces of him, there is a side to him that I've never seen before. I'm naturally seated beside Ben with Alexander across from me. Vivian is directly across from Ben. Doctor Ford takes the head of the table.

"So, Alexander," I ask, "what is it you do?" Placing my napkin on my lap, I check to see how many forks there are, two. Good stuff, easy peasy.

"I work with Benjamin, actually. I'm one of the Head Editors for *The Manhattan.* I helped Benjamin get his job there in the art department."

"Yes, my Alexander," Vivian coos. "Always do take care of things, don't you, dear. Cleaning up the messes."

Ben squeezes my leg hard, and I look over at him. He's staring at his salad plate, his eyes dark and his jaw tight, but he doesn't say anything.

What the heck was that about?

"Katarina," Roland breaks the tension, "when do you plan on going back to Canada?"

"Um. I'm not sure, actually. I'm really enjoying New York. I feel like I'm fitting in well here." I smile at Ben and give him a squeeze on the leg.

"Well. You'll never fit in, dear." Vivian chuckles. "But I do know what you mean. I used to travel, didn't I, dear?" She stares hard at Roland. "Indeed, I did, and I know the feeling of excitement a new city brings a young girl." She picks at the salad plate Nancy has brought out. "I once travelled the world. Did you know that?" Her gaze is solely on me, and I shake my head, afraid to eat or even move.

"I did. And it was glorious!" Fork in hand, she's swinging it around. Her eyes are aglow with the memory. "I travelled with like-minded artists. Dancing on stages that you could never possibly fathom." Shaking her head, she returns to her meal, scraping her knife on the plate as she cut.

"You were a dancer?" I squeak out. "That must have been exhilarating, Mrs. Ford."

"You have no idea." She makes a point of passing me over one more glare before turning back to her plate. "You have no idea what kind of strength it takes to walk away from that, only to be disappointed, in some cases. Just disappointed." Her gaze settles back on Ben.

He stops eating and his entire body stiffens. I can feel it from where I'm sitting. The room feels like it was hit with an iceberg.

Glancing at Ben and trying to break the tension, I focus on his mother again. Turning to her I say, "Strong mothers make strong sons. Seems you have not one but two incredible sons here." I motion to Ben and Alexander.

She closes her eyes with her utensils in hand, a look of annoyance on her face. The men continue to eat quietly until she snaps, "Oh? What do you know?" Her face is ice-cold as she looks at me. "Are you a mother, Katarina?"

Roland reaches out, taking her arm as she stares directly into my eyes, making me very uncomfortable.

"No, no I'm not," I whisper with my head down.

"I see. Well until you become a mother yourself you will not understand strength." Her voice raises. "The level of sacrifice you must make, putting all your dreams aside. The obligation you instantly have for another human being you didn't ask for!" She practically spits out the last part.

"Dear, it's fine," Dr. Ford says quietly. Ben and Alexander exchange glances, then look to their father and mother.

"Mother." Ben's voice sounds strained. "Please don't do this." He stares at her, his hand clutching his knife, knuckles turning white. "Don't be rude to my guest!" he growls.

"Benjamin!" Roland says. The room goes silent for a split moment, but Vivian's expression is spiteful and angry, staring at Ben full of anger and hate.

"Oh. I'm sorry, Benjamin. I just don't have the energy to pretend to like you today." She continues cutting her food, harshly scraping the plate. "Or your little girlfriend." The word 'girlfriend' came out as a sneer, and she rolled her eyes.

"Mother. Shut up! You don't know what you're talking about. But thank you. Thank you for breaking me to the point I had to put myself back together again. By myself!" Ben is glaring at both his mother and father.

"Benjamin, I am warning you right now. Do not speak to your mother like that. Don't get out of hand, here! You caused this. Your decisions, remember?" Roland is pointing his finger at me, and I'm suddenly wondering what my role in all of this is.

"Benjamin, calm down," Alexander joins the conversation, his eyes pleading.

Standing up, Ben pushes his plate across the table, and it collides with his mother's. Things start to fly—glasses are knocked over, and utensils go everywhere.

Vivan has some nerve, I'll give her that. Without flinching, she says, "What? Did I strike one of your nerves, Benjamin? You know you'll never be any different, no matter how much you try." She returns to the plate that miraculously stayed on the table, food intact. "This is who you are—a mess. The same mess you've just created on my dining table. Now sit down and eat."

My jaw drops to the floor. Did she just say what I thought she said? I understand now why Ben is so rude to his parents, especially his mother.

Turning back on me she says, "Why would an educated girl like you ever want to date Benjamin? Do you know what you're getting yourself into? Has he told you?"

Swallowing, I must look confused. *What the heck is she talking about? What is happening right now?* The entire room implodes. Ben is irate, and I've never seen him like this before. I'm scared and can only sit and watch what's about to unfold.

"You know, Mother? It's because of you I'm like this. It's your fucking fault! Why the fuck do I have to take fucking pills? Because of you. I can't take you anymore!" Ben is towering beside me now, leaning on the edge of the table, his fists clenched. All I can do is stare up at him, his eyes are as dark as night, and he's staring at his mother, spitting his words at her.

His father starts to stand but his mother continues to talk. "Thanks for sharing. We're all impressed by your twisted point of view. Roland? Please sit. Benjamin knows he's wrong. Like always." She matches Ben's glare with just as much spite.

"Do you really think you could bring this lovely girl in here and pretend? Pretend that you can be a good, what do you call it… boyfriend?" she mocks. "Do you think she's obligated to you? Come on, she's too intelligent for you, honey."

Ben lunges at her from across the table. He looks like he's going for her throat! His father grabs him by the shirt and cracks him one, right in the jaw. Ben's over the table now and starts punching Roland over and over. Vivan is screaming, Nancy is yelling at Ben to stop but seems completely enthralled by his rage.

Alexander starts to yell, "Ben! Holy shit. *Stop!* Ben, calm down!"

Out of nowhere, Geoff grabs Ben by the neck and pulls him off his father.

Before I even know what's happening, Alexander's hand is on my arm, pulling me out of the room.

"Wait! What? No! What are you doing?!" We are standing in the kitchen with the chaos on the other side of the door, his hand is tight on my arm like a vice grip.

"Come with me now. You don't want to see this!"

Nancy comes running in with my purse and a set of keys, handing them both to Alexander.

"Nancy, call me if he gets any worse. Not that it can get any worse. Fuck! You know what I mean! I have to get her out of here!"

Nancy nods, looking terrified but also a little angry. She looks at me, trying to smile.

"Come with me!" Alexander yells at me, and he flies me through the back door into the alleyway, not letting go of me.

"What the hell are you doing? I'm not leaving Ben! Hey, let me go!" I try to pry his hand off my arm.

"Just come. I'll explain in the car. You don't want to see Ben like this, trust me." He's pulling me down the laneway, practically running.

I stop fighting. He's right. Who was that back there? What was that back there?

Getting in the car, Alexander asks me where I'm staying.

"His place," I say.

"No," he looks at me, "you can't be serious?"

"I have a hotel, but I've been staying with Ben."

"Where's your hotel?" he asks.

I tell him.

"That's where I'm taking you, and you are not answering any calls."

Rattled, I remember my phone and pull it out of my purse. It's ringing.

Alexander looks at me and yells, "Is that him? Is that him?!"

"It's him." I look down at Ben's smiling face as the phone rings at me.

"Do not answer, for fuck's sake! He needs to calm down." To himself he says, "I need to deal with him. This is a fucking mess!" Gripping the steering wheel, he's driving a little too quickly. I'm buckled in, just looking at him and my jaw has dropped.

"Listen to me," he glances between the road and me, "you're smart, I can tell. It's not your fault. Tonight, I mean. But you're in social work, right? So, you must know a thing or two about mental health."

I nod my head yes, unable to find my words yet.

"You must know what bipolar is? Manic Depressive? Do you? Do you know?"

"Yeah. Yeah, I know." I swallow, nodding my head, my eyes wide as I stare at Ben's brother.

"Well, your boyfriend, my brother, is all wrapped up in that shit. Ben is a mess, a fucking mess! And I don't know what the fuck he's thinking being with you, but he's not boyfriend material." Alexander looks me straight in my eyes and delivers the blow, "He's not good with change, Katarina. He will destroy himself and you in the process."

My heart plummets to the ground. All I can do is stare at him in disbelief. This can't be happening.

"How long have you been seeing him? You haven't noticed?" he asks, clearly confused at how blind I seem.

No! Shit, no, I hadn't noticed. Ben was fine when he was with me. Kind, open, loving, and funny. Erratic… possessive… unpredictable… I stare at my hands, embarrassed. *How the hell had I not noticed?*

"Have you slept with him?" he asks, and my head jerks up to look at him, scared, and I begin to shake.

"Don't be coy, have you?!" he bellows, and after seeing my shock, softens his facial expression to more kindness and concern.

Embarrassed, I look away and slowly shake my head yes. *Fuck, yes.* A hundred times, yes. My eyes well up with tears.

"Jesus Christ! Fuck!" He hits the steering wheel, and I jump. Finding composure again, he breathes in deeply. It's clear he's handled his brother before.

"Ok, listen to me. He's never had a girlfriend, but he is heavily, and I mean *heavily* influenced by other people." He pauses for a moment, as though gathering his thoughts. "He's an addict and has an addictive personality. I'm sure he's going to be absolutely obsessed with you, which is going to drive him even more crazy. He's never brought a girl home, he knows better. Bringing you home… Something's not right." Turning to me, he says, "You need to stay away from him. *Stay away from him!* Don't answer his calls, nothing. Do you understand me?"

Fear ravaging through my body, I nod my head. "Uh-huh. I do. I do. I. Sorry. I just don't. I um… I didn't know." *How the fuck did I not know?* I contemplated my reflection in the spotted sideview mirror. *Objects are closer than they appear. Are they? Are the answers really right under my nose?* In that split second, I see her. The girl I'd been trying to find is in that reflection waiting for me. Her eyes, my eyes, staring right back at me.

Arriving at the hotel, I stumble out in my fog and make my way around towards the entrance when Alex leans out the window. "Katarina!" Turning, dumbfounded by his voice, I hear him say, "He will destroy you, Katarina, and himself. Please. Just trust me on this. Ignore him. Forget about him."

His tires peel off into the night air, as I burst into tears.

Chapter 28: Katarina

In my hotel room I'm pacing the floor, and my head is spinning. What's happened? Who is this man I fell in love with? I'm sobbing. The pain in my chest is choking me! Oh, the fucking pain in my body. It's so deep in my gut I can't breathe. I'm screaming and tearing at my clothes as the tears gush out of my face relentlessly.

Falling to my knees, I crawl to the corner of my room, tears streaming down my face. I'm bawling so hard my throat hurts. I feel incredibly stupid, used, and alone.

I thought I knew you! You fucking asshole, I thought I felt you, Ben!

I grab at the pain in my heart, the place where I thought I felt undying love for you and your truth.

Have you hurt me? Yes! Yes, you have!

Did I hurt you?

Do I want to?

You lied to me. You showed me a side of you that wasn't real. Not really. It wasn't the whole you! You didn't tell me! Why didn't you tell me?

Oh god, why didn't you tell me?

Looking at the ceiling with tears streaming down my face, I use the sleeve of my track suit to wipe my snuffles of anguish. I shake my head, unable to grasp what happened tonight.

We talked, Ben. We talked and talked and talked!

Was it even you I talked to? Was it even you? You who I fell in love with?

Who the fuck are you? How did I *not* see this?

Angrily, I wipe at my eyes—the tears refuse to stop.

Standing, I look at myself in the mirror by the door. I don't recognize the mess staring back at me. My eyes are red with anger and pain, raw cheeks stained with mascara. My nose is running, and I can't control the spit in my mouth. I pull at my hair, trying to calm my look of absolute anguish.

You've changed me.

I place my hands on either side of that shitty little mirror, anger overtaking my eyes.

You made me whole and now I can't be with you? You destroyed me. What we had, everything, was a fucking lie! Dishonesty of truth, the truth of who you are.

I'm so livid I sense my eyes getting darker. My brain starts to scream at me. *How could you be so fucking stupid, Katarina?*

So now what? What's next? How do I walk away, Ben?

Turning, I throw my arms up in the air in confusion and defeat.

How the fuck do I walk away? It hurts so bad I want to throw up. Sitting on the bed with my head in my hands, I wonder how to move forward.

Where were you? Where did you go? Where did you really go that time? Was it a bender? Who were you with? Why?

There are too many questions without answers and the hurt bubbles up inside me. *The shit you've put me through—again!* I am so empty it's agonizing. My heart bleeds raw, so fucking raw. How do I survive this?

How do I give you up?

Chapter 29: Benjamin

I'm screaming and can't stop. My hands are clenched in fists at my side as I try to organize the flurry of emotions in my head. I ran all the way home and my lungs are raw. I'm so fucking tired.

"*Katarina!*" I'm absolutely manic to find her. I search everywhere in my apartment. *Make the pain stop, Kay, help calm me down!* I need to grab her, love her.

She's not here and I'm scrambling. I've got to fix this. *How do I fix this?*

I've fully exposed myself! *SHIT!*

She's seen the bad part of Ben now. It came out of me so strong. *Fuck! Where is she?* I'm frantic. Things are flying through the apartment, and I don't know why. Is it me? My destruction? Cushions are everywhere, records shattered on the floor. I can't recall how it's all happened; all I know is she isn't here with me.

I fly through to the bedroom and stop short when it's empty, I crash to me knees and sob.

"No, no, no Katarina. Nonononono! Not like this, not like this!" I crawl over to our bed—our empty bed—pull up on the sheets and cry, stretching out where we would make love. It's too big and too cold without her. On my back, I bring my knees to my chest and grab at my cock, stomping my feet on the bed.

"*Arrrgghhh!*" I'm so fucking angry!

"*Fuck you, bitch, fuck!*"

I need you baby, right now!

"It's the most important time!" I whine. "When I need you the most! You. Said. You. Wouldn't. Leave. Meeeee!!" My body is flailing around, and I don't fucking care.

My heart is bleeding. I'm suffering without you.

I need you in my bed, you understand my needs. Where the fuck are you? My mind is raging fire. I cringe, by body hurts so much! The pain is excruciating. I'm sick and so empty. I can't do this alone! Nope, I shake my head, not alone. Not alone again like all the time alone.

Alone. Alone.

My hands are on my head as I sit on the edge of the bed lost, something shifts. An inner sound is made and in the mass of all the other noise it whispers, *Yes, you can. You have to.* Hanging my head in defeat, I snuffle my cries and try to listen to it. *The time is now Ben, stand up and get your shit together. No one wants a mess like you, so figure it out for the girl you love.*

I can't listen to it anymore. *I'm just not strong enough, she numbed all the pain, you have to understand. She's the one that makes all the bad stuff stop, and I need you to hear me. I need to talk to her so you can see, see what I see. You can't help me little voice, but she can. She can be here and love me.*

That's what I'll do.

Jumping up, I grab my keys and bolt out the door. There's no time for elevators, and I fly, swinging off the railings of the staircase, bursting outside. Running down the street, I start waving taxis down frantically, grabbing the first one that stops.

"Hotel at Times Square," I breathe out. "Quickly please!" I throw the cabby a fifty.

Chapter 30: Katarina

BANGBANGBANG! BANG! BANG! BANGBANGBANG!

Snapping my head up from my hands, I am startled by the loud noise. *What the heck?* Who is at my door, practically banging the damn thing down?

Shit, I know exactly who it is.

"Katrina! *Katarina*! Are you in there? Baby? *Just talk to me*!" He sounds frantic, his voice high and scratchy. He's breathless, and it terrifies me to hear him like this not knowing his state of mind.

Shit! Shit! Shit! I approach the door and, goddammit, I want to open it, but I'm so confused. My head is pounding from all my crying, my face full and raw, and I can barely breathe. I don't know what to do or what I *can do.*

I want him! I want to hold him; I want his arms around me…

I also want to punch him but maybe kiss him, smooth out his hair that I imagine must be crazy right now. But I don't do anything. I just put my hands on the back of the door and whimper.

"Ben?" I whisper. My voice is low and broken. He did this, he did this to me.

"Katarina? Kay! Baby, it's me." His voice is right at the door; he must be leaning right up to the doorjamb. I move closer and his breath is there, so close to mine.

"Please listen to me, Ok? I'm sorry! Really, really sorry! I—" He stops.

Fuck, what can he possibly say to me? He won't tell me everything now, will he? Do I even want the answers?

"I—I, should've told you, Kay. I'm so sorry… I—I love you!"

I can sense he's losing control, and I'm getting scared. I start to whimper as he whines and begs. I hear his hands on the door scratching for me to let him in.

He's upset. I can hear it in his pleas and feel it between us. My heart is burning out of my chest, it hurts so bad.

I'm resting my forehead on the back of the door when he yells at me, "Open the damn door, Katarina!"

I start to cry and paw at the door with my hands. I'm desperate to hold him in his pain, but I can't let go of mine, and I can't do this for both of us.

He has to get control of himself.

"I love you, Baby. I love you. Please open the door," he begs. "Let me tell you everything. You... you make me whole!"

I'm looking at the door like he can see me, I feel him on the other side.

He sighs in exasperation. "You make it ok. You make me ok. Kay? Pleeeeaaasee!"

I respond with silence. I won't open the door.

"*FOR FUCK'S SAKE OPEN THE FUCKING DOOR!*" He punches the door, making it shake in the frame, and I jolt my head back. Grabbing for my phone, I'm ready to call security and it destroys my heart.

"Ben, I can't open the door. I… I want to… I do," I tell him, terrified.

"I love you," he whispers.

My heart jumps a little skip.

"I-I love…" I start to say.

"Babes! Just let me in, then! Come on!" he cuts me off as he continues to try and coerce me.

"Let me touch you, please. Let me fucking hold you. Will you?" Scratching at the door, he's begging me to let him in. "Let me fix it, let me fix it. I can, I can do it."

I have to get him to leave. I'm not ready for this. I need to organize my thoughts, and apparently, I also have to figure out how to deal with him while not completely screwing him up.

I didn't sign up for this. I had no idea I fell in love with an emotionally delicate—hell—emotionally damaged person! Addict? Jesus. I start shutting down with the realization of how damaged he might possibly be. How fucked up is he?

Trying to reason, I say, "Ben, I'm not going to open the door. Alex told me, he said I shouldn't see you, and I think for right now that's what we gotta do."

Silence.

"I think we need to get some sleep, maybe *some space?*" I choke out the last part through my sobs. "I love you, Babe, ok? But I gotta… figure some stuff out." Resting my hand on the doorknob, I'm tempted to tear it open.

His rage explodes.

"ALEX TOLD YOU WHAT? WHAT DID ALEX TELL YOU?" He screams through the door, pounding on it like he might break it down.

Uh oh. That was stupid, Katarina.

Closing my eyes, I raise my voice and cautiously explain, "He… he told me about your condition. That maybe I should stay away from you. Ummm, maybe he's right on this one? For a bit, anyway." Biting my lip, frightened of what's going to happen next, tears escape down my cheeks and my hands shake.

"DON'T FUCKING LISTEN TO ALEX! HE KNOWS SHIT!"

Shit, Katarina. What is wrong with you? I lean my forehead on the door, only to have it knocked back again.

He starts kicking at the damn door, and it pisses me off. This is his doing, not mine, and while my rage is brewing, he's yelling, "*OPEN THE FUCKING DOOR, Katarina!*"

I'm about to call the police when I hear another male voice over his yell out very sternly, "*Sir*! You're going to have to leave these premises *immediately*!"

I crack open the door just enough to see what's happening outside, Ben's back is towards me, and there are two security guards with their hands resting on their billysticks. Ben looks like he's trapped between them and my doorway, and I know enough that anyone feeling trapped while in an outraged mental state is not a good thing. My beating heart begins to race even faster.

He has his attention on his aggressors, and I hear him mumble, "No," while shaking his head. It pains me to see him this way as the two men start to move forward.

"Sir, you need to leave!" says the big one, slowly inching towards him. He's much bigger than Ben, and I am scared he's going to get hurt.

"Katarina!" He yells out, "You said you'd never leave me!" The pain is evident in his voice.

Holding onto the door, I cry and shut and lock it. I break down. Weeping against it, I'm bawling and can't control my shaking as I fall to a heap on the ground. *Fuck me, Benjamin! Why did you do this to me?* My body burns while he continues his rampage outside.

After some time passes, I regain my composure and force myself up to standing. It's been silent for a few minutes now, and I decide to take a shower, try to wash all this shit away.

There's a light tap at the door. It must be security; great I'm probably getting kicked out too. I look out the peephole. Not security at all, worse.

Opening the door, I look at Max through blurry eyes, and he says, "I told you to be careful with that shit."

I shut the door again without a word, and I hang my head.

Fuck me. He did too.

Chapter 31: Benjamin

Slamming my hands against the door, I punch it, kick at it. I'll break the fucking thing down if I have to! The security men grab either side of me, and one of them hooks his arm around my neck. The other guy hits me in the side. Dammit that hurt, and I buckle.

Pinning my arms, they pull me backwards as I continue to yell, "*Katarina! YOU PROMISED!*"

They have me, and I'm fucked. Pulling me down the hall, I'm seething, foaming at the mouth in rage. There's an old man that holds the elevator door and looks at me with sadness in his eyes. Do I see empathy? I recognize him as her neighbour, and I feel a glimmer of hope. Does he know how I'm dying inside, and can he get that message to her? My eyes plead with him as I struggle to break free. "Please!" I muster out through my spit. "Tell her, please!" *She has to know.* He leans on his cane and stares silently at me. The doors shut. I've failed.

I failed my Katarina.

Back at my apartment, it's pushing midnight. I have no real recollection of how I got back here, but I know my side hurts, my hands are bleeding, and my heart is shattered. My stomach is so twisted, and I am fighting myself from throwing up.

I'm sitting in the middle of my couch with the lights off—the artificial light hurts my head. I decide to light a few candles instead. I need to calm down. I rub my thighs with my burning hands and breathe forcefully out of my mouth. I feel like I've made huge mistakes tonight.

Calling and texting Katarina is no use, I've tried enough times that she must have turned her phone off. 'Hey, it's Katarina. Leave a message,' comes on instantly when I call her number, but I keep calling anyway just so I can hear her voice. Alexander texts me, and then calls.

Texting him back, I tell him I'm home, and to come check if he feels he needs to. Yes, I will talk to him in the morning, and yes, I am going to work. I am trying, and it is brutal.

Someone is at my door. I hear it unlock, but I'm too exhausted to move. My heart sinks, terrified of who is coming for me now.

Why can't you all just leave me alone?

"Ben? It's me, honey. Are you in here?"

Looking up from my self-loathing slump, I squint my burning eyes at the front door. A woman peeks her head inside, and I notice the kind eyes and soft hair. Immediately, I sense the feeling of calm and comfort.

"Nancy is that you?" My voice cracks.

"Yes, honey it's me." She's standing in the shadow of the doorway. "I'm coming in now, ok?"

I nod in response.

She flips on the cabinet lighting in the kitchen, creating a harsh glow that stings my eyes. Seeing me on the couch staring into nothing, she approaches quietly and gently sits beside me. Her hand gingerly moves the hair off my face as I rest my head on the back of the couch, staring into empty space.

"Ben, honey. You ok, dear?"

I feel my face start to crack. She's so nice and soothing, but I'm so bad, such a bad boy. I don't deserve her kindness.

"I screwed up," I whine, exhausted and defeated. Immediately, her arms open, pulling me into her as I fall sideways, resting my head on her shoulder. Her fingers comb through my hair.

"Hey, hey, hey. Shhhh. It's ok, Bennie. It's ok," she soothes, and I feel like I'm seven again.

"No. No it's really not ok," I respond. "I don't care about my mother or father. I don't give a shit about them! But what about my Katarina? She won't talk to me!" I cry, my throat stinging with tears. "I don't deserve her. I don't deserve her to love me. Nobody should." I bury my head into Nancy's arms.

"Listen, honey. You listen to me right now, ok?" She takes my head in her hands and raises my face, so I have to look at her. "You screwed up. You did. You know you did, and you know why you did. It's ok!"

She is staring me down, insisting everything is fine.

"The important part is that you keep moving forward. Do not let this define you. You have a choice here, you can either plummet or you can soar. What are you going to do?"

I lower my eyes—no one has said anything like that to me before. Normally I'd be scolded for my behavior, made to endure session after session of therapy, and explain where and why I was wrong.

"As for that sweet girl of yours," she casts me a teasing smile, "I'm so proud of you, Ben! She is absolutely stunning inside and out, and she compliments you so well!" She grabs my knee. "And you. You compliment her, too, you handsome devil!"

I sheepishly smile, but only for a second. "She won't talk to me, Nancy."

I'm tired, so tired.

"She will." She nods her head, assuring me. "You're gonna turn it around. It will all turn around, and you'll figure it out." Holding my head against her shoulder, she strokes my hair while I slump against her.

"I saw the way she looks at you, Ben. If that isn't true, powerful love, then I don't know what is." Jokingly, she lightens the mood adding, "Geoff looks at me like that every day! He's still smitten after thirty-five years of marriage." Pulling away from me, she turns to face me.

I stare, somber and ask, "Why am I such a mess, Nancy?"

"No, Ben. No, no," she soothes. "You're not a mess, you're in love. Love makes us all crazy. It brings out the best and worst of us. We just need to figure out how to navigate through it. I promise. Just one day at a time." She taps my knee.

I lean on her shoulder, and my silent tears trickle down my nose.

"This is what we're going to do. You're going to wash your face, so you don't look like a dump truck hit you tomorrow morning. Let me see your hands." I let her take them in hers. "Yep, a few cuts. I'll clean those up. You'll be good as new." She heads towards the kitchen, yelling over her shoulder she starts rummaging through the cupboards. "You need a good meal to calm those nerves, looks like toast and honey will have to do. Do you have any tea, here?"

"She bought us stuff," I whisper. "I don't know. I don't know if I have anything."

Nancy, searching the cupboards, calls out, "You have a pot, good enough to boil some water, and… looks like you have tea. Earl Grey! Ooh, I like her," she mutters to herself. "Now, you go splash water on your face. I'll make tea and toast and when you come back, we'll chat. We'll just chat about puppy dogs and ice cream, ok? Get you calmed down enough to go to bed and get some sleep before work tomorrow, yeah?"

Standing up, I realize my entire body is sore, and I start to shuffle towards my bedroom. My empty, lonely bedroom.

"Yeah, ok," I mumble.

"Oh, and Ben?"

I turn in the hallway to listen.

"When you get there, you look at yourself in the mirror, and you tell yourself that you can do this. Even if right now it's only for her. You tell yourself you can do this. I believe in you, Ben. Now hurry back."

I do as I'm told.

I wake up the next morning to the noises of Nancy banging around in my kitchen. She must have stayed on the couch, either because she wanted to or because she was told to, I have no idea which. When I open my eyes, the little plant Katarina bought is sitting on my side table. It is green and bright, and the black bird on the side of the pot makes me smile. Nancy must have put it there beside a cup of hot black coffee.

I peel myself out of bed. It's six-thirty, and I'm not getting any more sleep anyway—lucky to have gotten what I did get. I drag myself like a zombie over to the shower, our shower, and turn it on. Instantly, tears of my despair and disappointment start to form and fall. The stream of the water washes them away as quickly as they fall.

How am I going to stop this? I have to, but my heart and soul are so broken I just don't know if I can. *I just miss her so much.*

Padding out to the kitchen in my robe to the smells of eggs and bacon, I imagine I'll see Katarina standing there. I don't, of course, but it is nice seeing a friendly face.

"Ah, Ben, I was just about to wake you. We need you to have a good start before heading into work. Geoff is going to pick you up in Alexander's car and take you in." Nancy is gliding around my kitchen, making it her own.

"Alexander's car? Why?" I stumble onto the stool and wrap my hands around the fresh cup of coffee she poured. Thank god. Coffee.

"Well, let's just say we're staying there, now." She stops, looking confused, and says, "Probably, for a while. Maybe forever if Alexander will keep us."

"What? Why? I don't understand?"

I notice how serious she is when she turns to face me. "Well, Ben, your parents and I had a bit of an argument last night after everything went down. It was an argument I should've had with them years ago."

Turning back to the stove, she continues over her shoulder, "They've been selfish and cruel."

Raising my eyebrows at her back, I'm surprised.

She turns off the stove and serves up a plate of breakfast she puts down in front of me. Resting her hands on the counter, she faces me square, clearly emotional as she sniffles, and tears form in her eyes.

"I'm sorry, Ben, I'm so sorry I didn't do something sooner. I was terrified of losing my job, our security. I thought that as long as I was there, I could help protect you, give you love and a good life." She shakes her head. "I failed you and your brother. Your parents failed you. It's not your fault, the way you are. You have a condition Ben, and that's okay. It's manageable, but you are not a little boy anymore, and you have to find a way that works for you. It's never going to go away, and no one can save you from it. But I promise you, you can live a good life if you choose to."

Stunned and silent, I don't fully comprehend what she is saying. Could she be right? I hold the power within myself to be the man I want to be? That all I'd been through, all that I'd done, was in part because of the way I was handled as a child? I hadn't been taught that way, and although I know she is trying to help, I am more confused than before.

She continues, "I told your parents last night. I told them what I thought about what they did to you. Both you and Alex. It wasn't well received, and they fired me. Or, maybe I quit, technically. Your parents were as shocked as I was at my outburst, but I'm proud of it and wouldn't take it back in a million years. It was long overdue.

"We have nowhere else to go, so we are at your brother's for now. We're working it out, but I want you to know your father won't be contacting you. I have his keys and together you, me, Geoff and Alex, we're gonna fix this. You have to be strong and do the work, but the first thing you're going to do is eat, so let's go."

I look down at the plate in front of me, it has two eggs and a bacon smile. I laugh out loud and so does she. Today is the first day of Ben 3.0.

Chapter 32: Benjamin

When I am home, so is Nancy. She never leaves me and lets me talk when I want or stay silent when I need to. I try to be strong and work out the shit in my own head, but it's all I can do not to unravel.

Every morning and every night I send my heart to her, my Katarina. She doesn't respond, and I am trying hard not to get angry about it.

Every day, I stare at my pictures of her, all the beautiful pictures I have. I'm not sure if seeing her smile, her naked body, and her laugh as she tried to block my shot helps, or keeps her too real, making things worse.

By the time the weekend comes, I am numb. Nancy says time and space are what girls need. Ok, time and space are what she'll get. When it's time for Nancy to leave, I will be staying on my own and I'm petrified.

Nancy and Geoff have moved in with Alex. Apparently, Alex has a secret girlfriend, for about two years now, and they are going to live together, keeping Nancy and Geoff employed. Nancy needs time to organize their new space so she's leaving me for the weekend. I never knew Alex was dating anyone. I guess, like me, he had to keep it a secret, afraid of it being ruined.

Why hadn't I just kept her a secret?

She'll come back around all in good time, Nancy assures me.

Well, I don't have time. As it stands, I am still on the lease, but with Father's name attached, I have to get out of the apartment and find my own place soon. Without her, I'm just not sure I see any point.

Waking up alone is not a good thing. My chest heaves and my throat burns, the cold and empty bed causes my brain to think about her too much. All I feel is that loneliness, that void. I can feel my pain morphing into frustration which spirals into anger, and those little doors start blasting open, and the little guys begin to party.

I have to find control, figure out a way to put them back in their closets and cope on my own. Jumping out of bed, I decide to run them out of me and out of my brain. I stuff my broken body into my gear and head out. The tranquility of the park and the memories of our times there bring a smile to my face, and the slight chance I might see her creeps into my thoughts.

Taking a cab to 59th and 6th, where we first met, I pop in my earbuds. I know this is becoming borderline obsessive, and I tell myself I'm not here to look for her, but I am. As I run through the park I check every tree, bench and hidden corner. I even go into the women's bathroom at the Bethesda. I don't see her, of course. She isn't hard to miss—I can sense her anywhere.

I find myself outside Gloria's. Probably not the best idea, but all I want is to talk to her. See her and touch her.

Yeah, I want to touch her. There's nothing wrong with that, right?

Using Gloria's back bathroom, I clean myself up a bit and cool off. Deciding I am going to see her today, I head to her hotel. She can't hide from me forever.

I need something. A reason to see her, a reason for why I am searching everywhere to find her without exposing the craziness that is building up inside me. Heading towards her hotel, I stop at my favourite bookstore, knowing how much she loves to read. The perfect gift. An easy way to start a conversation and see what she's been up to. Who she's been up to.

Wait, what?

My body stiffens. Who is she spending her time with? *Better not think about that, Bennie, that's a disaster waiting to happen.* Shaking it off, I figure if I show up with a gift, she'll talk to me, right?

I stop at Argosy, a famous bookstore I frequent whenever I am in the area. It also happens to be right around the corner from her hotel. The bookstore, old and unique, has seven floors specializing in anything from historical first editions from the nineteenth to twenty first centuries to rare and unusual books from the seventeenth to twentieth centuries. I wonder if she's ever been here before.

It is right up her alley, and I head to the basement with their general interest books and poetry, which is where I am hoping to find her something special. My father introduced me to this place when I was a child, using their services to appraise some of his old books and restore some of his others. Despite my feelings towards my father, I still love the store. I decide on a book of poetry, hoping that some of the poems will explain to her how I feel.

Sitting on the floor at the base of the book aisle, I dogear a few pages and clear the mix of emotions off my face before approaching the cashier. This has to work; I just need to get her thinking about me.

Arriving outside her hotel, I panic. What am I going to say to her? How can I get it all out before she decides she doesn't want to hear anymore? Or maybe I'll say the wrong thing and make everything worse. I don't know how to do this! These relationships. Terrified and afraid of failure, I call a cab and go home.

Chapter 33: Katarina

By Saturday morning, I realize I have to find a way to move on. I make a call to Monica. She knows right away that something is wrong.

"What is it? I can tell by your voice, so don't even try to skirt around it. Talk to me," she orders from the other line.

"I guess we broke up?" Without telling her the details why, I sob, the gush of tears starting again, my poor pillow soaking up the mess.

She is sincere but has no idea the pain I am in. No one in the entire world, especially a girl like Monica, can relate to the love I have for this man and the darkness his absence is causing in my soul. She tries her best once she realizes I am inconsolable. "Oh, Hun, this guy really got you, huh?"

I continue to sob, my throat too tight to answer her.

"You know what you need? You need a distraction, and so do I. I'm coming to see you!" she proclaims. "I'm going to clear my schedule and grab a flight. Don't worry about me, I'll figure out how to get there, just make sure you're home when I arrive, and we'll do something to take your mind off all of this, ok?"

Meeting Monica in high school practically saved my life. I'd made the decision to change schools mid-year and walked in not knowing another soul. When she'd bounced up to me with her Cheshire grin, we were instant friends. Not in the mood for company, but at the same time knowing her presence will occupy my mind—and I need the distraction—I agree. She'll be here early the following Thursday for a Girls' Weekend.

I drag myself through the rest of the week. I know I look like shit and am working like a robot, but at least I didn't give into the need to brood, close out the world, or—the very worst—see Ben. The staff sees my various mood swings and learns to stay clear. They keep their distance, and I do my job, which for me is an accomplishment.

Even though I try, I can't stop thinking about him. It feels strange being in the same city, yet so far apart. It is as if my soul is searching for him, unable to rest. Finding myself at The Meadow, a smaller park by his apartment, our apartment, I convince myself I'm not there in the hopes of catching a glimpse of him, even though I've brought a blanket and a light lunch. I hide under a tree for what feels like hours.

I finger the apartment key in my pocket—it has been four days, and I still don't know what to say to him, how I feel, or what I am going to do. One thing I am sure of is I'm not going back to Canada. With or without Ben, I've found myself here, and the city is becoming my home. I belong here.

It is a large city crawling with different personalities, and I realize I can help these people, people like Ben. The homeless population in New York is massive and knowing that the majority of the homeless suffer with mental illness, I decide to look into local support centres, hospices, and hospitals.

Almost forty-five percent of homeless men and women show a history of mental illness, and although I missed some signs in my relationship with Ben, I am confident that I've done some things right. If what Alex told me is true, and I'm sure it is, I think I can help Ben. When we were together, he was kind, calm and sweet. Maybe we can build off of that. If he can find a way to calm the chaos outside, I wonder if he can calm the chaos inside? But what will it do to me? I know I have a talent for helping people feel safe and secure, and plan on using that strength to do good in the world. When I tell my mother my plans, she groans, concerned about money and how I am going to live and eat. I downplay the idea, telling her it is simply an idea and start looking for work in my field anyway.

That evening, I stay in and enjoy dinner at the hotel bar. I am becoming quite comfortable in my own skin but getting a little lonely and bored. The thought of asking Max if he wants to go to a Broadway Show crosses my mind and I laugh, like that is going to happen. The two of us, slowly becoming two peas in the same pod of loneliness. Either way, all of these things are stepping stones I need and want in the quest to find myself.

Thinking of the little girl in the yellow flowered bedroom of her mom's home back in Kingston, I can't even remember her, let alone connect with who she had been. I drink a little too much wine and head back to my room by eleven when the piano guy finishes his set. Having not seen Max over the last few days, I find myself wondering if he is ok. However, upon noticing the empty bottles outside his door, I smile. I guess the girls remembered his coffee packets this week.

I awake to the sound of tapping at my door. The clock reads 1:00am, so I ignore the tapping and turn over, but it is incessant. The thought pops into my head that it could be Ben and fearing another scene from a few nights ago, I get up to see who it is. Looking out the peephole, I see Max, hunched over staring straight at the door. I open it.

"You have a visitor," he says, staring at me expressionless. Peering over his shoulder, I can hear the piano coming from down the hall. If Max is standing here, then who is playing the piano?

"You better get down there before security finds out he's here. Hurry on, go." Max moves over to let me pass.

I grab my robe, snatch my room key off the side table, and make my way down the hall towards the most beautiful, agonizingly sad sound. Peeking in the doorway, I see dark curls moving gently as Ben pours his emotions onto the keys.

I stand in the shadowed doorway watching the top of his head move along, imagining what his soft hands and long fingers must look like. There is a package in brown paper on the lid of the piano. Not knowing what to expect, I walk into the bar, the night air sweet and still, unsure what state he is going to be in. We are all alone here, just the two of us on the roof.

"Ben? What are you doing here, Babe? It's one in the morning." Straddled sideways on the bench, he twists his body to be square with the keys. With his head down, I have yet to see his face, unable to search his eyes. He stops playing but doesn't turn toward me.

Tightening my robe over my short night dress, I move in a little closer, stopping at the end of the bench. Finally, he turns, head still down, to face me.

"Ben? You, ok?" Of course, he isn't ok, but I don't know what else to say.

He takes a deep breath, and his eyes turn black with primal passion. I smile at him, and he smiles back, his eyes softening, his expression both sad and gentle. As broken as I feel, as angry as I'd been, the sight of him in the flesh helps to heal my bleeding heart.

"Hi, Baby," Ben whispers, low, and he rests his hands on his knees. "I brought you something." He inches closer, finding my gaze. "I thought of you and know you like to read. So… it's a book of poetry… I'd like you to have it."

"That's really nice of you, Ben, thank you," I reply, feeling myself thaw at the gesture.

He isn't drunk. He isn't high. And he isn't manic. He is quiet and sad. But other than that, he is the Ben I am in love with. My heart melts, and my body quickens at the sight of him.

"Will you sit with me for a minute?"

"Yeah, I'll sit with you." Straddling the bench, facing him, I gather up my robe and stuff it between my legs. Practically naked underneath it, our knees are touching, and he makes no attempt to move back, giving me space. Instead, he looks down at them, and as we're close, my hips start to weaken, moisture starting between my legs.

Chapter 34: Benjamin

Her knees are touching mine. Naked and soft, making me tingle, jolts of electricity coursing through my veins. My heart is in my throat. Suddenly, I'm unsure of what I've come here to say, and now that I have her here, her attention, I am choking on it. After what feels like minutes, all I can think of is, "I love you, and I miss you at my place. What I thought was our place."

I feel anger rising, replacing the sadness. "You said you loved me? I believed in that!" I spit and screw up my face, lowering my head to stop from tearing up. My anger is mounting. I have to keep that little guy locked down. With my hands resting on my knees, I start touching her skin just a little with my finger, instantly feeling myself soften again.

"My god, Ben, I do love you! Don't think I don't!" She grabs my face and makes me look at her. "I do! It's just…"

She's lost her words and starts looking at the stars like they are going to give her the answers. Lowering her hands, she hangs her head, and whispers, "I've died every day without you, Ben. I want to be with you, but…"

She returns her eyes to mine, and I can see the tears forming, I've broken my poor baby's heart.

"I know, I know." I sigh in grief. "I'm no good, Kay." Maybe, I just don't have this in me.

"No, that's not it. That's not true. It's us… We can't do this."

She looks lost, faraway for a moment, so I put my hand on her thigh and squeeze. It feels so good to be close to her, to touch her.

"No, Ben. No." She shakes her head and pulls back, but I just move in closer, tightening my grip.

Good Ben or bad Ben, I just want her skin, so I pull her in closer, looking in her eyes. "Yes, Ben. Shhh. Tell me yes, Ben. Let me show you we can. I can," I quietly plead with her. "I know I've hurt you, and I'm so sorry… but no one loves you like I do, Kay. Don't you understand?" I'm so confused at this point, but she makes me want to try harder.

Her eyes begin to soften, I'm breaking her down, so I persist, "Everything reminds me of you. I can't move around the apartment without seeing you, feeling you. You've changed things in me, no one needs you like I do." I tighten my grip on her legs, sliding up towards her hips as her legs voluntarily open wider. "Don't you get that? You take care of me, Babe. You didn't waste your time on me, I swear. I can be good, and we can be good together."

Finally, my lips are on her neck, and I begin to nibble. I wrap my arms around her waist and hold her as she begins to fall.

I had missed her touch so bad that when her hands start to trace the muscles on my back, I'm in heaven. They are warm and soft. They belong there. I squeeze her legs, pulling her in closer to me. My eyes are pleading with her, begging her, pushing her at the same time as she pulls my heart out.

I dive into her neck and bite her, softening the sting with my lips. She jumps at first but leans into me, a little moan escaping her throat. She tightens her grip on me and kisses me, the two of us clawing at each other as we explore the bodies we've missed. I stand, bringing her with me. We face each other. This is who we are, together as one. Her knees start to buckle as I feel her going limp into my arms, but I won't let her fall.

"Come," she says, pulling me towards the doorway. I reach back in time to grab the gift I'd brought her off the piano. Stumbling along, I follow her.

Reaching her room, I push her body against the door, my hands on either side of the doorframe. I have her pinned while she is trying to unlock it. My face is in her hair, lost in her incredible scent.

As I nibble on her neck with my teeth, I can feel her pressing her ass into my crotch, making me so hard. Opening the door, we stumble in, and I aggressively spin her to face me, grabbing at her robe and pushing it off her shoulders. I pull her into me by the belt of her robe, twisting it around my hands so she has nowhere to go. She catches her breath and a dart of fear shoots through her eyes until I smile mischievously and begin kissing her bare shoulders.

Opening her robe, I wrap my hands around her waist, and slide them down to her ass, grabbing it, lifting it and giving her a quick pinch. She gasps and smiles. Pulling back, I see she is wearing a black spaghetti strap nightdress that hugs her curves and makes her shine. My dick instantly comes to attention. I grab her back in again and kiss her hard.

She backs up and as I follow her lips, she turns me around, so my back is to the bed, her hands pushing on my chest. Edging me with her body and her kisses, I match her eagerness right back, the two of us grinding, demanding and desirous. Damn I've missed her. I stumble back when my legs hit the edge of the bed and fall, landing on the edge in a sitting position. She straddles me, and while I place my hands onto her grinding hips, she takes my face and starts running her hands through my curls. I close my eyes; I love it when she does that. She starts to cry. I can feel her tears on my cheeks, and when I open my eyes, her tears are streaming down her face.

"It's ok, Baby," I whisper. "It's ok. I'll take care of you, I promise." Taking a deep breath, she tears my shirt off over my head and goes immediately to my pants. She is hungry. I am famished. All I can think is *thank god, I need her so badly*. Her hands are all over my chest, playing with my rings like she always does. She devours me, my mouth, my neck, pushing me down so she can kiss my chest, my nipple rings.

"God, I love you, Kay. My baby, my baby." My hand is on the back of her head while she kisses me, my body propped up on my other. Sitting up fully, I push her back and lift her nightgown over her head, exposing her perfect breasts to me. I take them, push them together, putting them in my mouth and suck on her nipples. She cries out and holds my head in place as I ravish her tits.

"Oh Jesus, Ben. I love what you do to me," she huffs, reaching for my belt. I help her undo my belt and maneuver out of my jeans, not letting her get off my lap. As she settles back down, my cock swoons in the folds of her wet pussy.

Whimpering, her tears shine in her eyes but don't fall. She grabs my cock, putting it inside her, and I bite my lip to stop my tears from exiting my eyes. I need her so badly I can't breathe, but I don't want her to see my weakness. I want her to know I'm strong and will take care of her. She starts moving and weeps, her tears now falling down her cheeks. Taking my thumbs, I wipe them away.

We mold together, and we hold onto each other for dear life, making love, sweet powerful love. Wrapping her legs around me, she continues to rock against me. Holding her tight, I stand up, lifting her and spin her around. Laying her back down, I'm on top of her and our eyes meet. Moving as one body and holding our gazes, I never exit her. I smother her; she takes me and holds me, moaning my name over and over again.

"Ben. Make love to me, Ben," she says.

So, I do.

I feel and hear her breathing getting quicker. "Are you there, Kay?" I ask.

She nods yes with her eyes closed, and I grind in deeper and deeper. She cries out, entering her orgasm, and as she contracts, I let myself go too. Groaning into her neck, goose bumps rise all over my body. Laying down, I rest on her, her legs bent on each side of me. Taking my hands, I rub up and down her thighs, caressing them and hold her close to me.

The silence starts to suffocate the room, so I whisper, "You said you wouldn't leave me."

"I know," she replies but doesn't say anything else.

I let it go, just happy to be with her. How much time was she going to need?

"You have to go now."

She turns away from me, facing the wall.

I squint my eyes, anger rising in my chest. "I know," I say and get out of bed, dressing slowly.

Before leaving I lean in and whisper, "You won't stop thinking of me." And left the room with a soft click of the door.

I should go home, but I know I won't sleep now. It's late, two thirty in the morning, and I know exactly where I can go. I haven't been there in years and know I shouldn't go there, but I need to be in a crowd, any crowd. I need to disappear.

The club is hard to find unless you know what to look for. Underground, it is a simple black door with a blue "X" on the top of the doorway. I know it well. Hovering at the door, I can just hear the deep dark vibes on the other side. At this time, only the regulars will be left. The die-hards. The druggies. Dark people. My people. I tap the door with my ring, and the window slides open. I recognized the face right away—Stella.

Her icy blue eyes are open wide, her pupils large, even for this low light. Her blonde hair, cropped and dry, makes her look even paler than she already is. She is way too thin and gaunt, her pierced nose making her face look even more harsh. Stella stays here at the club. This is her home, my home, and the only place I need to be right now.

"Ben, good to see you buddy," she purrs, deep and smoky. "Where ya been, Sugar?"

"Let me in, Stella, just let me in," I grumble.

"Glad to." She smiles her arrogant, evil smile, opens the door, and stands back, letting me pass inside. All their eyes focus on me. I'm not safe here, but I'm not alone. I'm surrounded by people that need something from me, and I need something from them. It's a bad idea, but I do it anyway.

Chapter 35: Katarina

Waking up, I am a mixed bag of emotions. My head is killing me, my face is sticking to the pillow, and the tears form the minute my eyes open. I love him, I hate him. I hate myself and never thought the process of self-growth would ever be this complicated. The heart is a tough little bitch, and she doesn't give you much rope to play with.

Nothing much changes in my day to day, other than time making it a little bit easier. There is no doubt about what we have together, and in one way, I know he is meant for me. It is just figuring out the road and what it looks like, how we fit in. The rest of the week I'm not myself, and as I attempt to move on, stepping back to allow the universe to do its thing, the confusion it causes is shit. Just plain shit.

I am making some headway with local homeless shelters and mental health facilities in the city, and it keeps my mind occupied. Feeling productive is a plus, and at least I'm not drinking myself through my misery. In the end, I am glad Monica is coming. Her visit gives me something to do and look forward to.

Ben called me at four thirty the following Monday morning, again at six, again at eight fifteen, and then three more times before noon. I didn't answer. I feel like a heartless bitch, but I am trying to do what Alex had told me. We both need space, and regardless of whether this is going to work out or not, it isn't going to be today.

I try not to think about what, or who, he might be doing and assume Ben is home. Not sleeping, just like me. Running out his pain, anger, and confusion, just like me. Sorting himself out, just like me.

Unfortunately, by the time Thursday arrives, I have barely eaten all week, dropped five pounds, and have dark circles under my swollen eyes. This is probably the hardest thing I've ever been through.

If I have to guess, I think Ben must've called me fifty times in the last four days. When I didn't answer the phone calls, he started texting Monday evening. Some of them aren't very friendly, to say the least and, of course, I didn't respond to those either. The emotions are mixed; some angry, some apologies, hearts and angry face emojis, and so many begging me to talk with him. I leave them all alone. I have to help him break his habit of me, so I ignore him, trying to forget about him. Like I was told to do.

"Weeeeehoooooo! Girl, this is amazing!" Opening the door, Monica's hands are straight up in the air with a bottle of champagne and cheap plastic glasses, probably from the plane. She's wearing a massive grin, pink crop top and matching shorts, heels, and has enough luggage for a three-week residency.

"Shit, girl, come in. You're pumped up." In contrast, I'm wallowing in my grey sweatpants, without makeup, and at least two days of dirty hair. Picking up one of her bags, she bounces in, waiting for me to grab the rest.

"Yeah, man! It's *New York City!*" She goes straight to the window and peers out before turning back on me. "What's up with you? Come, hug me!" She grabs me, lifting me off the ground, and I can't help but smile. She smells like way too much perfume, her curls are way too big, and her laugh is way too loud, and I love her for all of it.

Holding me at arm's length, she comments as only Monica can, "You look like shit Katarina. We can't have this. Give me your face, let me see you." She grabs my cheeks as we sit together on the bed, turning me side to side. "Oi, good thing I brought everything I own." Her face scrunches up in disgust.

"Gee, thanks, Monica." I roll my eyes, unimpressed by her rubbing in the fact that I look so bad.

"Hey, don't pout. Listen, let's have a drink. We'll have a little buzzy, zip zip!" She stands up, wiggles her hips, pops the cork, and pours out two glasses. "And then, we'll have a little smoke! Hmmmmm?" Her eyes sparkle with mischief.

"How did you get that on the plane?" I ask.

"I didn't. Grabbed it from some guy when I landed," she exclaims innocently.

"You're fucked up." I laugh at her and take a sip of my drink. It feels good to laugh, and I start to relax for the first time in a week.

I get dressed and Monica fixes my face, so I look human, and we head to The Square. I get a kick watching her reaction to it all, taking me back to weeks ago when it was all brand new to me, too. Frowning for a moment, I get lost in my thoughts; it feels like so long ago. A lifetime ago when my world seemed simpler. I feel much older now, more mature than that Canadian girl with the crazy dreams and goofy smile. But that's exactly what I am here to do, grow.

She is making me laugh, and I am allowing myself to be a girl again. A silly, stupid, giddy girl with her bestie taking on the world. We walk the streets, and of course she wants to go to Fifth Ave, thinking she can shop there and quickly realizing a hairdresser's wage is not going to cut it.

We are back at the hotel for a rest and a bite to eat by six. Monica loves the piano bar, saying it is one of the coolest places she's ever been. We eat and start drinking wine—too much wine. We laugh and laugh and then I find myself crying about Ben, trying drunkenly to explain how I'm not going to see him anymore and how it's killing me.

"Honey, honey," she slurs, "It's ok. Maybe you just keep him casual, you know? Nothing wrong with having fun for yourself as you need it." She simultaneously winks and hiccups. "That's what I do. No connection, no broken hearts. We're young. Screw it!" She splays her arms outward, nearly falling off the stool.

I laugh at her. In the moment, it sounds like a great idea.

Unfortunately, I know that won't be a viable option, especially with Ben.

"Know what we're gonna do?" She straightens up on her barstool. "We. You and me," pointing at me, then herself, "we're gonna go back to your room and smoke a joint." She looks at me sideways as she drinks out of her fingerprinted wine glass. "And then, we're gonna dress all pretty and hit that Square at night. Find a bar. Come, let's go."

Ok, why not? Let's just fucking go.

Giggling like schoolgirls, we venture, more like stumble, out of the hotel and down to the Square. We are high and silly, and I am spinning—spinning in a good way. We stay out until two, never finding a bar to stay at that she likes, and finally she says screw it, "Let's go back to your place. We'll try again tomorrow."

Perfect. I'm ready for sleep anyway.

Friday morning starts with a bit of a headache. Dammit. We had fun though, and I am happy for it. I hadn't realized how much I needed to let loose a little.

"What do you wanna do today, Booboo?" Monica asks me, her face still in the pillow.

"Well, we can do Central Park? Or the double-decker bus? What do you think?" I suggest.

Muffled, she says, "Let's do the park tomorrow. My feet hurt, and I want to find a bar for tonight." Flipping over, she smiles. "I didn't just come here for you, you know. I need a boy toy. Come on, it'll be fun!" There's friskiness in her stare.

Rolling my eyes at her, I say, "I definitely don't need a boy toy," I throw her a sweater to cover up, "but we should go to a bar. It's only fair—I get it. Let's do the bus tour today. You can see the rest of the city, and we'll nap this afternoon. Then I'll ask the doorman about any good bars around, ok?"

Lifting her head, makeup all over her face, her hair a rat's nest, she grins. "Deal! I'm showering first." She throws the sweater back at me and jumps out of bed.

Round and round, I show Monica all I know about New York. We enjoy ourselves, and before heading back to the hotel, I take her to Gloria's so she can see where I work.

Ben has only called three times. One text. A heart with an unhappy face.

"Oh, so cute! I love the little cookies. What drink should I get?" Her eyes scan the menu board.

"I've grown to like the London Fog, especially if you wanna rest later." I point it out.

"Order us two. I'll grab a seat." I place our order.

Turning around, I'm juggling two drinks and two of the little cookies Monica is so smitten with. She is talking to someone, and I roll my eyes. She is such a flirt. I swear I can't leave that girl alone for five seconds without her accosting some hot young guy, no matter where we go. Focusing on her newest prey, I nearly drop our London Fogs. I have never cared who she starts to talk to, but from the back I notice the hair—Ben's hair, undeniably. I'd know his hair anywhere, and there is no doubt about who she is talking to.

I swallow hard and make my way over to the two of them. My feet are like lead, my hands clammy, and I have a sick feeling in my stomach. He turns, and we were face to face. The entire world stops moving; it stands still while the ground crumbles around us.

"Hey," he says.

"Hey," I say back, putting our drinks and cookie bags on the table. My heart is hammering with the love in my chest, panic is burning in my gut.

"I thought you might be here... just thought I'd see how you are." He reaches out as though he is about to touch me but stops and jambs his fists deep into his jeans.

"I'm good." I nod my head, dodging his gaze. "Yep, good. You?" He's staring at me, and I can't help but look up at him, straight into his eyes that know me so well.

"You don't look like you've slept," I say, trailing off and whispering. The only reason why I might look like I have is due to Monica's miracle face mask.

"Been busy. You know, work," he responds. Maybe he's sleeping like a baby, and I'm just a blind idiot...

"Yeah, me too," I mumble at my shoes.

Monica is staring at us and our awkward exchange with a smile on her face, seemingly awestruck by Ben. I offer her a half smile.

"So, you know this guy, Katarina? You gonna properly introduce me?" Monica perks up, breaking the connection and looking at me strangely when her eyes aren't fixated on Ben's face. I mean, whose wouldn't be?

"Yeah, sorry Monica. This is Ben... my... friend. My friend Ben." I stumble over my words.

"Yes! I've heard about you," she practically squeals, sitting straight up in her chair, giving me a big smile and poking Ben in the thigh.

"Hi. Nice to meet you, Monica." He looks decidedly uncomfortable. "What are you girls up to today?" he asks, running his hand through his hair aggressively and sighing loudly.

"I'm in from Canada for a weekend visit, Katarina's hometown," Monica pipes up. "Surely she's told you about me?" Monica continues to eye the both of us, her gaze shifting back and forth as Ben and I awkwardly look at each other.

"Oh yes. Yes, yes of course. Monica, you two are good friends. That's nice," he says, his eyes are glassy and a little shifty. I squint, sensing something is wrong beyond the absolute awkwardness of our conversation.

"We were just going back to our hotel. We're going out tonight." Monica laughs and winks at me, raising her eyes with a smile. "We're going to hit up some bars. You know of any good ones?" She leans closer to Ben and rests her chin on her hands, staring at him in awe.

I know what she's up to, thinking she's helping, but honestly, *what are you doing Monica?*

Ben's face creases into a grin. "Yeah, yeah," he nods, "there's a place I go to. I mean, I've been to before."

Monica is staring at him with her big smile, and I'm cringing inside.

"It's cool. It's hard to find, blue sign, small black door with an X. Over on West 17th Street." Ben gives me a pointed look, knowing I know exactly where that is, right near his apartment. "You should check it out." It feels like he is only talking to me as his gaze pours into mine with intensity.

"Thanks! Sounds great eh, Katarina?" Monica says, looking from Ben to me and back again.

"Yeah, good. Maybe. Maybe we can check it out." I offer her another smile that feels like a grimace. We cannot check it out, there's no way.

"You should." He leans in and kisses my neck, just below the ear, and I can't stop the quiet moan that follows.

"Maybe I'll see you guys there. Have fun. Later." He turns and leaves, and I close my eyes with a sigh. *What just happened?*

"*Katarina!*" Monica croons in a deep stunned voice. Her eyes are as big as saucers, staring at me, as she smacks the table. "That," she points in his direction as he walks out the door, "is Ben? Are you kidding me? I don't care what the fuck is going on with him, keep him! He's fucking *hot!*" She leans back, fanning herself with the cookie wrapper. "Katarina, don't be an idiot. You don't want him? I'll take him! What the hell!"

"Why was he talking to you?" I ask, terrified I won't like the answer.

"Talking to me? He wasn't. I saw that specimen of male sexiness, and I barely had time to say hi. Literally, you just came over as I was saying hello. Girl, you're lucky you already have him, or I'd steal him in a heartbeat."

Chapter 36: Benjamin

I battled with myself the rest of the afternoon and evening about coming here. The fact I even said anything to Katarina and her friend about it is dumb enough on its own, and the simple answer is to not even go.

But my body aches for her, and I can't stop pacing the apartment thinking about her, so here I am. I came early, not knowing if the girls would start or end their night here, and now it is pushing one thirty Friday night—Saturday morning, technically. This is early for New York, early anywhere, but I'm impatient. Where is she? Katarina and her slut friend, Monica. I can still feel her whore stares all over me from the café, and I don't like it.

I don't understand why Katarina is friends with her and her cackle laugh. I didn't like how she smelled. Like problems and drama. No class. The only person that's important to me at all is Katarina. I need her—her soft sweetness on my skin, her hands in my hair and on my body. *I need her now, right fucking now.*

I am situated in the bar at the best table to see the front door. The bar is dark and sultry. There are battery operated lights on the tables.

Candles flicker fire everywhere on shelves or nooks in the black painted walls, illegal but mostly everything here is. People are smoking, lounging, enjoying more than the alcohol that's on display at the bar. For a price, you can get just about anything you want. The bar level is separated by a low railing that you can lean on while looking out at the rest of the club. The second level is separated by a long series of bench seats, like a wall. It's sectioned off to provide seating for five to six people, each bench with a large round black table in front of it, open to visitors—I'm sitting at one of these tables, patrons dancing on the dance floor behind me. It is busy enough, but not overly crowded, yet. There are quite a few people here, the kind of people my parents would not approve of. Most of them artsy, wearing lots of leather and chains. Women, men, non-binary, trans. Whoever they are, it seems everyone wants to be at my table.

People lean against the cushion in my corner, just to be close, so fucking close all the time. Extra chairs have been brought over to us, surrounding me and blocking me in.

I am uncomfortable, but can't move, can't get away. Having not been here in years, I am the centre of attention. The prodigal son has returned. Activity surrounds me, drinks are being passed around, and there's so much talking, laughing and touching, but I just stare at that front door with only one purpose. *Katarina.*

These people are my people, old friends that defined me for years. I'd wrapped myself into this world to hide, run away, partied and eventually they are what I became. They wanted me to themselves, put me up high on their pedestal, and spent my money getting me high, getting themselves high, and calling us friends. I brought enough customers to stay and drink that the bar staff never bothered me. Every night that I came here, I owned the bar.

Stella is on my right, her brother Simon on my left. Both blond, they are parasites taking care of the guest list at our table. I am high as fuck, thanks to their attentiveness.

The bench seat is covered with black leather, tight and smooth. It is hot and sticky on my legs and back. Squirming, I don't like the way it feels on my skin. At times it feels cool to my touch, and I finger the seam with my clammy hands. It is a strange little bench I float on. Hot, cold, hot, cold. My clothes feel too tight, hugging the right areas, but hover off my skin like they're loose. I grab at my shirt to get a sense for how it moves, and my skin feels numb to my touch.

My eyes are buzzing, and I can't seem to find any saliva. I look back down at my shirt, it is black and see-through, sleeveless, exposing my naked arms. My chest is visible through the mesh fabric, showing off my nipples and their rings, making them available to see, touch, and grab. Simon likes that and tries to play with them like old times. "Piss off, Simon!" I nudge him with my elbow. Always leaning in close, too close.

Stella passes me a drink, some kind of dark liquid. I don't ask what is in it. I don't care. I drink it. I drink it all, and she passes me another one. Simon and Stella keep me here in this little box of mine. People come in and sit, laugh, drink and smoke, snorting off my table. The flurry of activity feels like a film on fast speed, and as the clock ticks along, I stare—just stare at that fucking door.

The bar is up there against the left wall from where I am sitting. If you need a drink, that's where you have to go, that bar. No matter what I may miss at the entrance, I'll see everyone at some point getting a drink. Everyone drinks at a bar.

Bitches and dykes, fags and gents, come in the door all night. They are all sexy, wanting to fuck, drink, smoke and get high, like me. I take a huge breath and blow it back out forcibly. My impatience mounting, all I want is her. Blackness begins to creep in, and everything narrows. So tired, so fucked.

Jolting up, my body twitches, and I wonder what I've missed.

Where am I?

Oh, I'm at the table. Good. What time is it?

Panicking, my eyes dart everywhere through the bar. I think I passed out for a moment, and I'm terrified for what I may have missed. I'm dizzy, confused.

Where the hell is she?

Simon's on me like a cat in heat. Searching my surroundings and trying to get my bearings, I check the nearby tables. Behind us are more tables, two or three steps lower than this level, scattered around with low black armchairs. Peeling Simon off me, I turn and search, but Katarina isn't at any of them. My eyes bulge trying to keep up with the lights bouncing to the beats the DJ is producing. The music is deep, filling my body and making my fingers twitch. I need to move but want to stay by the door and bar so I can see when she comes in.

Simon, fuck!

I try to shove him off with a flick of my elbow, but he leans right back in. He's always wanted to fuck me and won't stop grabbing my nipples. His face is in my neck, his squirmy little tongue licking my ear, begging for my attention with his raw, ugly little hand on my thigh. I am already claustrophobic, and the seating arrangement isn't working for me. I grab his fingers too hard, turning them back. He squeals like a hurt little puppy and finally backs off.

"What's your problem, bitch!" he snaps but stays right beside me like he always does, hoping for my scraps of attention. Rubbing my thighs, I start to groan, my sweat is cold as my body tries to regulate it's confused temperature. The darkness inside envelopes me, the heavy music is loud and sexy, making everyone act the fool. That and the drugs getting passed around; cocaine, ecstasy, and anything else you could pop or sniff without getting caught. The bouncers leave me alone, of course, and my table, that's why everyone is here.

Partaking in my fair share of the goodies, I figure fuck it, I've been here for hours, waiting. I smoke and drink, sniff whatever powder is on the end of Stella's finger. She knows. She knows what always makes me stay, despite my years of absence. My face is numb, my body is numb, and my mind… *oh Jesus, my mind! Where the hell is it?*

Fixated on Katarina is where it is.

With her in my skewed vision, I turn my head towards Simon, confusing him for the thing I really want. Leaning in towards him, only realizing at the last second how wrong I am, I groan and slide back into my own space. He smiles and then frowns, disappointed he didn't receive the little scrap he was hoping for. He scowls and I grin, pleased in my vengeance like the asshole I am. Settling back in, I am sweating so much my hair falls into my face as I bend my head down and take a line of something blue.

Take it in, Bennie. Yes, that's how it feels. Remember? Remember the high of powder in your face? Pick it up off the table, it's fine. Suck it off your finger. Yep, just like that.

Instantly, I think of Katarina, my fingers on my tongue like they were when I tasted her, smelled her. *Oh Babe, I haven't tasted you in a week!*

I can't feel anything at this point, and I don't care. I welcome the numb feeling. It is either that or pain and heartbreak, emptiness. I need her hands on my chest, on my heart, to slow it down and make it calm.

Panic creeps in when I sense the eyes all around me. Watching. I can feel them. In the city that never sleeps, everyone is alive, wide awake. Stella is always watching me, even when she's engaged with her friends, she always stays close. Laughing and controlling who and what is allowed at our table. She thinks I am her property, wanting to fuck me since the day we met. Long ago, when I would take a different girl to the back room, she'd glower and get bitchy for an hour. But all I had to do was give her a smile and a kiss, my needs having been met by another, and she'd set me up another line. Her jealousy didn't last long, and she'd take whatever she could get.

There's a blip of light from the front door, the city street behind, proving someone is coming inside. The doorman moves, blocking my view. Conversation, ID maybe, and he moves to the side, motioning the newcomers up to the bar. "Get a drink," I bet he said.

They must be girls. The doormen are always nice to the girls. Yep, there they were. Two, I squint. Two, maybe three? No, definitely two girls, walk in as the men at the bar turn and stare. One is in a tight, black dress showing off most of her leg and bare shoulders. Her hair is short, exposing her neck. I could lick that skin, bite it. Pull that dress down so those tits pop out of that dress. Give them to me! Something small and tight around her neck, leather? Yes, leather collar. I could grab that, pull and choke. She'd moan, she'd like it. Me. She'd like me. The other one breaks my stare. Red, loud, blonde, boisterous. *Ew. No. No like. No, no.*

They come in closer. Closer, closer. I squint. *What am I looking at? Who is that?*

Stand. I must stand. I try.

Nope, nope, nope. Dizziness takes over. I wobble. *Simon, move! Let me out. Fuck off.*

Pushing past, I stagger to my feet and stand up. Holding onto the bench, I take a deep breath in. Ahhh, fresh air! I can still barely see, but there she is.

Katarina. Finally!

I've been waiting for you.

She looks good, really good. I plan to walk towards her, and I can't help but touch myself, taking inventory that I'm still in one piece and my parts are all where they should be. I feel tingly, and I look down, my body not feeling like my own, and I wish I hadn't gotten myself so fucked up.

Taking another breath, I close my eyes. I must stop the spinning. Music fills my ears, making my brain vibrate. Breathe in, breathe out, breathe in, breathe out. Swaying, I stumble just a wee bit as I try to make my legs work.

The song playing is one I like. It's sultry and sexy, just like her. I can feel the vibrations enter my ears, travel through my brain waves and go through my body, filling it with its warmth. I'm buzzing, and I can't quite feel all of my face. I look down at my hands, and they feel disproportionate to the rest of me. My hair is hurting my scalp, and when I shake my head my vision cracks and everything starts to shudder. Refocusing straight ahead, I wonder, does she see me? I stumble and trip, grabbing onto a stranger. "Watch it!" she yells.

"Ssshhorry," I mumble. My mouth is dry, and my tongue feels thick, but at least I'm standing. I hear voices, and I look around me. *Who is that?*

It's just us, Bennie, we've got you, I hear in my head, and I nod. Ok. Teetering, I can breathe and open my eyes, my hands are spread out at my sides for balance. Concentrating, I pull sobriety up from my toes and begin to walk.

Approaching her, she turns towards me. I'm staring at her like a mad dog ready to pounce and attack. Do I do to her what she's doing to me? Can she feel that? The electricity between us? My body is drawn to her, and I can't control it. I'm not numb anymore, I'm on fucking fire! She's at the end of the bar and our eyes are glued to one another. Everything else is black. The world around us fades, the tables, the dancers, the DJ.

There's a soft glow around her silhouette, she stands there, beautiful.

Her eyes dart away. *You feel it too, don't you, baby? You feel me even when I'm not touching you, I can tell.* I can see her body composition change, and I can feel her eyes on my soul. *I'm still your favorite guy aren't I, Katarina?*

I'm walking now, drawn to her like a marionette. Up the steps I float, closing my eyes, hoping I won't fall. Up and up and I'm good. Landing on the same level, I breathe a sigh of relief. My legs have left me, but I find myself in front of her now. Monica is there too. Ew, Monica.

Facing them, I grab Katarina's arm with my left hand and sparks fire, it burns. I squeeze, oops, maybe too hard, she winces.

"You look good." I stare at her, not able to hide my obsession with her, my crazy. She stares back. I've said all I can think to say. My hair falls, and I realize my head is drooping. My mouth locks. My mouth won't work. She looks up at me. Disgusted? Confused? Scared? Not a happy look on her face though, that is certain.

"I'm glad you scamezzz." I fumble. *Fuck*. She looks mortified, disgusted, and my heart crumples. Then she turns away, and I feel my rage start to boil.

Monica's loud high pitch hurts my ears as she shouts, "I'll grab us some drinks, Katarina?" Motioning towards me she asks, "You, uh, want something?"

"Water," I spit out without breaking my stare on Katarina.

Monica goes. Good she's gone.

I close my eyes and squeeze onto Katarina's arm. I tell myself I'm sober. Urging my body to cooperate, I find my lips and my saliva so I can speak to her. I grab her other arm and hold on for balance. She looks down at them, back to me, and then looks away. Dubious.

"Ok?" she says. I can feel Stella watching. Judging. Hating from the corner. I have to get us out of here, away from prying eyes, and as I start to freak out, I grab Katarina's left hand, and I pull. She stumbles and tries to break free, but my grip is too strong, I pull her towards the red exit sign beside the bar. There's a hallway that leads to the side delivery door. It's private, there's no reason for anyone to be there, hidden away from all these eyes, away from Monica.

I pull her into the black hallway and throw her a little too hard against the wall. She reacts, pushing my shoulders back, and I stumble but regain my footing. It's dark in this little hallway, and she's searching my eyes, hers filling with tears and probably a lot of anger.

"What's your deal Ben?" she spits at me. "Who the fuck are you, and what's your motive here?" She waves her arms at the darkness.

I'm trying to figure out my excuse and the best way to answer her. I'm angry, she's angry, and we're both becoming increasingly aggressive. She's never seen this Ben before and should be scared. Heck, *I'm* scared.

I can't stop my actions, and I lurch towards her, grabbing her arms and pulling them down, pinning them against the wall on either side of her hips. Holding her wrists tight, I take my hips and pin hers against the wall so she can't move. My body begins to flush, fully pressing on her, my blood is boiling with sexual tension. I'm inches from her face, and she's searching mine in terror. It feels like my eyes are huge, dark and cloudy, sparking like they might catch fire. I find my words and drill them into her. "Why won't you talk to me?" I beg "Why won't you take my calls? Why won't you see me? Why are you doing this to me?" My eyes are burning, tears brimming. I'm mad, frustrated, and just fucking angry, out of control. The dudes in my head are scrambled, screaming all sorts of possibilities I don't want to hear.

"I don't know you like this, Ben!" she squeaks out, turning her face away from mine, terror taking over her.

I grab her cheeks and her jaw, forcing her to look at me. *Look me in the fucking eye, bitch!* Instantly, she tightens up, trying to push me off. Right, I forgot how feisty she can be.

"You know *me*!" I growl at her through clenched teeth as I take my hips and thrust them into her, my cock hard as rock in between her legs, making her skirt roll up her thighs.

"You fucking know *me*!" *She fucking knows me!* I tell myself and get angrier. I growl at her, my face right in hers, my eyes watering.

She gasps. *Fuck me, her hips!* My hands have a tight hold on them, and they open like a can of pop. She might not know me in the state I'm in, but her body does, she can't deny that. Her body knows me like I know hers, and right now, as much as she might be terrified, her body is betraying her. I can feel the energy electrify between us, and I know my body can do anything it wants to hers, and she'd take it gladly, every time.

But I'm afraid of myself, my mind. I don't have a good grasp on my temper, and there's no way this Ben has anything to say right now that's going to make anything better. It will make everything worse and in fact, it already is. She pushes me off her, and I'm so fucked up that I stumble as she twists off the wall, away from my grasp.

"Not now!" She glares at me. I'm bent over, she'd practically kneed me in the nuts, and I glare up at her, holding my stomach. It's twisted up so much it hurts. My hair is all over the place, and I feel dark, cloudy, menacing. If I can't have her, no one else can and torturous thoughts are clouding all sanity. Angry tears drip down my face, and I'm seething. I spit and hear myself yell, "*Don't you fucking leave me, Katarina! Don't turn your back on me!*" Drool drips down my chin. The music is too loud, and she's backed away from me towards the bar.

Terrified, but glaring, she turns on her heel and runs back into the open where I can't get her without making a bigger scene then I already have. Just as she turns her back on me, Stella shows up in the doorway, casting Katarina a nasty look, and moves in towards me. She grabs me and puts her face in mine. *Fuck me!* Squirming, I look past her and watch Katarina, my Katarina, walk away.

"It's ok, Sugar," Stella soothes. "Why so angry?" She's grabbing the sides of my head, brushing my hair back off my face, and helping me stand. I have nowhere to go, Stella blocks me, still talking, but I don't hear a word of what she's saying.

Chapter 37: Katarina

I don't know what time I get home. Monica connected with her boy toy for the evening, promising she'd find her way home in the morning. I wasn't overly supportive of the decision, but she's a grown woman and can do what she wants. I couldn't have forced her to leave even if I'd tried, and I knew I had to get out of there. I assured her I was ok and wished her better luck in love than I was having, and I'd see her the next day. Getting off the elevator, I'm a whirlwind of emotions. Rubbing my wrists, I look down and whimper. I've ruined this man. He's ruined me. How could I let things get so out of hand? I pause at my doorway, hearing the faint sounds of the piano, Max's piano. Contemplating only for a moment, I turn and head towards the bar. It's just what I need, actually.

I check my cell. Besides the missed calls from Ben, I see that it's almost three in the morning. The bar is long closed, but if Max is there, he'll have booze, and I need a drink. A stiff drink and a miserable old jerk so I can feel better about my shitty little life. Shrugging my shoulders, I make my way down the hallway.

"Hi," I say, leaning against the piano. He looks up from his slouch on the bench, his drink sitting on the grand lid.

"Katarina," his face is shadowed, dark and moody, "I thought I'd be someone you'd aim to avoid. What do you want?" Sitting up, he stretches his back with a groan.

"A drink." Hanging my head in my hands, my elbows rest on the piano. Max grimaces at me, obviously surprised by my presence and attempt to engage with him. I think he knows enough not to say anything, and definitely knows not to turn my hand away when I grab his glass of Scotch off the piano and finish it.

"Good thing I brought the bottle, huh?" Looking at me with interest, he grabs the bottle he's hidden at his feet and pops the lid.

"Yep." My nose burns, but I stretch my arm out, eagerly awaiting a fill up.

"So, what brings you down, Miss Life is Fucking Wonderful? New York reeks of roses?"

Looking at him with a glare and a twisted smile, I turn my eyes away when they start to water, avoiding his gaze.

"I made a mistake, Max. A big fucking mistake," I whisper as the sting of tears starts in my throat again. I take a swig of my scotch, it's awful, and I turn my attention back to his dark seedy eyes.

"Now I'm stuck in it and have to get out of it and don't know how. I don't want to, but I have to, and I don't know how to live with myself." I choke on the last part and look away as I take another swig of the poison.

"I destroy people, apparently. That's what I do." My head collapses onto my arm on the piano lid.

Raising his brows, he clears his throat and responds, "Well, you definitely haven't destroyed me. I did that all on my own." The last part he whispers to himself. "Stop giving yourself so much credit and tell me what this awful thing is you did."

My tears hover where they've been for weeks, and with my glass empty again, I tell him my painful truth.

"I fell in love."

"You fell in love?" He chuckles, his eyes wide and mocking. "Well, isn't that the tragic story of the decade." He rolls his eyes. "And how, may I ask, is that destroying someone and yourself at the same time?" Clearly, he's not concerned, he's not even remotely serious, which infuriates me.

"It's destroying me, old man, because it's the only love I've ever felt. That he's ever felt!" I splay my arms out as my voice gets high and pitchy through the tears and too much booze. "It's unexplainable! I can't even understand it." I point at his face. "But we feel it, him and I. Oh, we fucking feel it."

I redirect my gaze towards the exit sign above the doorway. Maybe coming here was a bad idea after all, but I continue. "We can't control it, or each other for that matter, and he's sick. He's not well." I look back at Max for any sign of compassion. "His family doesn't want me near him, they say I make him sicker. So, I try to stay away, and he's angry at me. He wants to talk to me, and I want to talk to him."

Max continues to watch me and listen to me whine.

"My body needs him." I sniffle. "I've lost all control, and there's no future. I've broken his heart and my heart, and the only thing I've learned here is how to love someone so deeply it destroys you and them in the process!" My voice begins to rise again. "The only thing I've learned is that I'm a weak coward and a goddamn bitch!" Breathing heavier, I stare at him, awaiting a response.

Max sits forward, leaning his elbows on his knees and says, "Well. Pity. Poor fucking you."

I squint my eyes. *Are you kidding me right now?*

"The only thing I see is a quitter. Someone who needs to find her fucking balls and stand up, fight for what she wants." This sounds suspiciously like a dare. "Mistake? You've made a mistake? The only mistake you've made is giving up. Your decision." He sticks his angry wrinkled finger in my face. "You decided to fall in love with your entire being, your entire soul. That's something most of the world never gets the chance to do." His chuckle is sour. "It chose you, love did. It chose you and whoever this guy is and that's a problem for you? Do you know how fucking lucky you are?" He leans in and pinches my thigh.

"Ouch!"

He pokes me again as I look at him in disbelief.

"This love is not the mistake. It's only a mistake when you don't follow through with it. That's the fucking mistake!" While I silently stare at him, he grabs his glass out of my hand and starts to pour.

"I told you to be careful with this shit, remember?" He sucks back his shot and pours another.

Agitated, I defiantly explain, "He's sick, Max. His head. You know?" I tap my own with my forefinger. "It's sick. This love is destroying him. Makes him lose control. *I* make him lose his control! He was a fucking mess tonight! Unable to socialize because he can't function. Not to mention, he's probably using again."

BONG! Max slams his hands on the piano keys, the loud sound makes me jump.

"So, take the fucking control, Katarina! Take the fucking control and help him function." His eyes are wild, and he's increasingly angry. "If you're the stronger one, be that. Exactly that! Strong, for fuck's sake! Do you think abandoning him is going to help him? If he's sick like you say he is, do you even know what that means? You not being with him is what's destroying him."

Staring back, there are tears in my eyes while I shake my head. *Is he right? Actually?*

"Fuck his family! Families don't know shit." Snapping me out of my internal thoughts, Max continues his rampage. "They don't know shit! Look at me." He's spitting and waving his hands like a madman. "Where's my family? Fucking gone, is where. When my lover died, it destroyed me!"

Sitting back, he shuts his mouth, realizing he's exposed himself, making himself vulnerable to me. My jaw drops, and I remained silent. Is he going to tell me the story? His story, his fall. The one story most of New York City is dying to know.

He quiets down, shifts his gaze, and starts to whisper, "I replaced my love... my pain... with Chivas Regal." Looking at his bottle, he grimaces before continuing. "I lost everything when he died. And you," he raises his gaze, his eyes cutting and judgemental, mean even, "your love is still alive, and you won't take it? Won't have it? *Won't hold onto it?* For the love of god, Katarina, don't be a fucking idiot. Mistake? No, you haven't made a mistake, you're making one now. Fix it before you're too late!" He nods his head disapprovingly as he scolds me like a young child.

Looking down, I'm defeated. "I don't know how."

"Ok." He perks up, straightens his back with a painful scowl, and says, "Listen to me good. I'm not Dear Molly for Christ's sake." Watching me closely he says, "We're far from friends, but I can tell you're a girl with her shit together even though you don't realize it. Are you ready? Listen up."

I'm not going to say no. I grab a chair from one of the tables, scrape it across the floor, and plop my sad ass down. Here we go. Opening my ears, I anticipate the words that will be coming at me. I can only hope they're words of wisdom, old man wisdom and experience.

He throws back another shot before clearing his throat and begins to talk, "When I had love, I… well, he was sick too. Like your guy, whatshisface." He pours another drink.

"Ben," I offer up.

"Yeah Ben, whatever. My lover's name was Mark." He stops pouring for a moment, seemingly lost in thought. A few tears well up in his eyes, and he returns to sip his Scotch. Afraid he may not continue; I don't make a sound.

"He... struggled. Couldn't always cope, not every day. But when we were together, he was ok, better. It wasn't perfect, little girl." He cast me a sideways glance. "No relationship is. And was it harder than most? Yeah, maybe. But so worth it, girl. So fucking worth it." Nodding his head, he's clearly reminiscing to himself.

"His family hated the fact that he was gay, wouldn't accept it. Thought it was my fault, that I was encouraging it. He listened to them, and it tore him up, screwed him up even more, and he turned himself away from me."

Speaking almost to himself he continues, "When I got him back again, his sister approached me. She lied to me. She told me that he was going to see a doctor to help him, help all of them accept that he was gay so we could have a future together. I needed to leave him alone, she said, not talk to him for a bit. So, I did." Shrugging his shoulders, he reconnects with my eyes and says, "He called and called, and then one day he stopped calling. I was waiting, Katarina. I was waiting for him to be ok and to come back to me. What I learned then…"

His eyes darken, the darkest I've ever seen, and his face contorts in anger, pain.

"What I saw was a notice in the paper. *The goddamn fucking papers!*" He bellows and slams his fists on the piano. *BONG!* Making me jump, sorrow and pity for him in my heart. His glass empty again, he takes a swig of Scotch from his bottle.

"He'd killed himself," he growls, fighting back tears that have been shed thousands of times, and I gasp. "Friends I had at the time called me and told me, too. Fucking phone wouldn't stop fucking ringing with the same news over and over and over. It drove me crazy! His family had taken him to a sexual rehabilitation center. Can you believe that? When he couldn't have me in his life to help him make it all ok and accept himself for who he was—who he really was and love him—when he didn't have that, he had no one! He was told it wasn't right, he couldn't have that. So, he saved up his sleeping pills and took them all in one night. Weeks after being in the center."

His eyes now brimming with large tears, he looks at me. "I listened to his family, my own family. They said it would ruin my career being with someone unstable." He hangs his head in shame, shaking it side to side. "He wasn't unstable, Katarina. All he wanted was to be loved and the whole world was telling him he couldn't be. Not the way he wanted to be."

Looking up again, he asks, "Do you have any idea how it feels to not be allowed to be with the one you love, Katarina?"

I nod my head, whimpering. *Yeah. Yeah, I know.* I hang my head with my own pain, my own sorrow.

"Ok, then. Don't do it. Simple." His voice is devoid of emotion.

"What about the side of him I don't know? The one I don't understand?" I beg for guidance.

"You will. You'll figure it out in time together, and you'll love that part just as much. Look at it this way, you've got two, for the love of one."

I have to think about that.

Chapter 38: Benjamin

I peel Stella's sticky hands off me and rub my face. My skin is crawling. I feel like I am drowning, and my mind is muffled and confused. I need to get out of here.

As I grab my stuff from the table everyone begs me to stay, pulling on me and pleading. Ignoring them, I tear myself away. Even the lure of self-medicating can't make me stay.

As I walk out of the bar, I cast a glance at Monica flirting with some guy. It doesn't stop her from catching my eye and glaring as I push through the bouncers. Katarina has clearly left, and I am glad Monica can see I am leaving alone.

Outside, I can feel my head clear a bit. I so badly want to go after Katarina, but I know I've made a huge mistake. Did I do this? I've been trying so hard to be good, but she is testing my patience, and I didn't have much to begin with.

Back home, I can't seem to straighten out my emotions or my thinking. What I need now is coffee and cigarettes. Actually, what I need is Katarina, but right now I will have to settle with coffee and cigarettes. Grabbing the coffee pot, I attempt to fill it with water. Blurry and stumbling about, I'm not doing so well connecting my hand to the pot handle, which infuriates me.

My patience thin, I try again. This time I connect with the pot, but it throws me off guard, and I stumble back, hitting the corner of the counter with my lower back. Knocking me off my feet, I slide down the island, whacking the back of my head on the counter's lip. *Fuck, that hurt!* Now I am mad, frustrated, and in pain. Not the best combo.

I hurl the coffee pot against the wall. It lands in the front hallway and shatters into a million little pieces. Pretty, almost like snow. That feels better. Yes, that feels much better, indeed.

After pulling myself up with the counter, I stumble into the hallway to take inventory of my beautiful destruction. As I brace my hand on the sliding hall closet door for balance, it slides open and I fall headfirst onto the floor, face planting into the pretty shards of snow and, really, the only thing I can do is laugh. *How did I get here, again? Oh, who the fuck knows.* I lay there, my eyes falling on the baseball bat propped in the corner of the closet. It gives me an exceptional idea. I scramble to get my ass up off the floor, my pounding head figuring what a great way to let out some steam.

Yes, I think so! Bat in hand, I use my newfound friend for balance. I name him Bob. Bob The Balancer and I have a mission, and that is to keep me on my feet, "Isn't that right Bob?" I ask him and the sound of my voice is unfamiliar. It throws me off, and I start to frown and sniffle. The back of my hand wipes at my nose but the motion feels slow and jittery. I shrug it off and refocus on finding my cigarettes. Guess I'm not having that coffee. Right. *Fuck! Where are those cigarettes?* Rummaging through my jackets in the closet, I can't remember what I had been wearing. What am I wearing now? Looking down at myself, I see I still have pants on, no shirt, no shoes, and I'm definitely not in service. I laugh. *Ha! Fuck me I'm a funny guy!*

Funny and handsome you little devil! I hear someone pipe up.

What was that? Oh yes, hello there, brain buddy! You've come to join the party too, have you? Well, come on then join the rest of us, but watch out for Mr. Angry, he's particularly agitated today. We have Mr. Angry, Mr. Funny, Mr. Sad, and Mister… well, let's just call him Mr.

crazy! Ha! Come on guys, let's go!

Bob the Bat, myself, and everyone else continue to search for my smokes. Walking barefoot throughout my apartment, I stop dead in my tracks in the living room when I notice the couch where we made love.

Mr. Angry starts to bubble up, and I tilt my head towards the chair where she first tasted me, then all the other chairs where I held onto her naked body. It makes me furious, her memories, and I raise the bat over my head before bringing it down onto the glass table, shattering it. Taking a deep breath, I rub my face with my arm and feel tears, or snot, or something all over my cheeks. Fuck it, who cares. She's a fucking bitch anyway. Where are my fucking smokes?

Must be in the bedroom. Stumbling down the hallway, I pause at the doorway, quickly realizing how much I hate this room. It smells like her, and this is where I always loved her most, morning, noon, and night. This is where I met her needs, exceeded them, and she transcended mine.

Now Mr. Sad pops out, making his appearance well known. I grab my head and Bob hits the ground. I start pulling at my hair, tears streaming down my face as I sob. All my other little Misters retreat back inside their doors as I relive what I've done tonight. They don't like it much when I see myself this way. This failure and weakness. Negative thoughts are crawling under my skin, and I grimace, hitting myself in the head repeatedly. Somehow, I need to get these voices to be quiet and stay quiet, shut their doors so I can fucking think.

Shower maybe? I enter the bathroom and stare at myself. The water is running, and my forehead is bleeding. How did that happen? My head hurts, and I start to see stars, grabbing the sink without any luck, I slip and fall hard on my ass.

Not feeling the best, whatever's in my stomach rises to the back of my throat, and the harsh taste of stomach acid lands on my tongue. Swallowing it back down, I start to crawl my way back into the bedroom. Locating Bob, I grab onto him, using him to help me stand. It takes me what feels like an hour to get back on my feet, but I do it.

Unfortunately, the process makes me so irate, the next thing I know, I'm standing up swinging. I clear the candlesticks off the dresser first, then I smash holes in the closet doors, and finally the mirror in the corner of the room shatters under my rage. It's quite satisfying. I whip Bob against the wall and then begin to pull out all my dresser drawers, ripping through my clothes to find those fucking smokes.

I can't find them.

With Bob the Bat back in hand, he cracks down on the headboard of our bed multiple times. I hate this fucking bed. I hate it! Throwing the bat down the hall, I go back to the kitchen for the knife that I know is in one of those drawers. Ripping every drawer out, I grab the largest knife I see and scrape it against the walls for balance as I rage back down the hallway.

I stab that bed mercilessly. I stab and pull. Stab and pull. Stab and pull. I ravage that bed until there's no sheets, no pillows, no fluffy blankets that smell like Katarina. Picking up my carnage, I open the patio door, and hurl it over the edge, getting a clean whiff of nighttime air, and I smile just for a moment as I look to the sky. Back on track, I continue to throw all the bedding and clothing out the door and over the railing. Over, over, over. Hating how it smells because I love how it smells.

Where are my cigarettes? Going back into the living room, I reconnect with Bob and pick him up before hurling him one handed at the TV, creating a massive hole in the center.

My feet are sore and slippery on the floor, and I start to slip around trying to maintain my balance. I look down to see a dark liquid, like paint of some sort, following me wherever I go, making me slip. I don't need this added stress.

Crawling on my knees instead is a simpler solution. I don't know where this paint is coming from, but there's a lot. Pulling myself up on a dining chair, her face enters my vision yet again. I remember what we did on this chair, and that chair, and that chair. On every fucking chair. Angry, I pick up the chair I've been supporting myself with and throw it at the window.

It doesn't break as I'd planned, making me more annoyed and agitated. *Fuck you, window.* Picking up the chair again, I continue to berate it with my rage, using my tufted dining chair as my tool of destruction. I end up destroying the thing before there's even a crack in the glass. Using the splintered leg of the chair, I go after everything that is left. The couch, the other chairs, the walls.

I throw tables, and the ones I can't throw, I push over. Grabbing wine bottles and books, I start hurling them across the room. I still haven't found my cigarettes and realize they must be in the kitchen. Wiping the paint off my hands, I find them in the freezer. Right. That's where I keep them. Silly, Ben. Calming down a little, I rest myself against the fridge and try to focus.

Oops. Ben made a mess. A big fucking mess. In the middle of the carnage and the glass and the red paint I notice our little plant. She's just sitting there looking at me on the edge of the kitchen island. She's so perfect and smiling, my little green plant with soft spikes.

Picking her up, I hold her close to my heart, my little Katarina. She's got soft little spikes to remind you not to mess with her, ready to defend herself but only when needed. On the inside she's soft and smooth, wanting to be loved just like the rest of us. She's so innocent and whole, and it makes me sad that I wrecked her home. My eyes well up, and my nose starts to fill. My head hurts so goddamn much.

I have nothing left, nothing.

Maybe she needs some water, a quick little drink. Turning on the tap, I hold her head under water but the paint on my hands makes her slippery, and I drop her. She cracks in two, and I gasp! My heart sinks as I stare at her, broken, the water and the red circling down the drain.

My eyes are so sore, and I start to whimper, smacking myself in the head. You're no good, Ben, no good at all. See? Everything you touch turns bad. You break everything! Look around you, you idiot. Just look at what you do. Imbecile. Like anyone is capable of loving you, loving this. Give up! Just give it up.

Flustering through the cigarette pack, I drop at least four before one makes it into my mouth. There's no way I'll be finding a lighter in this mess, and I'm too exhausted to move anyway. Stove. The gas stove will work. How do I turn this fucker on? *Here, let me. I got it.* Oh, Mr. Helpful, thanks for showing up finally. Right? Yeah. Bending over, I light my smoke, filling my lungs. It burns and tastes awful, but the flame is so pretty. Jumping up on the counter, I position myself between the stove top and the fridge contemplating how the fuck do I fuck up so much shit?

I start to laugh, then start to cry, but there's just no more tears left. I've spent days self-loathing, self-sabotaging, and there just isn't anything left. How do I feel? How can I feel the pain I deserve? What can I do to replace the pain in my heart, my soul? The burner beside me starts to smoke, as the flame flickers away. I'm mesmerized by its glory, its lack of control, the ability to dance around as it pleases with no judgment and no one to make it stop doing what it's made to do.

Hovering my hand over the burner, it's hot, and as I play with the flames, testing my own resilience, an idea comes over me. Test yourself, Ben, how much pain can you really endure? Placing my hand on the burner, I hold it there and scream. Now that's pain! I scream and scream and scream. Yelling echoes in my head, and I can't tell if it's me, my Misters, or someone else. Everything turns to black, and I start to slip.

As I'm falling off the counter, I finally hear nothing at all.

Chapter 39: Katarina

Back in my room it is around five thirty in the morning. By the time Max had finished berating me, I realized that I am an adult, Ben is an adult, and if I want to have twenty of his screwed up little children, we are going to do just that.

I am glad about my decision to rectify things between us, knowing we'll need to take some serious measures if we are going to make it work. But he is mine, and I am his, and that's all there is to it. It isn't going to be easy, but I love him, and I'm not going to walk away. At the same time, I feel that there is something terribly wrong. I can feel it in my gut and don't want to wait until morning—well, until later in the morning—to reach out to him.

"Hey, it's Ben. You know what to do." *BEEP.*

I call again.

"Hey, it's Ben. You know what to do." *BEEP.*

Shit, his phone is off, and I can only hope he is home, sleeping off whatever he took last night. I call Monica, she picks up.

"Ya, lady, ya. I'm good you?" she mumbles half asleep.

"I'm ok. You sure you are?" I laugh. "Where are you? You haven't seen Ben, have you?"

"Naw, he left. Right after you. And then I left. He was alone, I know that much. I'm at Noah's but should leave now. Man, this is gonna hurt. See you in a few." The line goes silent, and I realize she has hung up.

Forty-five minutes later Monica is walking in my door, shoes in hand and clearly ravaged. Her hair is a mess, her makeup is smeared all over her face, and she is wearing a massive smile.

"Had fun, huh?" I smile at her.

Grinning from ear to ear, she replies, "New Yorkers are something!"

Girls' weekend is over for me, and as much as I love Monica, I can't wait for her flight the next morning. We groan out of bed midafternoon and grab all her shit, throwing it into her bag with her insisting I keep the black tube dress and face mask products. We head out to grab something to eat, and for her to at least see the Park before heading home.

The entire afternoon, I keep checking my phone, but there is nothing, no calls, no texts, no emojis. Every time I go to reach out to him something stops me; I just can't do it over the phone. We finish her trip at the hotel bar, grabbing a drink and dinner before calling it a night.

Max hangs his head at the piano, but there is a different vibe between us, and as I walk out the door that evening, I cast him a glimpse that I am sure he responds to with a slight smile and a wink.

Sunday morning can't come soon enough. Monica has to be gone by six to make her flight on time, and I help her down to the front lobby with her three weeks' worth of luggage. I give her a big hug, her hair in a ponytail, and looking comfy in a tracksuit. She turns and is gone, back to her Canadian boy toys.

Back in my room, I feel dizzy, not having slept well the past few nights. I wonder if Ben is home or somewhere else. It's unusual not to hear from him for this long, and I am getting worried. I could go to his apartment, but I'm an absolute wreck and need to get some sleep if we are going to have any sort of meaningful conversation. Sitting on my bed, I try Ben one more time.

"Hey, it's Ben. You know what to do." *BEEP.*

Shit. I lie down on my bed, and my body finally succumbs to the last few days, passing out in seconds.

When I wake up, it is four in the afternoon, and I instantly check my phone in a panic, but there are still no calls from Ben. There's a call from my mother and a text from Monica telling me she is on the plane, but that is it.

I shower and dress, call Ben again, but to no avail. I need food, so I decide to leave to get something to eat. I should just go to his place, right? I can't do that though. I don't know why I don't have the courage, but I just don't.

I'm worried, doubtful. What if maybe the roles are reversed, and now he doesn't want to talk to me? Maybe my final rejection at the club was the last straw for him, and he is over it, over me.

Clearly, he was a mess and my ignoring him has made the whole situation entirely worse. The thought that maybe he has picked himself up, shaken himself off, and decided I'm not worth it brings a lump to my throat. I am doubting myself, making me freeze in my tracks, unsure of what move to make next. So, I wander around aimlessly, ending up at the local Barnes and Noble, waiting. Not entirely sure what for.

Every time I go to pick up the phone, I put it back down again. I want to talk to him face to face, but it is now late Sunday, and he still hasn't called. What did I expect? I pushed him away. It was up to me to fix this, and a phone call isn't going to cut it. I might even need to grovel and beg, but we both have work tomorrow and the timing has to be just right.

Finally, I decide I'll go to work in the morning and then go straight to his place afterwards. I'll let myself in, make us a nice dinner, and when he gets home, hopefully, he'll be happy to see me. I can only hope I am right. In order to sleep, I smoke the joint Monica left for me and reluctantly shut off my phone. Sleep first, work second, Ben directly after that.

Chapter 40: Katarina

"Someone was here for you last night, real late," Max grumbles. Already in the elevator, the both of us are heading down for a coffee. The maids must have forgotten his coffee packets again, so he is pissed, not as pissed as usual, but definitely annoyed. I think I'm rubbing off on him a little, and maybe he is softening up. Well, around me, anyway.

"Someone was here? What do you mean? When?" I ask, overly eager.

"It was midnight or so, I guess. Not Ben. Don't get your titties worked up. It was some guy, kinda looked like Ben. You sure know how to pick 'em. Short black hair. He was asking for your room number, and of course, they wouldn't give it to him."

"Maybe his brother?" I ask.

"I don't know, little one, I'm not a detective, jeez. Wish I'd never told you now," he mutters, stepping off the elevator and continuing to grumble as he hobbles to the coffee machine, cursing at the staff walking by. Forgetting about my own coffee, I go to the front desk to ask about the mystery guest, my heart beating out of my chest.

"Excuse me, was there someone here looking for me last night?" I squeak out.

"I'm sorry miss. The staff change happened thirty minutes ago. I just got here, and no one said anything. I don't have any messages either," the concierge says.

"Thanks," I whisper. Disappointed, intrigued and confused, I skip my coffee and head straight to work. I'll get one there and if I start early, hopefully Gloria will let me leave early. Fingers crossed.

Chapter 41: Benjamin

The authorities called my father. By the time anyone arrived, I was so incoherent I wouldn't have been able to argue or put up a fight anyway. Neighbours had placed calls when bedding started flying past their windows. The fire alarm going off in my apartment gave security the obvious location of the culprit. It didn't take long to put the two together, and they hammered down my door with a battering ram. Finding me in a slump, bleeding and burned, it took them less than two seconds to make the call.

The whole thing is a blur, and I'm happy to keep it that way. The moment I become lucid everything starts to crash, and I find myself sobbing like a broken child. There are glimpses of my family, Alex, Nancy, my parents coming in and out of the private hospital room, but Katarina only shows up when I dream. There's a lot of emotions bouncing off the walls from everyone, demands for answers to questions I don't have. I wish the bed would open and swallow me whole. Suicidal thoughts run rampant, and when I realize I'm strapped to the bed, confined to a room without windows, my reaction doesn't fare well with the orderlies. I assume I'm sedated at times, and I guess I can't really blame them. I am beyond repair, and without Katarina in my life, I don't really see any point to it anyway.

"Benjamin?"

I'm lying on my side, both hands cuffed to the railing. I open my heavy eyes and realize I can move my legs, and I let out a deep sigh, thankful for the freedom, as limited as it is. The voice is coming from behind me, and I have the suspicion it might be my father.

"Benjamin? Darling? It's us, your parents."

My eyes pop wide open. *Darling?* It's my mother. What the fuck is she doing here? Rage starts to boil inside me, and I try to release my hands. Panic sets in, and I thrash around until there's a soft but strong hand on my shoulder.

"Benjamin! Please stop!" my father shouts in his authoritative voice. "This will get you nowhere and…" he trails off, choking on his words, a small cry escaping his lips. "We, we're not here to hur-hurt you." He stutters.

What? My eyes start to shift from side to side as I try to figure out what's happening, where I am, and why things have changed. Because something has definitely, changed.

"Can I have use of my hands please?" My voice is hoarse and doesn't sound like my own. There's silence and shuffled movement. An orderly comes into my vision, and releases the straps, one at a time. Behind him stand my parents.

I sit straight up in panic, rubbing on my wrists, my eyes darting for the door. Two security guards stand on either side, and I know I'm outnumbered no matter what actions I choose next.

"Ben! Please!" My mother cries. "Ben, darling. We'd like to try talking. To you? Together." She motions her hands between herself, my father, and another man I don't recognize but is dressed in a shirt and tie resembling most doctors I've been in contact with before.

"Why would you want to do that?" I genuinely ask. Talking is not something we've ever really done before. More like yelling and scolding, ignoring and monopolizing, running... anything but talking.

"Well, son. We're ready to admit our mistakes." My father clears his throat and shifts his feet. My mother snaps her hand in his, tears in her eyes, and the doctor man puts a firm hand on my dad's shoulder. "Nancy found these letters with some bracelets you made under the bed." He holds the clear bags out towards me.

My eyes dart to my pictures of Katarina and a sharp pain goes through my chest. I start to whimper and panic at the same time. They hold my life in their hands. Quickly, I realize they now know just how broken I am and how they'd been the ones to break me. Hanging my head, I begin to cry.

All my life I've been troubled, or at least that was what I was told. As soon as I became a teenager, I became reckless, defiant, and moody. At some point, I was going in a direction that my family couldn't keep up to. I never knew the depth of what was really going on, avoiding it and any issues or feelings I did have. I suppressed everything and chose to run away from it and bury myself in the city's nightlife. My brother had been no help. I was the older brother, right? I should be the one to take care of us, not the other way around. Younger brother or not, he abandoned me just like everyone else.

"Ben, we had too many expectations of you. And we, well, we should have been more lenient. More… loving. More… understanding." My mother looks to my dad, saying, "I just wasn't raised that way." She turns back to me. "You have to understand, Ben. This... Who I am... I worked very hard to become. I wasn't allowed to be myself, either." My mother turns her head into my dad's shoulder and begins to cry. I've never seen her express any emotion except disappointment, and it scares the shit out of me. The doctor isn't saying anything at all, and my dad holds onto my mother's small frame. In that moment, I realize how weak she is, how frail. And how exactly alike we are. It gives me pause.

I knew enough from my mother's Ballet school that the strict discipline, beyond any natural means, wouldn't allow committed dancers to explore the world like their non-dancer peers. Expectations were set so high they were always unattainable; mistakes were not tolerated. The lack of affection and attention, striving to be perfect in order to feel any kind of love, that was never given regardless of how hard they tried. The shaming, constant shaming, if one little step wasn't right. This was my mother's world, and subsequently, mine.

"Benjamin. It's not your fault, what's happening to you here. I've mishandled your diagnosis from the beginning and Dr. Feinstein here has helped me, us, realize that."

The doctor offers me a friendly smile.

"You've been suffering from negative self-perception and control issues." Our eyes meet and for the first time I think my father actually gets me. "Your rebelliousness is due to you trying to find any form of something you think you can control. It's no wonder you have made these choices over your life, you're screaming inside."

I don't have much to say. I suck back my air and lay against the headboard of the bed. My anxiety, fear, and anger control me. But, when Katarina is around and loves me, I feel worthy, emotionally and physically needed by someone. They know that, too.

My parents are pieces of work. I never expected they'd admit it.

"We've got some stuff to fix," he says, coming closer and sitting on the bed beside me. My mother sits on my other side and brushes a curl from my face.

Hiding in my hair, my face cracks, and I begin to sniffle again.

"What about her? Will she ever be a part of me again?" I look at my mother, asking her, in my own way, if a woman can love a person like us.

"We're going to help you try," she says.

Chapter 42: Katarina

Getting to work early, I'm not focused on anything at all. Scatterbrained, I'm overly eager to talk to Ben and to try to sort out this mess we're in. The café is hectic, but I approach the counter where Gloria is in full morning rush, anyway.

Tightening my apron my head tilts down. Almost afraid to ask, I say, "Gloria? Big favour–"

"Katarina, stop. Just stop. Look at me."

Not fully understanding, I lift my head and look at her. She looks serious.

"I think your presence is needed elsewhere right now."

"Huh? What's up?" Following her finger, she's pointing to the corner table, our table, and I see Roland sitting with some crumpled up papers, maybe a book of some sort, and a bag full of string. In front of an untouched coffee, he's slumped, red in the face, and looking utterly defeated.

"Uh, ok? Um…" I witness the scene, still holding onto my apron strings.

"I think you need to go, Katarina. He's been here for an hour waiting for you."

"Uh. Ok. Ok thanks, Gloria. You sure?"

She nods, so I lift the countertop, enter the eating area, and head over to where Roland is sitting.

"Dr. Ford?" I approach cautiously. When he raises his head and looks into my eyes, I see he's clearly upset, my heart instantly goes to my throat. Oh no, what's happened?

He smiles weakly. "It's ok, Katarina. We need to talk. I need to talk to you, will you sit?" His eyes plead with me, and I bite my lip.

Hands sweating, I slowly sit down. The entire world is passing in slow motion, my ears are ringing, and all I can do is stare at Roland, waiting anxiously to hear what he's about to say. He's holding the torn and creased papers. I realize now the Ziplock bag is full of Ben's bracelets. They're a mass of different colors repeated over and over. I don't know why he's brought these things.

"Is Ben okay?" I whisper, my voice cracking out, not sounding at all like my own.

"Yes. Well, no. He's fine, he's going to be fine." He seems to be having trouble making eye contact. "We've had quite a scare. Big enough for us all to wake up." I start to panic when he continues. "Well, for me to wake up… and realize… realize that I've made some very big mistakes when it comes to my son. My *sons*." He whimpers a bit, tightening the grip on his papers.

Looking up at me, he takes a deep breath, tears in his eyes and delivers the blow, "Ben's in the hospital. He's ok now, but he's been asking for you."

My hand goes to my mouth and tears start to fill my eyes. What had I done to him? What had he done to himself?

I search Roland's eyes, trying to understand what he's saying. "I have it all here, Katarina. Here, in these papers, these letters he wrote to you. These are for you."

He pushes them towards me, and I take them. Ben's writing is manic and messy—little black drawings of emotionally tormented faces, spots of sunshine, small hearts and stars and dark scary faces. There's a lot to take in, but I can see his heart is on these pages.

"It will explain everything you need to know. I've been my son's doctor for the last twenty years, and he's never really opened to me. I never knew any of this, Katarina. If I'd just known, maybe if I'd just listened, he wouldn't be where he is now." He buries his head in his hands. "His mother and I have been to see him and the crisis doctor at the psych ward."

"*Psych ward!*" I'm insanely angry, unsure I even trust this man, this family at all. "Why have you put him there?"

"Katarina, please stay calm. I know this is upsetting, and we're not exactly your favourite people. But we all have connections to Ben. Alex reminded me of that after Ben's breakdown, and it was a breakdown. That's why he's in the ward. We're trying to help him."

"Help him? Now? I don't—"

"I don't expect you to fully understand." He cuts me off sternly, "I don't either, but I'm trying to put it together. And, you should know, we're trying to back off. Let the two of you handle it. Let him handle it like the grown man that he is."

Flipping through the mess, I can see Ben has bared his entire soul onto these pages. The way he feels, the way his family makes him feel. His mother. And me, how I make him feel. What he says he wants his life to look like. He's trying to accept who he is, trying to make sense of who he is, and it will take time, but it's all right here—he wrote it in a fucking book.

I start to cry. This is a lot to handle, and I'm terrified I don't have it in me. I don't want this! But I do want him. Underneath all the hard stuff lies a sweet soul, a man who would do anything for me, a man who loves me more than life.

"He is capable, Katarina. And he loves you. He loves you more than you'll ever know, I think. These bracelets are yours, too. They're for you. These are his pictures of you, so I think you should have them."

Looking at the bracelets, I can see the green ones that match the one I'm wearing on my wrist. There are so many of them: brown ones with black, white ones with pink and little bits of brown sugar.

"Oh Ben," I whimper, my face tightening when Roland takes my hand and looks at me.

"Please tell me you'll see him. Will you help him? Please tell me I haven't ruined him to the point where a woman, a beautiful, smart, and kind woman like yourself can't love him. Tell me, Katarina, tell me that you love him still. He's not that damaged, is he?" Roland's voice cracks.

Breathing in deeply, I will the room to stop spinning. "I… I don't know how damaged he is, Roland. Clearly you don't know, either. But one thing I do know is I'm not going to give up on him like you did." I match his stare. "I'm not going to abandon him and make him feel worthless like you all did. I'm not going to do that." He nods sheepishly in agreement.

"You're absolutely right, and I deserve that. I do. I'm going to try to fix what I can, but right now he's been asking for you for all day. He just wants his life back, Katarina. Will you come? Come with me?"

Standing, the chair scraping against the penny tiled floor I say, "We can't get there fast enough, where's the car?"

Chapter 43: Katarina

Standing in the hallway of the psych ward, I don't know how to enter. I don't know how to do this, nor do I have a clue of what to say. Feeling apprehensive already, and with the added pressure of what's expected of me, I'm discomforted by fears of failure. Am I stronger? Or does he make me strong?

I wish my father were here to tell me what to do. How do you feel when you're alone and just need to be loved? What happens when the thing you love is also a part of what's killing you? *What do I say now, Dad, and how do I fix it, so he doesn't hurt so bad?*

The last time I had entered a hospital room I was fifteen years old. My father was dying in that room. The situation was different, of course, as my father lay in bed, hooked up to machines that beeped and whirred, assisting him to breathe as he lay there waiting for his end.

But the feeling is the same.

Back then, I was afraid of the man my father had become, realizing I would never see him again. I stayed by his side but was afraid to walk out alone. Today feels no different. All I can do is hope that this time my love for someone will help keep them alive.

I can see Ben through the window of his private door. His silhouette is hunched in a chair facing the wall. He looks small, like a little boy, and I can tell that he's shattered. His body language shows how much defeat he must be feeling right now. It's painful to see him this way, and I let out a whimper, putting my hand to my throat, trying to muffle my tears. It stings as I swallow, forcing my own pain down so I can deal with his. He's broken, but so am I, and I'm not sure I can pick up these pieces alone.

Walking in blind, I'm afraid of what I'll find. Watching myself, I have the sensation of my hand leaving my body, reaching for the door. My wrist wears the green bracelet he made for me. I've brought one for him too, from the bag full of visions he made of me. Raymond told me the hospital staff removed his other ones, and I think he'll like having the new one.

My legs are in cement as I approach him. I'm not sure if we're strong enough for this. It's definitely not what I'd planned for my summer adventure in New York. Approaching him, all these thoughts scramble in my head, and I can feel his pain in my own heart, his desperation in my soul. Our connection is so strong, the twitching of his nervous hands become my own. Drawn to him, embraced by his aura, my soul connects to the one it loves, and I reach out mechanically, naturally.

I touch one of his curls on the back of his head with my two fingers, not even thinking. Quickly, I pull back, realizing my thoughtless action might upset him when he stiffens and sags, but my fingers return, and I continue to play, finding more of his hair until he starts to turn into my touch.

"Katarina?"

"Yeah, it's me." I'm standing behind him but enough to the side that I can see his profile. A security guard stands waiting at the doorway.

Ben grimaces and hangs his head as my heart plummets for him, with him. It's not the reaction I was prepared for, he'd been asking for me, after all. Suddenly, I feel very scared that this man sitting in the chair is not the man I am in love with and will never be again. I start to turn away when he reaches out his hand and grabs my hips pulling me closer to him.

Spitting out soft cries, he says to me, "I don't want you to see me like this." He buries his face in my stomach.

Standing still, I grab his head as he whimpers. His tears make my shirt wet, but he's quiet, not sobbing.

"It's not the same anymore, Kay. The way I am, you don't even know… I can't break this."

It's not what I was hoping to hear, and my world starts to come crashing down as I try to hold it together. I know that he's trying to push me away, even as he holds onto me, so I try to reassure him. "You've been asking for me, Ben, and I'm here. I want to be here; I want to help you."

Dropping his hands from my body, he turns his head away as I squat down in front of him, trying to see his face. He's hiding from me, and I need to see his eyes. I need for him to look at me so that we can connect, but he won't and instead mumbles into the chair, "I should be happy you're here, but I'm not the man you think I am."

Refusing to hear him, I shake my head. "Don't try to give me reasons not to love you, Ben. I know exactly who you are, and you know it too. Who I decide to love is not your decision to make. It's mine, and I choose to love you." My desperation rises and a slight pang of anger strikes my consciousness. "You made me promises, Ben, and no matter what you say now, I am still in love with you. You can't take that away from me," I whisper and lower my head as tears start to form in my eyes.

"How can you?" he spits out, glaring at me. Angry at me, or maybe himself, I don't know, but I'm shocked and at a loss for words.

"*How?*" he yells. "How can you want all of this fucked up?" His voice rises, and he's getting agitated.

Ignoring it, I force myself in and sit on his lap, so we're face to face. "I don't know, but I can't stop it. I can't just walk away." Our eyes search each other, and I feel him begin to soften as my heart beats out of my chest. "I won't let you push me away." Sighing. I shake my head. "You're right, it's not the same. Our life may have been simpler but neither of us were complete, not really. I wish you didn't need to get help—"

"But I do, Katrina! *I do!* You don't get it!" His yelling makes me lean back, but I won't leave his lap. The security guard moves towards us and the orderly pops his head in the doorway. I give a subtle shake of my head, letting him know we're ok in here. I've got this, so far, anyway.

"Stop lying to yourself!" His eyes are black and sparking like crazy. He may be angry, but I can see the scared little boy inside.

Holding my head against his, I softly try again to explain my heart and what I've realized over the last few days. "I'm scared, Ben. But my love for you is stronger than my fear of you."

The next few seconds happen so fast it catches my breath. His hands grip my hips and squeeze. I don't expect to be thrown across the room, but that's exactly what he does. My hip cracks against the hard linoleum floor, my sneakers screeching as I slide a few feet.

"*GET THE HELL AWAY FROM ME! Get out!*" he screams.

What the fuck just happened?

The security guard comes to my aide, but I hold him so he can't retaliate against Ben, "Sshh. Don't move towards him please," I whisper, and he looks at me. I give him the okay with my eyes, and he slowly gets up and returns to his station by the door.

The orderly has come running and the security guard stops him short with his outreached hand. I raise my own to say 'stop, I'm fine' and everyone settles back. Ben hasn't moved since he threw me; all is calm for the moment. Resisting flight or fight mode, I close my eyes and bury deep within myself to stay put. Regaining composure, I see Ben's hood pulled up and he's tucked into a ball, facing the back of the chair. In that moment, all sense of rationality comes bubbling up in my throat and collides with my intense anger and frustration.

"Fuck you, Ben." My voice is low and guttural. He reacts with shock in his eyes as I scramble to my knees and start slowly crawling towards him. "You don't get to do that! Push me away. *Me?*" I point at my chest and laugh. "The one person who knows you more than anyone in this whole damn world and is still here willing to put up with you and this shit?"

He lifts his head more, turning so his feet are back on the ground. His eyes are dark with anger as he watches me scramble up from the floor and grab my bag. Pulling out the papers he'd written, his mess of emotions, I crumple them tight in my fist. Standing up to him, but far enough away that he can't get physical again, I throw each page at him like shards of shooting stars, some hitting him in the face. He starts swatting them away, his eyes getting darker by the minute.

"This is what *you* said, Ben! This is what you said to me, your feelings! Who the fuck you are and why! All your secrets and how you feel about me! I am absolutely terrified about what a future with you looks like, but I'm not going to hide and pretend I could *ever* love *anyone* else because of a little hard work! Don't you dare self-sabotage this, and don't you give up on us! Not now!"

His face is pure shock, and I'm not sure if it's because I'm yelling, and he's never seen me yell, or if it's the fact someone actually gives a shit about him. Slowly, he uncrumples one of the balls that landed in his lap. He takes a moment, his eyes scanning the page, his mask of anger starting to fall away.

"I don't know what to say, Kay. I just figured…" he trails off as he continues to stare at the page.

"You figured what? You figured you could change my mind? Make my mind up for me? Well, you can't. You may be fucked up, but I'm not leaving." I'm breathing heavily, trying to get control of my anger.

"We said we wouldn't leave each other." Completely against all my social work training, I plop my ass on the ground at his feet. This is what I had been afraid of, my heart clouding any of my skills and throwing them right out the window. I have to separate my love and personal life from my professional one. This is what Roland couldn't do, and I have to be better. Better for him, and for myself. This will be the only way this is going to work. I can't be the one to help him or take this on alone, not if I am going to survive the process. Right now he needs Katarina his girlfriend, not another therapist.

He doesn't say anything. I didn't expect him to, knowing he needs time to process everything that has happened in his world the last few weeks. He has to make a decision about me, and he has to make it for himself. I don't expect it to be today, but I'll sit with him, stand by him, as his broken mind heals, and hopefully, we will heal together.

Minutes turn into hours, and as I get tired, I lean my head on the edge of the chair. When I feel his bandaged hand reach down and gingerly stroke my hair, I look up at him.

"Kay," he says, "why are you still here?"

Finally, his beautiful green eyes are clear and shining, the cloud of anger and confusion having disappeared. Opening my arms, I wrap them around his legs and hug him. He bends down and hugs me back. My heart aches, and I start to cry.

"Because I love you. I'm so sorry I was ignoring you. I've been confused too and still am. I had no idea you were hurting so badly." My tears start to fall, and I feel guilty for how I've treated him, wishing I'd known more and acted sooner. "I still don't know how this will work out, but I'll love you until the day I die." Whimpering, I cover my face with my hands.

Gingerly, despite his bandaged hand, he pulls me up. I sit on his lap, and he holds onto me, murmuring into my hair, "Oh, Kay. What have I done to you? I can't even touch you properly, I've hurt myself so badly." Pulling back, he shows me the extent of his bandaged hand. The damage of what his internal pain had done to his external self.

Taking his less injured hand, I smile and rest it on my face. "Yes, you can. See?" My tears fall freely into his hand.

His eyes shift again. The green becomes brighter, and the gold glows like the morning sun.

Then he looks at me the same way he did the first time we met, and he says, "Do you have any idea how much I love you?"

Reaching towards me, he kisses my forehead as I let myself break down. I hunch into him and cry and cry on his chest. He just holds me quietly and lets me.

"I'm sorry I failed you," I whisper.

Stroking my hair with his unharmed hand, Ben sighs. "You haven't failed me, Kay. I've failed me. I've failed me and you. I failed us."

"Do you think we can do this?" I ask him honestly. "Can you be who I need you to be for me?"

He stops and looks away, clearly thinking it through before making an answer. "No one has ever understood me or my monsters." He looks me in the eye. "You understand my needs and how to keep me grounded. I'm not easy, and I can't promise you everything... but I promise I'm gonna try for you."

I'm quiet, patiently waiting for him to continue.

"All my demons go away when I'm with you. My parents never understood. They didn't believe in me, so I never believed in myself, but then I met you." He hesitates for a moment, then asks, "Am I still your favourite guy?"

His pout and sincere eyes make me giggle and smile. "Yeah, you're my favourite."

He grins, pulling me in close to him and kisses the top of my head. Resting on his chest, his arms still make me feel safe. Remembering the bracelet, I fish it out of my pocket. "Here, I brought you this." I place the bracelet on his right hand and tie the knots to make it stay in place. "Now we match." I look up at him and smile, my tears dry.

He looks right back at me and says, "I'm going to tell you everything, Babe. Anything you want to know."

"I know. We'll be ok, we'll figure this out," I promise and lay my head back on his chest.

Chapter 44: Katarina

"Mom?" I'm quiet, my phone glued between my ear and my tear-stained pillow. Back at the hotel, most of my stuff is packed up and ready to go to Ben's apartment—our apartment.

"It's ok, Katarina. Tell me what's wrong."

I cry and cry, and she just listens and listens. "Mom? I... I gotta do some things. I gotta stay here... for a bit longer."

She sighs. "I know you do. I knew that when I talked to you a week ago. You just needed to figure it out for yourself."

"Really? Are you mad?" I ask, maybe looking for an excuse to bail and go home to her.

"No, Katarina, I'm not mad. You're a force to be reckoned with." The line is silent for a moment. "Just like I was when your father left. I'm heartbroken, but I understand. This is who you are, and this is what you need to do. Do you know what you're doing?" she asks.

"No. No I don't think I do," I admit.

"Can you fight it? The feelings?" she presses.

"No… I can't." Shaking my head, even though I know she can't see me, another tear drops out of my eye.

"Then, you're where you're supposed to be, Katarina." She sounds confident, making me think deeper into my decision to stay.

"But I'm not sure what I'm doing," I say. "I'm staying here for Ben." Is that right? Or am I staying for myself?

"Are you? Really? Or are you staying because you've found what is missing? You've found not only a purpose for yourself but also pleasure, and dare I say, love?"

When I stay silent, she blatantly asks, "Do you love him?"

"Yes, I do," I cry back, nodding my head. *I do! I do!*

"Then you know what you're doing. You have a gift, Katarina, and I know that gift can feel like a curse. Trust me, I know because we share the same one."

My head is pounding from my tears. Taking a deep breath to calm my nerves, I listen to her continue, "You have a big heart. Don't shut it out, afraid of what will happen. Embrace it and chase it! Take the bruises and bumps that come with it and keep going. We can't control what the heart wants or who we love, so don't even try."

I remain silent, trying to absorb what she's saying. I want to ensure I'm staying in New York for the right reasons, for myself, and not just because I'm trying to save someone.

A moment or two goes by and she says, "Outside of Ben you have friends, work prospects, a current job? You're standing on your own two feet, and you did it all by yourself. Katarina, I think you've found what you were looking for don't you?"

With that I realize, I guess I have.

Chapter 45: Katarina

Organizing the rest of my things, I take one final look around my tiny little hotel room. I find the book Ben bought me under the bed and open it. It is a book of poetry, a few of them earmarked, and I skim past them. I know they are meant for me, and I want to share these intimate moments together, hear the words he found so inspiring coming from his own lips. We'll read this together to further our already strong bond.

Alex arranged an extended leave from work for him, and we have four weeks together before he is expected back at work. During that time, he'll have physical therapy to work on his hand and a therapist to see once a week. That was dictated by the courts and a condition of his release from the hospital. Thankfully, I've found a great clinic in Soho that deals specifically with family trauma and dysfunction. He also has a psychiatrist who took a good look at Ben's cocktail of meds and made some necessary adjustments. Previously to all this, I had been speaking with the facility regarding employment opportunities for myself. That connection gave me the confidence to reach out to a female doctor who is willing to help us.

"You ready, Katarina?" Alex pokes his head in and grabs one of my bags to take back to Ben's place. He brought his girlfriend, Margo, along and we click instantly. I am thankful as I miss Monica and know I need to expand my friend circle. It is already a hard thing for me to do, especially with women, but Margo has a way about her that is calming and non judgemental. She is a veterinarian and anyone who loves animals has to have a heart of gold.

"Yeah, I'm ready. Thanks, Alex." Pausing to lock the door behind me as we leave, I notice a silent figure in the hallway to my right.

"So that's it, huh? Leaving me to put up with some new shitty neighbour. I was just starting to like you a bit."

Good ol' Max. He always has to get the last word in.

Turning my head, I smile at him. "Yes, sir! You'll have a new person to torment and terrify. Thought you'd be thrilled."

He hobbles up to me and casts a glare at Alex who stands awkwardly waiting for me.

"It's ok, Alex, you go ahead, I'll be down in a minute," I say dismissively.

Turning back to me, Max says, "These boys of yours, I tell ya, I can't keep 'em straight."

"Be quiet, you! That's Ben's brother, shut up!"

He winks at me with a smirk, and then his expression grows serious as he hands me a large, tattered manila envelope. It looks old, but in fairly good shape, and has the name 'Mark' scrawled on it in black pen.

"What's this?" I ask, taking it from him.

"I haven't opened that in twenty years." He glances towards it, leaning on his cane, his hands trembling just a little. "I hope it's still ok inside. I've kept it in the safe so it should be fine."

"Okay? What is it?" I question. Flipping it over. It's sealed, but I can tell it's been handled a lot over the years.

"It's a piece of music I started composing when Mark went into hospital." He puts both his hands on his cane, keeping his balance. "It's about us, my love for him. The love I believe he had for me." His eyes turn glassy, and he pauses for a second before continuing. "Our struggles are in those notes, our pain, our joys, and what I hoped our commitment to each other would become. The light I believed would be ours in the end."

Looking at him, I'm amazed he's opened up to me so much in the last few days. I feel he hasn't talked to anyone, really, in decades. I have no idea why he is confiding in me, but I am letting him.

"I never finished it. When he died I just couldn't." He hangs his head a little, turns away and walks to his room. He isn't done talking to me, so he raises his voice so that I can hear him still. "I want you to have it. I know Ben can play. I heard him that night, and he plays well. Very well. If he can play, he should be able to write. I want the two of you to finish the story. Finish the story for me but make it your own." He stops at his door and looks at me, a slight hint of kindness in his eyes. "Then I want to hear it. I want to know what my love could have sounded like just once. Tell me you'll do it."

I acknowledge him. "Yes. Yes, of course. I'll make sure of it."

Smiling with a curt nod, he opens his door and is gone.

Chapter 46: Maxwell Templeton

There is something about this girl I find intriguing. She is innocent but not naive. Maybe the fact that she is so virtuous—unlike the rest of New York and its inhabitants—is what stands out to me. She is smart. She is quiet, and she has eyes that know things, a heart that feels things. You can tell that she understands people and how they tick. Her intuition is strong, and she brings out the best in the people around her. She has brought out the best in me—a part of myself I thought was as dead and gone, as Mark is.

She isn't simple, and she isn't just another pretty face. Something has happened to this girl to give her an edge, but she doesn't let it control her. It protects her, gives her strength. She believes in the good in the world and isn't afraid to find it.

This girl has a purpose and a reason for being here. She may not know it yet, but she is going to do some wonderful things. Her heart is gold, and she is selfless. Watching her from time to time, I notice her determination when she runs down the hallway with her earbuds in at six in the morning. When she laughed with that friend of hers—the blonde, obnoxious girl—I could hear she was free. But it is when I watch her read in the lounge area, that's when she is the most interesting. Her facial expressions change and reflect what she is reading so much that I can guess what the story is about and probably be right.

When she came to me that night with her shoulders stooped so low, I sympathized with her. I felt her pain, knowing by her language that her anguish was the same affliction I had been carrying most of my life. It was then I decided to help her, I don't know why. That's what she did to people, made them their best. I felt the need to be the person for her who I had never had. It was selfless of me, and I'm not a selfless man. I hate the world and am angry it hasn't spit me out yet—sent its reaper to come pick me up and take me home. Home to my Mark.

I don't want her heart to be shattered like mine was. She is young, kind, and deserves better from the world. I am guarded, angry, despise people and they despise me. I am living with a ghost and just can't see her living this way.

When I opened up to her and spoke about Mark, I found myself silently reminiscing about the marvelous things I'd forgotten. The memories I'd left at the bottom of so many bottles over the last twenty years. I didn't share those with her, those are mine. But it did help some of the pieces stick together again. That is just what she does. I went home that morning and pulled out Mark's music. I almost opened it but couldn't do it. I placed it back in the safe and shut the door, passing out on my lonesome bed, leaving it in the vault.

When I heard her name at the front desk the other night, I stopped and listened. The man asking for her looked so much like her lover, but I knew it wasn't him. I told him—lied to him—that I would call him when I saw her. I don't know why I didn't call him, but I knew the lovers would find each other anyway.

She isn't going to stop loving Ben, and he isn't going to let her go, that much I know.

When I got wind of her moving out, overhearing her conversation at the front desk, I finally called that Alex guy. I'm human after all. I'm also pretty nosy. I wanted to know where my neighbour was going, without being vulnerable enough to let her know I care.

Going back to my room that day, my decision was made. My love story is dead, gone. But theirs is just beginning. Ben can play piano as well as anyone I've ever heard, including myself, and I figure he can change the outcome of the music I'd stopped writing years ago. For myself, I want that story to develop, maybe end up different. I don't need a happy ending, don't expect it. Happy endings are for fools.

What I want is completion. I want my music to live on in the world of others so that they know. So that they understand who Mark was, who we were, and the love we could have had if the world hadn't gotten in our way.

Chapter 47: Benjamin

With my girl by my side, I enter my home. Alex, Margo, Geoff and Nancy rallied around us, and I believe my parents are somewhere in the mix. Making sure we aren't alone, we have the support network we are going to need to be successful. I am excited for the future but scared.

It is getting dark by the time we get there, and the lights are off when we enter. Knowing there is nothing in there anyway, I'm not sure I am ready to see what my destruction has done to our space. This is our home, and I need it redecorated and reimagined as soon as possible.

Turning on the lights, I look into the space, afraid of what I'll see—our memories that were damaged by my rage. That's when I see the baby grand piano in the middle of the living room, by the window, where the dining table used to be. Clearly shocked and a little confused, I stand there, staring at the instrument.

Alex comes up behind me and puts his arm around me. "It's from Max Templeton. He stopped me in the hallway the night I went looking for Kat. He reached out to me. This is his old piano from his old home. It's been in storage, he said."

I simply nod, not fully comprehending why it is here.

Walking over to it, running my hand along its sleek blackness I pause, reading the small plaque on the fall board:

Ben,
Never let your music die.
M. Templeton

It feels surreal and the emotions have me choking back tears.

"Let's leave them alone for a bit," I hear Nancy say, and within a few minutes, the soft click of the door.

I am healing, most of my bruises and cuts have gone down, and the large bandage on my hand is now smaller, more manageable. I can walk without the pain from the cuts on my feet. It has been a long week, but I am beginning to feel like myself again. I back away and start taking inventory of the rest of the apartment. Playing piano was a bit of a nightmare for me as a child, other than the night I had played a little at Katarina's place, it just wasn't talked about. In the silence, anything can happen, but when her arms come around me, her head resting on my back, I know the silence will never be as loud as it used to be.

"Being here with you is good," I say and squeeze her arms. I look around and can see there's some damage to the walls and floors and kitchen cabinets, and I swallow hard. All the furniture is gone except the piano facing the window. It dawns on me again. *A fucking piano?*

"What do you think?" Katarina takes my hand and leads me over to the bench explaining, "It's a gift. For you. It's here to help you with your hand, get your feelings back... understand your new feelings. How the keys will feel under your touch." She pulls me closer, keeping her eyes on me.

I'm quiet. It's a beautiful piano, and I haven't had one in my space since I was living at home. I don't know how I feel about it but am desperate to get feeling back in my hand, even if it is just to fully feel Katarina's skin again. Sitting down on the bench, Katarina sits beside me, and my eyes are drawn back to the message on the fall board.

My eyes are wide, and I stare at Katarina.

"You've got to be kidding me?" I say to her as she smiles effortlessly, awaiting my approval. I'm astounded, a little anxious but excited. This is a generous gift—beyond generous.

"It's his own piano, Ben. He gifted it to you. But he wants something in return," she puts her hand on my knee, and it feels so good.

Running my hands over the fall board, I slowly lift it up, exposing the keys, along with them, I also expose the pain and torment, talent and triumphs I had had as a kid. The black and white little keys of my childhood stare back at me. As I sit caressing the keys, Katarina exits and comes back with an envelope.

"I haven't opened it yet." She sits back down beside me as the sun, just starting to go down, casts a glow that reflects off the floor.

"It's sealed, but I know what's in it. Max told me. I thought we should open it together."

I take the envelope from her with my good hand; it says 'Mark' on the front in black sharpie pen. Holding it for her, she uses her hands to open the seal and pulls out what's inside, and hands it to me.

It's sheet music.

"Max told me that it's a piece of music he was composing before his lover died. He wants you to finish it. Us to finish it. He said he wants us to take his love story and add in our own and when we're done, he wants you to play it for him. Do you know how to write music, Ben?"

"Yeah, yeah of course I do," I whisper, staring at this music stunned, my hands shaking as I hold the pages. I don't know if Katarina fully comprehends what we have here, and how significant it is. In my hand is Maxwell Templeton's own work. A piece of music that he's written and wants me to finish. Does she have any idea what the prominent New York music and art scene would do with this? Want, with this? Max Templeton is famous. There's no way she knows just how much.

"What does it say at the top there?" she asks, leaning over me to get a better look.

Max's handwriting scrawls across the top of the page, indicating the title of the music he's half written. I can't believe he wants me to complete it.

"It's the title of the piece he's written. He's called it: Two, For the Love of One."

I look at her and she smiles, laying her head on my shoulder, a tear falling from her eye. "Fitting," she says. "Fitting, don't you think?" Lifting her head, she looks back into my eyes.

Chapter 48: Katarina

Remembering the words of advice that Max had given me, I smile. He really is a difficult guy to read, Max is, but he is a personality I've learned to respect, maybe even care for. Just like a father, really, my father. He'd been difficult too, but I loved him anyway.

I want to continue Ben and my love story all the way to the end. I know we can be together, and I know I'm not going home, —I am already home. Maybe one day we'll need a second bedroom or a change of scene, but for now I just want to furnish the space we have. Having purchased a bed to sleep in, I take Benjamin's hand and guide him down the hall to see what I picked out.

The couple I hired painted the back wall black, and the rest they repaired and painted white after my design direction. They installed two brass reading lamps on either side of the bed and fixed the damage that had been done in the bathroom. We needed a new mirror, new shower door and a towel rack. The bed is in the middle of the black wall and compliments the soft, tufted white headboard. The sheets are black linen, with a mix of large black and white pillows, making the bed a cozy space to lay in and read a book. A crisp down-filled white duvet covers the king bed with a soft grey throw blanket draped at the foot. There are large letter Fs embroidered on two of the accent pillows.

"What's the F for?" he asked me

"It's for Ford, silly. Your name. Is that okay?"

"Oh. Yeah... That's not what I was thinking," grinning, he gives me a mischievous look. I had missed his body so much.

"Giving you any ideas, Benjamin?"

"Yeah, lots." He moves towards me and gently grabs my waist, kissing me. My knees start to buckle as shock waves go through me, and I'm instantly wet. He tastes so good.

"Mmmmm, Ben," I breathe into his mouth. "I've missed you so much. I'm glad you're home again." I begin undoing the buttons of the black dress shirt I'd brought him to wear home. We had a good chuckle when we realized he wasn't going to be able to work the buttons alone.

I take it off him, my hands touching his shoulders and stroking down his arms, landing, as usual, on his nipple rings. With the pressure of his kisses, he moves me towards the bed. Raising his bandaged hand, he asks me, "Can you take your clothes off for me, Baby?"

"Yeah, I can do that," I whisper, my breath quickening.

He stands back and watches me undo my own blouse, button by button, my eyes cast down to see what I am doing. Slipping it off my shoulders, my red bra with white polka dots becomes exposed and my lips curl into a sly grin. He likes polka dots. Undoing my black capris, I keep my eyes locked on him and slide my pants down my thighs.

He steps in and grabs me around the waist, leaning down for another kiss.

"You left on the hardest thing for me to take off," he says, referring to my bra.

"I thought maybe you could wait a little while?" I tease him sheepishly.

Shaking his head, he takes hold of my chin, and our eyes connect, "I'm not waiting anymore, Katarina."

I step back and reach behind my back, unclasp the hold on my tits, and let the bra fall to the floor.

"God, you're beautiful, Kay," he says, staring at my nakedness. I undo his belt, lowering his jeans and boxers in one movement. I go down on my knees to help him step out of them. On my way back up, I lick the inside of his thighs, holding onto them for balance and nuzzling into his cock.

I had missed the warmth of his body and the smell of his skin. The spicy, woodsy smell that was all over him and on everything he owned. I lick him like a popsicle. Putting his dick in my mouth, I feel felicitous. Turned on and fully aroused, wetness begins between my legs as I suck and suck. God, I love sucking on him. My hands hold him to me, his skin warm and soft with his hands playing in my hair. Voracious and thirsty, I can't stop from moaning. He is moaning too, of course, because I make him do that, and I am ecstatic and proud that I gratify him. Stopping with a final lick, I stand up so I can kiss his chest and pull him onto our new bed.

He leans into me, kneeling and grinning as he stalks me down onto my back. His hands are on my hips, the good one wrapping around to my ass and squeezing as I prop myself up towards him. I stare into his eyes and pull him down on top of me.

I am fully open to him, his body on top of mine, the sheets cool and cozy on my back but quickly heating up as we move. He's so close to me, his body and his love smothering me to a point of ecstasy I'm trying to grasp. I want his whole body inside mine, moving together forever as one being. We're getting hot and his hair is falling in my face as he speeds up, slows down, speeds up again. Grabbing his hair, I pull on it, taking his head back so he has to look at me.

"You ok, Baby?" he asks

"Yeah, I'm good, real good. Just don't stop, Ben. I like what you're doing to me."

Rocking his body on mine, my breathing is getting quicker, and he knows all too well what that means. "Will you get on top of me?" he asks. "Please?"

He flips onto his back, settling into the fluffy pillows around us. My skin glistens with sweat right between my breasts as I straddle on top of him and start moving up and down. Whenever and however he wants, I am his forever.

With my head back, the feelings intensify, and I arch backwards, placing my hands behind me on top of his thighs for balance. He sits up and grabs me, his chest against mine and holds me close to him. I wrap my arms around him and my pussy contracts as I cry out and start to come. I hear him let himself go, unable to hold on any longer, as we find our joy together.

We fall down, and I land on top of Ben breathless. My body is euphoric, my head intoxicated. I know what I want and this reconnection in our new bed confirms it. This is where I'm supposed to be, In this space, in New York, and with this man.

Removing myself from his body, I flop down beside him, pulling the soft throw blanket over us. He wraps his arm around me, and I nuzzle his hair, resting my head on his still heaving chest. My eyes fall on the small table I placed temporarily beside the bed, the one I'd put there to house our little plant. Nancy had been able to save it and fix it, just like we were able to do for ourselves.

"We have a lot more memories to make," I say, stroking his chest. "A lot more, to replace the old ones." Raising my head, our eyes meet.

Ben grins and says, "We sure do, Red."

Confused, I ask him, "Red? What do you mean by Red?"

"Red Shirt, Short Hair. The day my life changed for the better."

I smile and nod, the two of us falling silent in each other's company. As we stare at the ceiling, I'm overjoyed for not giving up on us.

Chapter 49: Katarina

Well, here I am. Fairly successful in my quest, if I do say so myself. I can sit here and give myself a multitude of labels, personality traits that make up the woman I've become. But that's not liberating at all, is it? All I know is that I am a woman on the brink of becoming another woman, and another woman after that. I am light years away from the girl who arrived in New York City.

Coming here has been the best thing for me, and as cliche as it sounds, I recommend anyone who has a dream to chase it. There may not be a pot of gold at the end, but there's always another rainbow. There's a shit ton more work, not only on the horizon, but also all the way down to the end of my road, and I'm committed to take it all on, the good, the bad, and the ugly. And do it in style.

If we're lucky, we'll find someone to take the road with us. A part of us is always alone, and always will be. No one can truly understand us because we are all divinely different. I can't get into your head, and you can't get into mine. But what we can do is find the one person, or maybe multitudes of people, who want to explore our intricacies and have fun along the way. It shouldn't be as scary as it all seems, but I realize it is. The best thing we can do is believe in ourselves, love ourselves, and trust that the Universe will stay true to the path it's laid out for us. As a young, independent woman, I believe in the famous words of the exquisite Audrey Hepburn and carry them wherever I go:

"I believe in being strong when everything seems to be going wrong. I believe that happy girls are the prettiest girls. I believe that tomorrow is another day, and I believe in miracles."

The road ahead is going to be a long one, but I believe in the love that Ben and I have found in one another. We'll continue to grow together and find ourselves, picking each other up and brushing ourselves off to try again. We'll celebrate our triumphs and our failures together. In the end we'll write our own song and as one, never let our music die.

~ The End ~

Acknowledgements

If it wasn't for my friend and fellow writer, C.H., I have to admit none of this would have happened. When I reached out to him blindly (we didn't know each other personally at the time) I was looking for validation. Can I even write a simple sentence? Do I have something here and if so, what the hell is it? After reading over the beginning of my work, he said to me, 'I must tell you honestly, I am really digging it. This is interesting stuff.' How he continued to support me in all my mood swings of doubt is what perseverance and real friendship looks like: I still remember when he told me, 'Meg, remember you are a writer. Keep going, Meg… keep fucking at it… this is very interesting work.' It had shocked me, literally made me stop and evaluate myself. I realized then that at some point I had to believe in my work, and much like Katarina, I had to believe in myself. C.H., Thanks for the conversations, they are some of the best I've ever had in my life.

Next, I need to thank my Beta readers. There were a few, and I appreciate you all, but in particular, Lianna and Joan. You two ladies are full of talent and intelligence, able to look at my words objectively and give honest feedback I could work with. You made points that were relevant and constructive without changing the story that was pouring out of me. Your time and effort meant a lot, and I'll be ringing your bell for the next novel.

To my friend Monique. Oh, the hours we spent together smoking cigarettes and drinking wine while I would read random scenes to you that I was working on! At that point in the journey, I was too protective for anyone to even touch my new baby—you were patient and accepting in my weirdness. After listening intently, you would explode in an excitement that is all you. Genuine, authentic, and perfectly best friend material. Thank you for encouraging me. I am honoured you think so highly of me and my writing, and I will forever be grateful to you and our friendship.

To my sons. I know it can't exactly be easy seeing this side of your mom. It takes great strength to separate your mother into two roles, that of your mother, and that of a woman who has intense stories to tell, filled with imagination that can sometimes be uncomfortable. I hope I've taught you to follow your dreams and not to let the opinions of others stand in your way. Do not shrink yourself to appease others, and don't you dare worry about what they think. If your hearts and minds are pure, and your intentions solid, push forward. And if you dare to leave the world with a piece of work that inspires or helps another person, then be true to yourself—always. Not everyone will support you, but the people who love you always will.

I can't forget my editor, Jen. My god, woman, what I've put you through! *No freaking out* The laughs we've shared will always be my favourite. I have learned so much from you during this process, and I am eternally grateful. Thank you for believing in me and my work and the countless hours you've spent guiding me towards something great. You are a talented and selfless woman navigating through my words while allowing my work to stay as my work. It's a true talent, and I'm never letting you go.

My beautiful cover design credit goes to the super talented Jo. Thank you for bringing TFTLO to life in the form of her book cover. I am amazed at your talent and how well you depicted the concept and plot of the story so eloquently.

And lastly, my husband. Remembering our nights talking through TFTLO and how it started to unfold will always be some of my fondest memories of our times spent together. We got through some of the hardest times of our lives. During those talks, you helped me find the part of myself I needed to imagine a new world. Thank you for letting me be me and loving me anyway. Thank you for allowing me to find myself and loving the new version just as much. Thank you for always, always supporting me, and for doing all the dishes. I can't wait to mold *The One I Hurt* and other worlds together as we sip and smoke, and runaway to another exciting place.

Before I go, one thing I must say to my mom. You never saw it finished, but I know you knew I'd get there. You didn't raise a quitter, and as Queens crowns go, you always made sure mine was straight-even if you had to slap it into place. I am who I am because of you—all the good, the bad, and the ugly.

And I love you for it.

Meg Lush

Meg Lush is a content creator for Best Version Media. Her work has been featured in *Liberty North Neighbours* and focuses on highlighting human experiences and the arts within her Ontario community.

She is a wife, mother of two, and shameless servant to three black cats. After a diagnosis of Multiple Sclerosis in 2017, Meg refocused her energy into her writing career. Her debut novel, *Two for the Love of One*, explores themes of heightened emotions, mental health, and complicated relationships.

Coming soon from Meg Lush …

The One I Hurt – Teaser

She's a glimmer of Starlight in his world of torturing darkness...

Forbidden past...

The next day he came back. Only, this time there was no hiding, no games, no cupcake. This time he strutted right up to my secret spot, parting the bushes like he owned the place. It aggravated me, but I didn't make a move to leave, either.

"Why are you here, D?" I asked without looking up.

"D? What's that all about? No one's ever called me that before—I like it. Maybe I'll keep coming back just to hear you call me that." He leaned against the roof right in front of me, blocking me in. I suppose I should've been a little scared, but I liked the feeling of being trapped by him.

"You said you make those bracelets for the kids at the hospital, eh."

I looked up at him, wondering why he cared.

"Yes. I figure it's the least I can do for kids and teens that don't get to go outside and see the world like I do. Kids that are sick and scared, instead of being healthy and scared." I laughed, knotted in my final bead, and looked down to admire my work.

"Can I see that?" he asked, taking it from my hand before I could answer. He plopped in front of me, our knees touching. "Did you know my sister died of cancer?"

He said it without emotion, just clear as day, and it took me by surprise. The guy baffled me. On one hand he was cold and dispassionate, on the other he made my blood boil and my emotions swirl. I wanted to pin him down like one of nature's experiments and dissect him piece by piece. Knowing at the same time, no matter how threatened he may feel, he'd only share with me what he wanted me to know, if anything at all.

"I didn't. I'm sorry, I—" I stuttered.

"Don't be. It's how life works, Starlight. One day at a time, and some of us have more days than others. Don't be so serious."

"Serious? Me? You think I'm serious?"

"No. I think you're too serious. You're also a brat. I doubt you ever do what you're told."

Holy shit. Who was this guy?

"If you think I'm such a brat then why do you continue to come here? You weren't invited, you know."

"I don't need invitations little kitten. It's an open space."

"Yes, well…"

"Ok, ok. We're getting off on the wrong foot, here. You intrigue me."

I raised my brows. "Intrigue you? How?"

"Well, we established that you're pretty, or at least I think you are. But there's more to it than that. I need to know what makes you tick. You and all that darkness. Why do you live with your demons instead of letting them out to play?"

Who the fuck was this dude.

I scoffed. "You're making me much more interesting than I am, I assure you. Also, I am not your kitten or your Starlight or whatever, so stop saying that."

"Hmm… see? Feisty. Why so angry with me? You don't even know me."

He was right, and I hated it. I had no idea who he was, why he was here, or what he wanted. He was putting a wrench in my unhappy little matrix of life. But for some reason, I didn't want him to leave. I wanted him to stay and hold me in those big arms and touch me with those hands and stare at me more than he already was. I wanted to know if he could make me feel on the outside as much as he was making me feel on the inside. I wanted Dominic Adams more than anything in the damn world, but he was a Ken doll, and I was the Loch Ness Monster. We didn't fit. Would never fit. And I didn't trust myself around him.

I didn't trust I wouldn't fall head over heels with the enemy. It was easier to think this way. Thinking any other way would only lead to disappointment, hurt and pain.

When I saw Dominic at school, we didn't talk with our mouths. If he happened to notice me lurking in the hallways, we spoke with our eyes. He knew we were from different worlds just as much as I did. He told me he understood with his look and reassuring smile. Maybe that's how I started to fall. When his eyes told me everything I couldn't say, and for the first time in my life, I felt seen, really seen.

Over the next few weeks, he met me every day at The Spot. Morning, noon, and after school we spent together and before I knew it, I was reading him my stories. I was letting him in, and he was taking everything he could get.

We talked about dreams and fears and who we wanted to be in the world. I told him about how I wanted to open a Jewellery store and design my own pieces using nature's gifts of crystals and stones, creating pieces of beauty with the purpose of healing. I talked more to him than I'd ever talked to anyone, even Janet. With Dominic, I could share my soul.

He told me things too. Things like how unconnected he felt from everyone, even his friends. He told me how losing his family created an inability to relate to others who didn't share the same darkness and loss. He told me that he felt safe with me, unjudged and not alone. And that's when my heart started to let go.

As the earth around us started to die, and the ground got colder, our space in The Spot only got warmer and more full of life. I was secretly falling in love. People can't ruin secrets, and our secret was one everyone wanted to tarnish. We were special. We were polar opposites on the outside, but on the inside, we were one.